The Social Hour

Coffee Book 3

Sophie Sinclair

Natalie.

thank you so much,
for supporting the series!

♡ Sophie Sinclair

THE SOCIAL HOUR

Copyright © 2020 by Sophie Sinclair
Print Edition

Editor: Michelle Morgan, www.fictionedit.com
Proofreading: Stephany Renfrow
Book Cover Photographer: Wander Aguiar
Photography Model: Forest Harrison
Book Cover Design: Carrie Guy, Shawna Montague
Formatting: BB EBooks

All Rights Reserved

This book is dedicated to all the wild magnolias just waiting to bloom.

You'll never do a whole lot unless
you're brave enough to try.
– Dolly Parton

Prologue

Cameron

Six Years Earlier

THE POOL STICK slides easily between my fingers as the quiet click of the cue ball sends the eight ball into its designated pocket. I stand back up and arch my eyebrow at the redhead sitting on the edge of the pool table at the opposite end of me. She giggles and slips the last piece of clothing down her legs. I place the pool stick down on the table and stalk toward her.

"Well, that was quick." She smiles.

"And predictable." My lips tick up into a smirk as I grab her waist and push her back on the green felt. I run my fingers down her chest and over her fake tits as she opens her legs for me. I lean over her and my lips graze against her creamy silky skin following the path my fingers just took.

"Oh god, yes!" she pants as her fingers thread through my hair.

"Is this how you want it?" I murmur against her skin.

"God, yes!" she screams.

"Mom! Are you home? Dad, I think I heard her downstairs in the game room."

I immediately stop kissing her and look up, her wide eyes mirroring my own deer-in-the-headlights frozen stare. *Mom...Dad?*

"Are you fucking married?" I seethe as she scrambles out from underneath me.

"Shit, shit, shit!" she whispers. "They weren't supposed to be home until Sunday."

What the fuck?

She shoves my coat into my arms and pushes me toward the French doors leading out to the pool.

"Get out!" she hisses as she turns to quickly find her clothes and put them on. I'm just standing there slack-jawed watching her in disbelief. She growls in irritation as she lunges toward me and grabs the door handle open. "Get out before he catches us!" She violently shoves me out the door. "You're going to have to climb over the back wall. Now go!" She slams the French door in my face, the glass rattling.

My eyes try to adjust to the darkness as I look around the backyard. I'm tempted to barge back in through the door and get some answers from her, but I'm not so sure it's worth it...if she's worth it. Pitiful thing is, five minutes ago I thought she was.

I mentally shake myself and jog toward the back wall. I don't particularly want to meet the fist of a scorned husband right now.

I look up at the eight-foot stone wall. At least I'm used to rock climbing, although not the ideal time to be doing it in the dark, while wearing wing tips, my Dolce & Gabbana suit and Burberry wool coat. I grab the edge of the cold stone as my foot slips on the crusted ice. Dammit, this isn't easy. I get a better purchase on a different stone and heft myself up. I deftly climb up and over the top and jump down into mud.

Are you fucking kidding me right now? My Italian leather custom-made shoes are now ruined. Fucking Jessica. How in the hell did I miss the signs she was married? *With kids?* I wipe my hands off on my wool coat and gather my bearings.

I quickly walk to the sidewalk and spot my silver Audi R8 parked in front of Jessica's neighbor's house. *You're such a fucking idiot, Cam.* Didn't you wonder why she asked you to park across the street from her house? I look at the house in question. It's a sprawling two-story stucco home with a minivan parked in the driveway. I drag my hand down my face in utter disbelief at my stupidity. *Details, Cam, you missed the fucking details tonight.* Like why would a single woman live in such a huge house in an upscale neighborhood? And the fact she always insisted we go to my condo at night, making excuses for why she could never sleep over.

I've been seeing Jessica for the past three weeks, but we always went to my place after our "dates" of her hanging out at the bar while I finished up paperwork. I should have known better. Rule number one: Never get involved with the customers. Jesus, I can't believe I got duped. She probably isn't even an attorney like she said, probably just a bored trophy wife seeking attention.

I shake my head as I get into my car. My pride seriously wounded. I actually liked Jessica, maybe I was even falling in love with her. She was funny and smart, beautiful as hell. I start the car and the engine roars to life. I look over at the house one last time as I pull away from the curb. I can see her in the upstairs window watching me. I grind my teeth and jam my stick into gear, peeling away from the curb.

Never again. I will never let a woman make me feel this way again.

Chapter 1

Andie

Present Day

I RING THE doorbell and shift Enzo in my arms as I look down the street. It's a beautiful neighborhood with perfectly manicured lawns and fancy cars parked in the driveways. I look back at my economical Ford Focus sitting behind a Lexus and an Infinity SUV and already feel out of place. Enzo starts to fuss to get down as I punch the doorbell again. I hope I have the right house.

The heavy door swings open and a petite blonde with beachy-wavy hair and flawless makeup answers the door.

"Hi! I'm Melissa, are you here for *Moms Gone Wild?* Come on in."

"Hi, I'm Andie. This is my first time to a *Let's Meet* event."

"Oh well, welcome. If you don't mind taking off your shoes." She smiles as she looks down at my Converse, but her smile doesn't reach her eyes. "He's cute! What's his name?"

"This is Enzo, he's fourteen months old."

"Aw, great! We have some other moms here with little ones around his age."

My lungs quietly exhale as my anxiety slowly leaks from my veins leaving me less edgy than I was five minutes ago. We enter her family room and I see five women sitting around a coffee table chatting as their babies crawl or toddle around the room.

"Hey girls, this is a new member of the group. I'm sorry, what was your name again?" Melissa laughs lightly.

I smile around the room at the women. "Hi, my name is Andie and this little guy is Enzo."

The women smile pleasantly and greet me as I sit down on the floor with Enzo since there aren't any more seats left. Some women are dressed to the nines and some are wearing yoga pants. I'm feeling good, dressed in between in a cute top and jeans.

"So Andie, where are you from?" a nice woman across from me asks.

"I just moved here a couple months ago from Alabama."

"Oh, did your husband get transferred here? It's *so hard* starting over in a new town with a baby in tow." She gives me a sympathetic smile.

"Oh, um, no it's just me and Enzo."

"Oh…I'm sorry. Well, that's a shame. So you and Enzo's dad divorced? Long distance will be *so* tough on a little one."

"No, we never married. His dad actually isn't in the picture."

A woman to my left gasps as the one across from me frowns. "Wow. So, did you have him in-vitro?"

"Hannah!"

"What? I'm just curious."

"Um, no, I had him the natural way with my ex."

So much for feeling anxiety free. The other women eye me surreptitiously as they sip their coffees. Melissa puts down a fruit tray on the coffee table and the ladies dig in like a flock of vultures on a fresh kill.

"Did y'all hear about Stephie?"

"No! She's not coming today is she?"

"God, I hope not. Her kids are so awful, am I right?" The five ladies all nod in agreement as Melissa sits down next to me. I feel bad for poor Stephie being talked about behind her back, but I'm grateful they're no longer talking about me. "It took Theresa two cleaning companies to get the grape juice out of her white rug. I lied to her and told her you couldn't see it, but you totally can."

"I mean, who brings grape juice to someone else's house? It's chock full of sugar, and hello? It's *purple* and *stains*!" Hannah shakes her head in wonderment. *Note to self, never ever get Enzo hooked on grape juice. These women are kind of scaring me.*

"Anyway..." Melissa continues, "her twins were asked not to come back to St. Marks."

The lady to my left gasps again. "No!"

"Yes. And apparently her husband Brian is furious with her and called her a horrible mother who poisoned his boys."

"Wow, Brian sounds a bit unfair. I mean it takes both parents..." I look up not realizing I said that out loud as the room grows silent.

"She's one to talk. She doesn't even *have* a husband," the lady down the couch whispers loudly, but I can clearly hear her.

Melissa looks at me strangely and says, "Anyway, Brian said she better get those boys back into St. Marks or—"

"Yoo-hoo! You guys home?"

"Ssh! Ssh! Hey Stephie, we're back here!" Melissa shouts over her shoulder and rolls her eyes to the group.

Enzo totters over to another little girl around his age. She turns to him and pushes him down. He starts to cry so I crawl over to him. "Oh hey, it's okay buddy. She didn't mean to." I try to soothe him even though I clearly saw her push him without provocation, but I'm not about to call out this kid in front of these women.

"Is that Jessie crying?" One of the moms looks over in my direction but doesn't get up to help.

"Ah, no, she's fine. It's just Enzo."

"Jessie is a *boy*!"

The women murmur their disapproval as I silently pray to God to please swallow me up by the thick luxurious cream-colored carpet. I look over at the kid in question. I mean seriously, how the hell am I supposed to know? He's wearing pink and has long hair. Thankfully Stephie enters at this moment distracting the gossipers.

"Hey girls! How's it going?" She squeezes herself on the couch squishing the yoga pants mom over.

"Cute purse, Stephie."

"Oh, don't you love it? Got it at Marshalls! Can you believe it? Who knew they had Marc Jacobs at Marshalls! I take it with me everywhere, such a steal!"

"Probably a knockoff," someone at the end of the couch near me mumbles.

"Where are the twins?" Melissa asks as she hands Stephie a coffee.

She slams it down on the coffee table. "Oh, the boys! I almost forgot!" She leaps up and darts out of the room.

"No, she didn't."

"No freakin' way."

"Seriously guys, we need to ban her from the group."

I look around at the ladies shaking their heads as two five-year-old terrors come running into the house.

"Shoes! Take off your shoes!" Melissa shrieks at the two boys. One sits down and takes his shoe off flinging it toward the couch. He nearly misses one of the moms' heads by an inch. He throws the other shoe at one of the kids, not missing her. The other twin completely ignores Melissa as he dives straight for the fruit platter.

"No! You'll mash it into the carpet!" Hannah yells as she swoops in and picks up the tray. Melissa gratefully grabs it from her and takes it into the kitchen. Enzo watches the whirlwind of twin boys as they wreak havoc on the playroom. I'm beginning to see why the ladies aren't too fond of Stephie and her twins. Completely oblivious, Stephie giggles as she parks herself between two moms on the couch.

"So, did you ladies hear about Julie?"

"No, what?"

"She got a tummy tuck."

"She did not!"

"Yes, she asked me not to tell, so keep it a secret. Her husband got it for her for their anniversary, but I'm telling you, that is going to last a month before she's back to her regular weight. That girl can't turn down a French fry to save her own child."

Stephie, you're one to talk. I pop a grape into my mouth as my eyes nervously dart around the room. Thankfully no one is paying me any attention, which means I did not say that out loud. A toy goes whizzing past my head, thrown by one of the twins…or Jessie who has gotten in on the action. At this point I just want to protect Enzo. I grab him and army-crawl back toward the coffee table shoving a pacifier in his mouth to keep him from fussing.

"Oh, who are you? Are you a newbie?" Stephie perks up as she spies me.

"Uh, yes, hi, I'm Andie." I do a lame little hand wave.

"Nice to meet you, Andie. Aren't you pretty. Do you work?"

"Stephie, don't be rude," yoga pants lady whispers harshly.

"What? I'm just chitchatting."

One of her twin boys comes up to Enzo and pats him on the head and hands him something. I smile distractedly as I return my attention back to Stephie.

"Actually, I'm a photographer. I'm just starting out my business here in Nashville. I photograph weddings, fami—"

"Oh my god, I've *got* to tell you guys about our photographer the other day!" Stephie rudely interrupts. "So sweet Bentley was being a little rascal and sticking his tongue out every time the photographer tried to take a pic. It was the cutest! Anyway, Teddy kept running out of the shot and we were all dying laughing because he wouldn't sit still. But she managed to photoshop him back in, so it looked perfect. *And* she even did the 'aliens coming to take us' illusion in the background. You know, like the dinosaurs everyone is doing these days, but we did aliens. It was so perfect! Highly recommend her. I'll text you all her number." She winks at me as she settles her ample ass back into the cushion.

Jesus Christ, did she even take a breath during that five-minute monologue? I'm no longer feeling sorry for poor Stephie. In fact, I'm kind of hating her in this very moment since she completely took the wind out of my sails. One of the reasons I joined this group was to try and get my photography business off the ground here in Nashville, but in one fell swoop she completely drove that dream-bus right off the cliff. Not like I want to hang out with any of these ladies ever again, but I came here today hoping for some kind of connection...a possible friend, a play buddy for Enzo, and most importantly, some photography jobs.

The ladies chatter about different photographers they've used, because of course everyone raves about *their* photographer. A woman on the couch to my left gasps. I look up to see her pointing to the area of the rug to my left.

"Who did that?"

I look down at the cream carpet in horror. Someone has drawn a picture of a dog peeing on a fire hydrant with red marker.

"Oh my gosh, look!" The same woman points to me. I look down at Enzo and almost throw up in horror. He's gumming on a capped red permanent marker. That must have been what Stephie's little asshole handed him. I was so caught up in Stephie's question I didn't even notice. I quickly take the slobbery marker out of his mouth and chuck it under the coffee table.

"Did your son seriously draw all over my carpet?" Melissa screeches beside me, her hands clenched.

Shit! "What? No! He's only fourteen months, he doesn't even know how to draw."

"He was holding the marker!"

"Because Stephie's son came over and handed it to him."

"Are you accusing *my* precious Bentley?"

"I'm just saying, my baby can't draw and that is clearly a picture of a dog peeing on a fire hydrant!"

"My Bentley would never draw such a vulgar picture. Besides, he knows he's not supposed to play with permanent markers." Stephie narrows her eyes at me as she smiles sweetly. It's seriously disturbing.

"Same with Jessie."

I look over at the twin in question and notice he has red marker all over his traitorous little hands. I gather up my diaper bag and stand up tugging Enzo into my arms.

"Well, clearly it *wasn't* an accident *whoever* did it." Hannah looks around at the group like they're minutes away from solving a serious crime. Thanks for that keen observation, Sherlock Holmes.

"Andie, I think it would be best if you went home." Melissa turns to me, a frozen smile pasted on her flushed face. I can feel tears prick behind my eyes. She quickly walks me to the door. "Good luck with everything. And reach out to us if you need help..." She opens the door.

I turn around on the front step to face her. "I'm so sorry about your carpet, but you have to believ—" Melissa shuts the door in my face. I shakily walk down the front walkway, my ears burning because I just *know* they are talking about me. I drive to the park and push Enzo in a swing, his favorite activity, because even though I had a shitty morning it doesn't mean he has to. And even though those ladies were a pretty crappy bunch, it doesn't mean every mom in Nashville will be.

I observe the other moms at the playground and I so want to run up to them and ask if they need a fellow mom friend. I'm so fucking desperate I'm willing to throw myself down at their feet and tell them how lonely I am, how hard it is to be a single mom in a new town and how fucking crazy-scared I am. But I don't.

The truth is I want to fold. I want to throw everything back in my car and go back to my parents' house. I miss my best friend. I miss knowing everyone in my small town and I miss the judgmental stares, because even though they were disapproving, at least I knew the people who were throwing the stones.

Chapter 2

Cameron

"HEY CAM, I'M so glad we could do this!" My sister Kiki leans over and hugs me before sitting down at the table across from me. "But I must warn you, TJ is coming by in a little bit to join us. I need him to help me pick out some clothes for a super picky client after lunch. You okay with that?"

I quickly type out a text to my business partner. "Of course, you know I like TJ. He's like that weird cousin everyone likes to invite to the Christmas party to stir shit up."

Kiki smiles and snorts, "He totally is. Oh my god, I've had such a morning! Can I just say, I am so freaking happy you live here now?"

I smile at my younger sister and set my phone down. "Yeah? Why's that?"

"Because I love you, and it's nice to just be able to grab lunch or dinner with you whenever we want. I hated it when you lived in San Fran."

"Yeah, I really like Nashville. I'm thinking about opening up a second location here."

I own a string of upscale bars in California, Chicago, and now here in Nashville called The Social Hour. They have been crazy successful, but a lot of work. My business partner Josh and I are in the works of franchising them. My plan is to sell off the California locations and just focus on the Nashville and Chicago bars.

"Really? That's amazing!" Kiki smiles as she peruses the menu. "I'm starving. Okay, okay, I want to hear more about this new location and what's going on with you, but I need to tell you some news first before TJ gets here because he can't keep his big mouth shut." She pauses to take a breath of air and I look up at her expectantly.

"I'm pregnant!" she gushes as she tears into a piece of bread the waitress just dropped off at our table.

"Wow, that's awesome! Congrats, Kiki." I get up from the table and give my sister a hug.

Kiki waves her hand. "Yeah, I know, wasn't exactly planned."

"Does this mean you guys are going to have two under two?"

"Close, but by the time baby number two comes along, Chase will be two and a half, so it won't be too bad. Right?"

I chuckle. "Why are you asking me? I don't have a clue."

"Yeah, so when are you going to settle down and have kids, huh? Chase needs more cousins."

"Chase has plenty of cousins with Brooke's boys and Sarah's twins. I don't need nor do I *want* to throw any more kids into that mix."

"Who's mixing it up with who?" TJ pulls out a chair and unwraps a scarf from around his neck. "Cam, looking as delicious as ever. Hello Kinksadoodle, you look fetching as well." TJ air-kisses Kiki and sits down.

"I was just asking Cam when he's going to settle down and start producing babies."

"Oh my god, you're pregnant again!"

"Wait, what? No! I did not say that!" Kiki slaps her hand down on the table. I smile as I pick up my menu because there's never a dull moment with these two.

"You didn't have to. I just know. Your cheeks are rosy."

"It's cold out."

"You're talking about babies."

"Because I *have* a baby—"

"You're eating bread like Marie Antoinette eats cake," TJ jokes and Kiki quickly throws her roll down on her plate. "Oh good, here's our waitress."

"Hi, welcome, what can I get you to drink?"

"I'd love a bottle of Taittinger, please. We're celebrating!" He snaps his fingers in the air like he's about to do the mariachi dance. The waitress smiles at Cam and winks.

"Congratulations, what are we celebrating?" She places cocktail napkins down next to our waters.

"Oh, just celebrating love. Kiki, will you need a glass?"

"You know I won't," she grumbles as she looks down at her menu. The three of us place our lunch orders. Kiki folds her arms across her chest and sinks back into her chair as she pouts. "I hate you right now."

TJ smiles cheekily at her. "I knew it. Can't get anything past Uncle TJ."

"Please don't call yourself Uncle TJ in the third person. It's creepy. Especially when the kids aren't around."

"Well someone needs a Snickers bar." TJ pushes the bread basket toward Kiki. "Here, have some more carbs. You're acting cranky already. When's the due date? Oh I hope it's a girl this time, Chase is a maniac."

"Oh, me too. I'd love a little girl to dress up and…" Kiki looks up at my bored expression. "Anyway, I'm only eight weeks along, so mum's the word, okay?"

TJ pantomimes zipping his lips. "I guess Cam and I will be drinking this delicious champagne alonesies."

"I hate you right now."

"You already said that. Is this how you're going to act for the next seven months? Geez-Louise, if so bring on the bread. So, Cam! How are things with you?"

"Things are good. I was just telling Kiki we're thinking about opening up another location. I'm actually going to call Connor and see if he'll partner with us on it. Think he'd be interested?"

"Totes! Oh my god, Cam, I know he would. So exciting! Can I plan your opening?"

I look over at Kiki who is giggling. "Uh, let's find the location first and then we'll talk."

"I'm thinking glitter, lots of it, an explosion of glit—"

"So, how's Lisa? You didn't bring her to the band's new record release the other weekend," Kiki pipes up cutting TJ off from any more party-planning talk or god forbid, glitter.

I sigh. "Lisa is no longer."

"What? Why?" Kiki whines. "Dang it Cam, I really liked her!"

"She was adorbs. She always gave me fruity Mentos when I'd see her." TJ sadly nods in agreement with Kiki.

I cut my eyes at him. "You want me to stay with Lisa because she gave you fruity Mentos?"

"I mean, is that asking too much?" TJ looks up hopefully.

"Right?" she frowns. "Why does he always do this to us? Especially to the ones I actually like!"

"I don't know. I just wasn't feeling it," I say as the waitress sets my lunch down in front of me and winks. "Thanks."

"That's because you're secretly gay," TJ whispers loudly.

"For the millionth time, I am not gay, TJ."

"It's okay, I'll wait for you."

"Uh, hello?" Kiki says. "You're married to Connor. Have you forgotten about that gorgeous man?"

TJ sighs and rolls his eyes. "I could never forget about him, Kinky. Puhlease, that man pushes all the right buttons. But I did tell Connor before we got married that if Cam decided he's gay, I'd drop him like a hot potato and never look back."

"What?! TJ!" Kiki shoves him playfully, laughing.

"Besides, Cam's my celebrity crush. I'm sure you have one, right?"

"Uh, I'm not a celebrity." I smirk.

Kiki looks over at me and laughs. "Uh yeah, he's called my husband."

TJ fans his face. "He is pretty smokin'. That would be the other guy I would leave Connor for."

"Hands off my man." Kiki giggles as she pinches him.

"Okay, okay." These two are starting to give me a headache. "No one is leaving anyone for each other's husbands *or* for me."

"When did Cam turn into such a fantasy fun-sucker?" TJ mumbles to Kiki.

"Ever since Lisa dumped him, apparently."

My jaw ticks in annoyance. "Lisa did not dump me."

They completely ignore me. "She probably took a selfie with his ding-a-ling and it got zero hits."

"Nope, ugh, no. Too far. I'm not talking about my brother's penis."

I grind my teeth. "Lisa didn't dump me, she wanted to take our relationship to the next level, and I wasn't ready. I'm too busy with The Social Hour and trying to negotiate all these deals. I'm not looking for anything serious right now."

What I don't want to share with these two is that Lisa was pressuring me about marriage and kids. She said her biological clock wasn't just ticking, it was ringing alarm bells. The next thing I know she's showing me wedding dresses and wanting to move into my condo. It was too much, too soon so I ended it. Devastated was an understatement. She showed up on my doorstep crying on several occasions or would drunk text me at all hours of the night. So yeah, I'm definitely not wanting to jump back into a relationship if that's how it's going to end.

"Cameron Forbes, is that you?"

I look up at the brunette who has suddenly materialized at my side. She's an attractive woman wearing a black shift dress and heels. I try to wrack my brain where I've met her before, but I have no idea who this woman is.

I smile at her and stand up. "Hi, how are you?"

She wraps me in a tight hug as TJ and Kiki look on. "Oh my gosh! It's been forever! Still hot as ever." She leans back and smiles at me, winking.

"Uh...yeah. How are you?"

Who are you?

She playfully slaps my chest. "Oh my gosh, silly, you've already asked me that. How are *you*? What are you doing here?"

Okay, someone from my past from California...

"I'm good. I live here now...so..."

Kiki coughs into her hand and TJ snickers. Assholes.

"Oh my gosh, what a kawinky-dink! Me too!" She laughs as she starts to rummage through her purse. "Here, um, let me give you my card...oh dammit, I brought the wrong purse." She grabs the receipt the waitress left for us and scrawls her number on the back.

"I've got to run, but call me! We could...hang out like old times." She winks at me as she taps her manicured fingernail against my chest.

"Sure, okay." I smile uncomfortably back at her, but she doesn't seem to notice.

She stands there with her eyebrows raised waiting for me to say something, hopefully not her name.

"I'll call you." I give her my charming smile and kiss her cheek.

"Okay!" She quickly waves hello to Kiki and TJ and then flits over to her table on the other side of the restaurant where her girlfriends are waiting. She points over to me and I give a halfhearted wave as they all smile and giggle and wave back.

"Who the fuck was that?" Kiki laughs.

"Definitely *not* Lisa," TJ surmises.

"I have no fucking clue." I look down at our receipt as I sink back into my chair and cringe because she only left her number and a heart. I show it to TJ and Kiki who start cracking up.

"Real smooth, Casanova." Kiki smirks. "Real smooth."

Chapter 3

Andie

I PLOP THE laundry basket on the floor next to the couch and flip on the TV. I'm exhausted after running errands with Enzo all morning. I tried to clean up my house while he napped, then I took him and our puppy Darth Vader for a walk before making myself a small dinner.

I flip through channels, but I'm not really seeing anything, my thoughts are elsewhere. I click the TV off and turn on some music instead. I'm feeling restless and I'm not sure why. I pour myself a glass of cheap red wine and head back into the family room and curl up on the corner of my couch.

A lone tear slides down my cheek and I'm surprised by it because I didn't even realize I was that sad. But I am. I'm sad and I'm fucking lonely. I swipe the tear away as I take a large gulp of my wine. Why am I wallowing, what's wrong with me? I have a beautiful baby boy, a roof over my head, a car that runs.

The truth is, I'm exhausted. Beyond exhausted. I'm zombie-walking exhausted. The kind where your head tilts to the side, drool comes out of your mouth, yet you keep on walking because there are brains to be sucked, or whatever zombies do. My brain has definitely been sucked. Enzo is my zombie keeper, and I am a slave to his bidding. He's an easy-going, amazing kid, but he's still a toddler and he's into *everything*. And he thinks he's kin to our puppy Darth Vader. I've caught him twice now trying to drink out of the dog bowl. I should be concerned that he acts more like a dog than a kid, but I'm too tired to be.

I look down at my chipped nail polish from when I had ten minutes to do my nails two weeks ago. I haven't showered in two days, my laundry is overflowing, and my fridge has one container of cold pasta, an apple, and some soon-to-be-expired milk. My bills are due and I'm on my last bottle of cheap wine.

I'm a hot mess and there's no one I can share it with. I mean, sure, I have my parents who are super supportive and great, and I have my best friend Mandy who I can always call up and whine to, but I didn't do myself any favors moving to a big city where I don't know a single soul and have no job prospects.

Well, scratch that, I know my neighbors, the sixty-year-old Millers and Becky, my fourteen-year-old babysitter who lives down the street. Shit that's depressing. I made a mistake moving here. I should have stayed in the sleepy little town I grew up in working at Dr. Shiller's dental office. At least I had insurance and free dental care.

But Mandy's right, if I want to go after my dreams, I have to make something happen. I can't just sit complacently waiting for it to fall into my lap. Pursuing my photography dream isn't the only reason I moved. Let's face the facts here, small towns equal obnoxious amounts of gossip. And when my now-ex-boyfriend Mason up and left me with a baby on my hip, the tongues were wagging faster than the time Edith Frye got caught walking down Main Street in nothing but her skivvies. I take a big swallow of wine and wallow.

Mason, that stupid asshole. How did I get involved with that idiot in the first place? His charming smile and good looks are what drew me in. He wasn't that smart, but he had great hair, a steady job, and he sometimes gave me an orgasm. Small towns don't have a lot of thirty-something eligible men to choose from, and as far as gene-pool selections went, Mason was a total catch.

We dated for six months when I accidentally got pregnant when the condom broke one night. But I don't begrudge condom companies or Mason's extremely superb sperm swimmers because God made us parents to the most adorable, love of my life, Enzo. Unfortunately, Enzo was a deal breaker for Mason. He decided he'd had enough. He was bored...restless...the baby cried too much, too many diapers, formula was too expensive. The complaints were never ending.

He was going to join the rodeo circuit and become a bull-riding star. I'd never even seen him on a horse much less a bull, but apparently one night he went to a neighboring town's country bar, Thorns and Roses, and rode a mechanical bull. He managed to stay on for *eight* seconds.

Whoopdee-fucking-doo.

He said he caught the rodeo bug. I rolled my eyes thinking he was an even bigger dipshit than I originally thought, until the next evening when I came home from Mandy's and there was a hundred bucks on top of an *I'm sorry* note. I'm sorry his nuts didn't turn black, shrivel up and fall off, but I've quickly learned we don't always get what we wish for.

His note said he didn't want a woman or a kid to hold him down because he had to pursue his dream, so he left. He just fucking left me hanging with everything. After being the talk of the town for four months—gossip ranging from, "Oh did you hear about poor Anderson Leighton Daniels? Bless her heart, leaving her all alone with a new baby," to "Andie Daniels, she must have been cheating on him, she deserved it," and everything in between. I just couldn't take it anymore and decided I needed a change. A fresh new city to get my photography career going.

I loved Alabama, but I wasn't flourishing there and I needed to do something so that Enzo would grow up being proud of me. I tearfully said goodbye to Mandy and my parents, packed up Enzo and Darth Vader, and drove out of Inkdale, Alabama and made the two-and-a-half-hour drive to Nashville to start over. That was six months ago, and eighteen therapy sessions.

I take another gulp of wine as I cry, curling myself around a throw pillow. I'd be kidding myself if I said I had zero feelings for Enzo's baby daddy. Even though I'd like to run Mason over with my car, I have to admit at one point I was in love with him. Too bad Mason didn't feel the same about us. I wipe away the damp on my cheek. I deserve better than him. *Enzo* deserves a better dad than him.

I get up to pour myself another glass of wine, but instead decide to just bring the whole bottle back to the couch and drink straight from it. Lauv's "Fuck, I'm Lonely" starts to play and the lyrics sting. I *am* so fucking lonely. It's just me and my little man against the world. Who the hell is going to want to date me? I don't have a career, I'm single barely making ends meet, and I have a kid. *Hot ticket right here!* No single guy is going to look at me and say *yes*, I just won the lottery with this one!

The song continues and I cry harder because even though Lauv is lonely, at least he has someone to ask to come over. I don't even have that! I will myself to silently bawl because I can't wake Enzo up in the state I'm in, but it's too hard so I muffle my face with my pillow. And I ugly cry like Enzo does when he doesn't get his way. I scream into my pillow because life is fucking unfair and it's freaking hard. I wail, because my heart is broken over the fact that I'm twenty-nine, alone, and I'm scared shitless. I cry until I can't cry anymore and I'm left spent and hiccupping. Vader's cold nose nudges my hand. I pet his silky fur and he jumps up on the couch next to me.

"At least I have you, Darth Vader." I sniffle as I stroke his fur. "You won't leave me, will you buddy? You don't care that I have zero dollars in my bank account and I have a kid. You love that kid almost as much as I do." I lift my t-shirt up and wipe my snotty nose on it. "Men suck, Vader."

My phone buzzes on the table next to me. I gingerly pick it up as my swollen eyes try to read the incoming text on my phone.

Mandy: *How do you get vomit out of Berber carpet?*

I swipe the tears off my cheek, missing my best friend so

much.

> **Me:** *Oh no, which dog vomited?*
>
> **Mandy:** *Not dogs. Kid. Everyone has the stomach flu except for me. I think Deacon is being the biggest baby of them all. Nothing like taking care of a thirty-two-year-old man baby. I just Lysoled his face. He's not happy.*
>
> **Me:** *I'm coming home to help you.*
>
> **Mandy:** *Don't you dare! Besides, you don't want Enzo getting this. It's nasty. You stay right where you are.*
>
> **Me:** *I think I made a mistake.*

My phone immediately starts buzzing. I answer it hesitantly, not really wanting a reprimand from her, but my need for a human connection trumps the wrath of Mandy.

"Hi." I sigh miserably.

"What's wrong? You're crying. What happened?" she asks sharply.

"Nothing, just feeling sorry for myself. I miss you, and Mama and Daddy. I think I made a mistake moving away."

"No, you didn't. Now you listen to me, Anderson Leighton Daniels. You got out of this crappy little small town to start over and pursue your dreams. You need to find a job. It might not be the one of your dreams, but it's a job and it will support you and that sweet little booger godson of mine, so you are going to put your big-girl panties on and look online and find something."

"But—"

"Now I miss you too, but that doesn't mean I want you back here. I need you there so that I have a place to get away from Deacon and the kids. I *need* to get away like nobody's business. I will come visit as soon as this godawful flu gets exorcised from the house. I'm bringing my cowboy boots, and I'm going to squeeze this sexy plus-size girl into my favorite tight-ass jeans and we are going to go out and listen to music and shake our booties. Okay?"

"Okay." I smile as I sniff. The picture of Mandy letting loose makes me laugh, because she is hell on wheels when she does.

Mandy's voice softens. "Andie, I know it's scary, but you're the strongest person I know. You can do this and you *will* do this. I believe in you. Now tell me what you've done to get your photography going."

"Nothing, I haven't had time. I've been so worried about getting a job that I—"

"Okay, well one thing at a time. Did you apply to that office job you were telling me about?"

I sniffle. "Yeah, I applied, but I haven't heard back yet."

"There's my girl! You will. Now you need to get on those mommy groups you were telling me about and sell yourself, girl! You're an amazing photographer."

"Those moms I met didn't think so."

"Puhlease. Those wannabe tiger moms wouldn't know their lattes from their assholes."

"Mary Kate doesn't think so."

"Pfft, Mary Kate is a twat. We don't care what she thinks. She's still jealous you beat her out of the homecoming queen crown…and because Mason chose you over her."

"I almost wish he had chosen her," I sigh defeatedly. "But then I wouldn't have Enzo."

"Your happy-ever-after is out there, Andie, you just have

to find it."

"I don't believe in happy-ever-afters."

Mandy sighs, "Do I need to get out our life aspiration posters we made in ninth grade?"

I laugh thinking about the posters we made in art class about where we want to be in ten years. Mandy's had Eminem quotes, pictures of dogs and Deacon. Mine had pictures of photography equipment, inspirational quotes, and landscapes of Italy. "You still have those?"

"Hell yes! Things happen for a reason. Whether it's good things or bad things, we choose how we react to them and we have to live with those choices. Mason was definitely a shit-head bad choice, and let's be honest, we never saw the rodeo thing coming, but you have a beautiful baby boy and you chose to start over in a new city. You did it girl! You got out of this one-horse town...don't give up now. You've come so far. *'Look, if you had one shot, or one opportunity. To seize everything you ever wanted in one moment. Would you capture it or just let it slip?'*"

"Did you just quote Eminem?"

"Yeah, it's right here on my poster. Ooh, this is a good one too. *'You don't get another chance, life is no Nintendo game.'* God he's brilliant."

I snort. "That was on your ninth grade life aspiration poster?"

"Yeah, I can't believe Mr. Perkins gave me a C on this. What the hell, you got an A?"

"I can't believe you kept my poster. Mr. Perkins liked me."

"Yeah, he liked looking at your ass."

"Eew Mandy, he was like eighty years old!"

"More like forty-five...hold on Andie...What?! Stop yelling, I can't understand you. Andie, hold on, Deacon's being dramatic *again*. You got what in your hair? Oh no, I've gotta go. Oh Jesus, oh lordy...Michael just puked on Deacon. Deacon, *calm the fuck down*, you're going to wake Everett!" she screams into the phone making my eardrum burst. "Ugh, that's pretty gross." She makes a hideous puking noise. "I think I'm gonna puke. Oh Mikey, don't cry, Daddy didn't mean it. Call me tomorrow, Andie!"

Before I can utter a word, the line disconnects. "Bluebird" by Miranda Lambert starts to play and I sit and listen to the lyrics. Miranda and Mandy are right, I've still got a wildcard up my sleeve. Things happen for a reason, but nothing can happen if you're complacent.

I look down at my phone and find the *Let's Meet* app and tap open my profile. I take another swig of wine and search local mommy groups in the Nashville area. I'm not going to let that first group stop me, I am taking back the reins on this shitshow called Life. I haven't had time to do this before, but I need to make the time and make connections. I can't give up now.

I take another chug of wine. Oh, there's a running with babies group. I ask to join that one, and there's a mommy and me. *Click*. Single hot moms, yup, I'm single, I'm hot...kind of, maybe? Lukewarm-ish, for sure. Huh, this one looks interesting, something about foodies. *Click*.

Satisfied that I've done all I can do, I let Darth Vader out to go potty and then shuffle into my bedroom, brush my teeth, and pass out fully clothed on top of my covers.

30

THE NEXT MORNING I wake up with a hangover of monumental proportions and a cranky Enzo. Nothing is worse than being hungover, eyes swollen from crying your heart out and having to take care of a toddler. I shuffle to the kitchen as I try to soothe an irritable teething baby. I reach down and grab a teether out of the freezer. Enzo gums it and then drops it on the floor. Vader trots over and sniffs the frozen plastic chew.

"No, Vader!" I bend down and swipe the teether before he can grab it. I stand back up and sway. Whoa. I need some coffee, some Tylenol, and a nap. My phone dings on the kitchen table. I reach over and pick it up. Holy crap, I have twenty notifications from my *Let's Meet* app. I put Enzo in his highchair and scatter some Cheerios in front of him. I tap open the app and my eyebrows go into my hairline.

Hi! This is Jennifer! Welcome to Super Moms! We can't wait to get to know you! What's your superpower?! Mine is changing a diaper in ten seconds! I timed myself. We're only two members strong right now, but the force is getting stronger! Let me know when you sign up for your first meetup with our group and I'll keep a lookout for you! It takes superpowers to raise your little, so may the force be with you!

She sounds very enthusiastic...she definitely likes her exclamation points. Weird, I don't remember signing up with Super Moms...I read the next message.

Hi, this is Paul. Welcome to Vriendly Vegans. Thank you for volunteering to host your first meetup at your house next Tuesday. You already have twenty coming! I'll help out and bring vegan mushroom tofu lemon balls. Vriendly Vegans can't wait!

Wait, what? Twenty people! When the hell did I volunteer for that? I'm not even Vegan!

Hi this is Cynthia from Hot Mamas. Please fill out this questionnaire for us to accept you in our exclusive meetup group. 1: What dress size are you? (For Hot Mamas t-shirts of course) 2: Do you enjoy shopping? If so, where? 3: Do you like sports? If so, which? We have an intense tennis group! 4: Is your child potty trained? (our group is so big we have divisions) 5: Please attach a recent photo if you consider yourself a hot mama.

Uh, pass.

Hi, this is Tom. Thanks for joining Single Moms and Dads. I've looked up your profile on social media, but we'll have to meet in person first so that we can chat and get to know our applicants. We can meet at my house tomorrow night if you so desire…a mixer of sorts of just you and me. My address is below. Can't wait to meet you in person, Anderson.

Eew, eew, eew…I do *not* desire. What the hell is wrong with these people?

Hi this is Denise from Running Mamas. Come out and

run with us anytime! I've already accepted you into the group so you can see the calendar of when we will run next. We have all levels of runners. Hope to see you soon! Cheers.

Finally, a normal one. I quickly peruse the notifications from Heels and Wheels, Doughnuts and Babies, Educational Mamas, Working Mamas, Single Mamas and Papas, Lonely Hearts Club, Singles and Mingles, ugh…the list goes on. I join one more normal-sounding local moms' group but delete the rest. Note to self, never sign up for a meetup group while drunk and lonely.

I check my other emails and see a response to my inquiry about the office manager job. Finally, some good news! I have an interview tomorrow afternoon at four. I excitedly twirl Enzo around the kitchen and his eyes light up with delight. He squeals and Vader starts jumping around my legs barking in excitement. Enzo fists a handful of my hair and yells, but I don't mind, because it feels like things are finally going in the right direction.

Chapter 4

Andie

"OKAY MRS. MILLER, are you sure you're okay to watch him? It should only be for like an hour, two max if traffic is insane. The puppy should be fine. He's in his crate, but if I'm not back in two hours can you let him out in the backyard?"

"Honey, it's fine. He'll be fine." My sweet sixty-year-old neighbor gingerly takes Enzo from my arms. I hand her his diaper bag and wipe my sweaty palms on my slacks.

"I'm so sorry again. My babysitter has become so unreliable lately. But I really need this job, so you're doing me a huge favor. Oh! I forgot, the pediatrician, vet, and poison control numbers are written on the fridge—"

"Ssh, ssh. It's alright, honey. We'll be fine. You better get going before he wakes up."

"Oh, okay, okay, you're right. Thank you again!"

I scurry down my front steps and get into my car. I can't believe Becky canceled on me *again*. She said her mom changed her mind and wanted her to study instead of babysit, but I know she's probably going to hang out with her friends. I was a teenager once. It's so damn hard to find babysitters these days. No one wants to work for ten dollars an hour. They want fifteen to twenty. Who can afford that?

I check my reflection before I pull away from the curb. At least my makeup isn't smudged and my hair is still pretty tame. I check the address one more time and put it into my phone. I can't believe I left a sleeping Enzo with Mrs. Miller, but I was desperate. She's never watched him before. She has three grandkids, so at least I know she has some experience. Right? Oh Jesus, maybe I should call her just to go over everything again.

No Andie, he'll be fine. Babies are pliable at that age. If she drops him, he'll be okay. I mean she wouldn't let him put things in the electrical sockets and walk away, right? *Right?* If she accidentally shakes him...I start to sweat. Maybe I should text her a link on shaking babies. No, just calm the fuck down. Fourteen-year-old Becky watches him. Becky who has braces and an iPhone glued to her eyeball all the time. She got chewing gum stuck in his hair the last time she watched him and the time before that I walked in to find her doing TikTok videos while Enzo was on the floor chewing on one of Vader's dog bones. Mrs. Miller will not drop him or shake him, and I can't see her doing some cheer routine to Lizzo. She's a grandma for fuck's sake.

What really has me on edge causing a multitude of insecurities is this job interview. I need this job as if my life depends on it, because let's face it, it does. My savings are depleted. I need to pay rent on my house, bills are piling up, I need to put gas in the car, buy some sufficient food besides mac and cheese, and find an infant daycare to help with Enzo. Oh, and I can't forget Darth Vader, the puppy Mandy begged me to take when her foster dog surprisingly gave birth to four puppies one afternoon. He needs food too. If it were just me, I could survive on crackers and peanut butter, but as it stands, I have two other mouths to feed.

I'm in my current predicament because of Mason. Just thinking about him makes me want to punch the steering wheel. My parents have been helping me out, but things are tight for them since my dad retired and my mom is only working part-time at the preschool. I've been making ends meet by cleaning the Millers' house, but they're an older couple who live alone with no pets. They don't need me every week, and to be honest it's not something I enjoy doing. I can barely keep my own place clean.

I saw this job posted online and I immediately called. Office manager for a busy stylist? If I could manage Dr. Shiller's dentistry practice for the town of Inkdale, I can easily handle a stylist. And it's right in the heart of Nashville, so a short drive from my house.

I PULL INTO a small parking lot next to a brick building that houses a bar called The Social Hour. Huh, did I get the address wrong? I double-check my email and sure enough, this is the address. I grab my purse, my coffee, and lock my car. I take a deep breath and check my silk blouse to make sure Enzo didn't leave any spit-up or gooey marks on it. I roll my shoulders back and pull open the front door. I walk down a concrete hallway with brick walls and see an elevator to my left and the glass doors to the bar on my right. I decide to check with the bar first before going up into an elevator to what could be someone's private apartment.

I enter the cool dark entryway and take in the bar. It's beautiful and fancy if industrial can be fancy. It's like modern industrial-chic. Is that even a thing? It should be, because this place is amazing.

It's small, but cozy with polished concrete floors and exposed brick walls. Behind the shiny bar is a wall of glass door coolers that hold every beer and wine imaginable. The Social Hour is spelled out in metal script across the back wall. To the side of the bar is a door leading to outside stairs and a patio. Wood beams across the ceiling hold steel light fixtures that cast an amber glow. My heels click on the concrete floor as I look around for someone to help me. I tuck my clutch under my arm and timidly step toward the glossy mahogany bar.

"Hello?"

"We're closed!" a man's voice bellows from one of the back rooms.

"Oh um, I know. I'm here for the interview?"

I hear a cuss word before a door slams making me jump. This is not what I was expecting. At all. I'm about to turn around and run the hell out of here as fast as I can in four-inch heels when a tall well-built man walks from the back hallway wiping his hands on a dish towel. He's wearing nice dress slacks, a white button-down with the sleeves rolled up and his shirt unbuttoned where his tie should be. His skin holds a deep golden tan like he just went on a beach vacation—somewhere exotic and expensive, because this guy looks like he doesn't settle for anything less.

He looks up at me and I'm speechless. The dim lights in the bar cast shadows over his eyes, so I can't read them, but his sinful mouth tilts down in a frown as he stares at me. His sharp jaw juts out a little as he sets his hands on his hips in a casual stance that's anything but casual. His dark chocolate-brown hair looks mussed as if he'd been tugging at it. He glances at an expensive-looking watch on his wrist before returning his attention to me.

"Can I help you?" He throws the dish rag on the bar.

My coffee tumbler slides out of my hand and crashes to the ground splattering all over my pants and shoes. I snap out of the trance he's put me under as I quickly regain my wits. *Shit, shit, shit.* I lunge for the cocktail napkins sitting on the bar top and throw them over the coffee pooling around the cup.

"Oh my god, I'm so sorry, I don't know what happened. It just slipped."

He crouches down next to me and hands me the dishrag. I look up into his eyes, completely mesmerized by their color. They are a light gray, the color of fog, and my knees weaken. "Use this, not the expensive monogrammed cocktail napkins." His voice has me drowning in its smooth deep baritone. It's husky, but rich. I could roll around in his voice…like rolling on cool silky sheets. Mmm, I could do a whole lot with this guy on silk sheets. I swallow past the lump in my throat, past the gut reaction to run to him. I steel myself against the sudden need to run my fingers over his expansive chest, down his well-defined forearms. I've never had such a visceral attraction to a man before. It was never like this with my idiotic ex.

"I'm so sorry..." I stuff the napkins inside the tumbler and wipe up the remaining coffee, standing back up.

"Listen, we're closed. So..." He takes the dish rag from me, throwing it behind the bar. He folds his arms over his chest in a show of impatience as he stares me down. I open my mouth to try and speak but it's like my vocal cords have suddenly been severed. I try again and fail. He arches an eyebrow. Jesus he's intimidating and sexy as hell.

"I, uh...I'm here for an interview?" I finally manage to rasp out.

"Are you asking me or telling me?" The left side of his lip curls up just the slightest. "Hopefully you're not applying for a waitressing job," he mutters sarcastically.

Jesus Andie, get a hold of yourself. He's just a man. A man you have no business ogling over. You're here for a J.O.B.

I clear my throat and try again, my voice coming out stronger and more resolute. "I'm here for an interview."

Deliciousness standing in front of me sighs and looks to the ceiling, his annoyance clearly written across his face. "So you've said. I'm not hiring."

I quickly look around the bar. "But you said to meet you here at four PM." I try and gather myself together, willing myself to not start crying as I think about the whole afternoon I wasted trying to get everything set for this interview. *Think, Andie.* The email did say four, right? I thought it was office manager for a stylist, but maybe it's for the bar?

"I'm so confused. You need a manager right?"

"Look ma'am, I'm not sure who you talked to, but I'm not hiring. I've got a lot to do before we open tonight so..."

My nose starts to smart as a lone tear escapes down my cheek. "Uh, okay," I squeak out as I quickly swipe it away before he can see it. What a fucking disaster.

I turn toward the door so he can't see my pathetic state, but I can't seem to move my legs. How am I going to pay next month's rent? How am I going to pay for milk and dog food? I need this job so badly. My whole world feels like it's about to crash down on me.

I hear him sigh. "Look, I'm kind of in the middle of something. I'm missing half a shipment of champagne for a big party tonight, and I really don't have time for this...so I'm going to have to ask you to leave...now," he says curtly as he starts forward.

He probably thinks I'm some crazy dingbat who's decided to pop a squat in his bar, but I don't really care because I can't seem to make my feet move. I quickly swipe my cheeks again of any stray tears before turning back toward him. I lift my chin in defiance as he steps into my space and gently cups my elbow, propelling me toward the door. I look down at his hand on my arm. Now under normal circumstances I would fling this guy's hand off and knee him in the balls for manhandling me.

But these aren't normal circumstances.

It's like I'm frozen in my body where I can hear everything happening around me, but I can't move or talk. His touch makes me want to turn into him and purr. He smells like delicious expensive cologne. Not overly strong, but just the right amount that makes me want to lick him like a rich chocolate dessert. I'm a hundred percent positive he'd call the cops if I did that.

He opens the glass door and gently pushes me forward. He gives me one last look before he walks back into the bar shaking his head. As the door slowly closes, I hear him mutter, "I needed that like a fucking hole in the head today."

I should be horrified by my reaction to him, and the way I presented myself in there, but I can't get over my instinctual attraction to him, or to the fact that he was kind of a jerk. Here I am, a damsel in distress, and he basically shows no concern or kindness and boots me out of the bar. My cheeks heat with utter embarrassment as I replay the last ten minutes over in my head. I turn around just as the elevator doors in the little lobby open up and another gorgeous man steps off.

Jesus, what is in the water around here? This man has jet-black hair and kind aquamarine eyes. He looks vaguely familiar to me, but I can't quite place where I know him from. He smiles softly at me.

"Can I help ye, Love?" He has the most charming accent and adorable dimpled smile that immediately puts me at ease.

"Um, I don't think so. I came for an interview, but I guess TJ changed his mind. He said he's not hiring." I frown as I point my thumb over my shoulder in the direction of the bar.

The prince in front of me smiles good-naturedly and laughs. "Aye, yer not gonna get a job over there. But if yer lookin' for TJ he's upstairs if you want to try again. Connor." He holds his hand out to me.

I breathe in a deep cleansing breath. Oh, thank god, I haven't totally screwed up my chance for this interview.

"Hi, I'm Andie. Nice to meet you, Connor. Thank you for being so helpful...and kind." I shake his hand and then I check my watch to see how late I am for my shot at a second chance. "I better head on up. Thank you again! Oh, and if you know that guy in there, tell him he needs to ease up on his attitude."

Connor laughs. "Aye, I'll let him know. Don't take it personally. He can be a real ornery arsehole sometimes."

I smile. "I like you, Connor. Cross your fingers I get the job!" I step on the elevator.

"Good luck, Love."

I ride the quick trip up and step off the elevator into a beautiful brick loft. The exposed walls are painted a light blue and the beautiful wood floors gleam with the fading afternoon sunlight. There's a large desk in front of the elevators piled high with magazines and a laptop. Music plays loudly from a room in the back and someone is singing off-pitch and loudly.

A large gray hairy cat jumps off the windowsill, saunters over to me, and meows as he headbutts against my leg.

"Well, hello there. How are you? What is your name?" The cat meows again as I glide my hand along his silky fur.

"I wanna be your love-uh!" A man sashays out of the back room screeching into a pretend microphone. He doesn't see me as he continues to belt out Prince's "I Wanna Be Your Lover." My eyes widen as he tries to do the splits on the hardwood, but can only get about a quarter of the way down. "Ow shit, I think I just pulled something. No wonder you had to take pain pills, Prince. RIP my man." He kisses his two fingers and points them to the ceiling as he thumps his chest two times with his other hand.

Well, this is weird and definitely awkward. The bar downstairs is starting to look a little less daunting as I take in the cute ginger-haired guy slowly trying to get up from his splits position. I start to quietly backtrack toward the elevator hoping I can get back in quietly. I cover my face with my clutch and coffee tumbler hoping he doesn't notice me. I just want to go home, have a glass of wine, and forget this whole afternoon ever happened. There's got to be other jobs out there.

"Aah! You scared the bejeeze juice out of me!"

Shit. I sigh as I lower my pocketbook and coffee, my wish to go unnoticed dashed away.

"Oh, I'm sorry. You probably didn't hear me with the Prince performance going on." I give him a lopsided smile unsure of what to think of this guy. I hold out my hand to him. "I'm Anderson Daniels, Andie for short. I have a four p.m. appointment with TJ?" *God, I hope this isn't TJ.*

He takes my hand and gently shakes it. "Hi Shorts, I'm TJ. I will be conducting your interview today. Love your Southern accent, a little twangy but so charming! Let's go in Sarah's office. She has a comfy couch and chair in there. The girls aren't here at the moment, but you'll meet them eventually." We walk toward the back and TJ turns down the music. "Did you happen to see the splits?"

"Almost as good as Prince."

"Really? Ooh, I like you already." He sits down in the

chair perpendicular to the couch. I sit down on the sectional and look around Sarah's space. She has a large table with mirrors and lights and a hundred different pots of powders and shadows scattered about. There's a black director's chair and several makeup cases. Another station has styling tools neatly lined up in a cart with a cushioned swivel chair like you would see at a hair salon.

TJ crosses his legs and sits up straight. He unfolds a pair of tortoise shell reading glasses from his shirt pocket and clears his throat. "Okay, let's get started. A little Q and A if you will. What's your fave color?"

Um...strange...but, okay...maybe he's easing me into this.

"My favorite color? Purple."

"Me too!" He shimmies in his chair as he scribbles feverishly on his notepad.

"If we asked you to go pick up food instead of calling Uber Eats, would you?"

"Um...you mean get takeout? Sure."

"Ah-mazing," he singsongs under his breath. *This is the weirdest interview I've ever been on.* "If you had to choose between eating completely naked at a restaurant or having diarrhea at a pool party, which would you choose?"

"Excuse me?" My eyes dart around the room as I look for a hidden camera. *Is this for real?*

"Stay with me here, Shorts. There's a method to my madness." He doodles in his notebook as he waits for my answer.

I drum my fingers on my leg. I really need this job. Stay focused, Andie. Maybe this has happened to one of their clients and they need to know I could handle something weird like this. Just answer the questions and then you can say you tried your best, go get Enzo from Mrs. Miller, skip the glass and just guzzle the whole bottle of pinot. "Um…both are pretty bad scenarios…"

"I know, right? But if you had to choose one…"

I shift uncomfortably in my seat. "Uh, if I had to choose, I guess diarrhea in a pool? Eating naked in public is pretty nasty. I mean both are nasty, let me clarify that, but if I had to choose…I'd choose the pool."

"Totes, me too!" He scribbles enthusiastically again. "Say you wanted to come up with new words. If your bestie was totally unsupportive of this, would you A: quit talking to the hater and find a new best friend, B: tell your bestie you're doing the best you can in life and if coming up with new words makes you happy, then dammit that's just the way it's going to be, or C: cry until you can't cry no more."

"Um…what do you mean by new words?" I ask.

"You know like…" He twirls his pencil around in the air as he uncrosses his legs and looks around the room. "Oh! Like you know when people say, that is *so* fetch, what if you came up with the term, that is *so* gogetters. Like for examps, I love your blouse! That is so gogetters, girlfriend!" He quickly writes in his notebook as I mull over the question. I would bet on my only strand of real pearls that he's writing down this new word. He looks up at me and raises his eyebrows.

"Oh…okay…I would say to my bestie, be supportive I'm doing the best I can."

"Exactly! Kiki just doesn't get it," he grumbles.

"Um, TJ? What exactly am I interviewing for again?"

"The office manager position."

"Oh, okay, I just wanted to make sure." I look around the room uncomfortably, deciding this probably isn't the right job for me. I mean TJ is nice and all...odd, but nice. But I was looking for something a little more main-stream...more professional. The gray cat jumps up on the couch and headbutts my arm. I absently pet his head as he climbs into my lap. He's so sweet as he softly starts to knead my leg as TJ finishes scribbling something down. At least the cat is normal, even if he looks like a thirty-pound opossum.

"Say we have a really finicky client. And she's demanding and rude and makes you feel like dirt. How would you handle that?" He looks up and his eyes widen as he sees me petting the purring cat. I immediately stop, afraid I've done something wrong.

"Um, well, as difficult as it would be, I would be kind and professional and try to get her whatever she wants. Clients come first, and you never know what kind of a day someone is having."

TJ stares at me for a beat. "You're like Sarah and Kiki all rolled into one. And I've never seen Oreo climb into someone's lap before. Are you opposed to cats wearing sombreros?" He shakes his head. "Never mind, don't answer that. Okay, last question. What's your stance on fire?"

"I'm not sure I understand the question."

TJ sighs like I'm the biggest idiot in the world, and to be honest, this interview is starting to make me feel like one. I gently scoot the cat off of me and cross my legs.

"You know, like, do you like to start them?"

I scrunch up my nose in confusion. "Erm, no? Unless it's in a firepit, but even then, I don't really trust myself."

"Perfecto." He checks something off on his notebook.

"TJ, I really appreciate your time, but—"

He stands, quickly pulling me off the couch and into a hug, cutting me off before I can take another breath. "I hope you don't mind, I'm a hugger! You're hired, Shorts! You are *so* adorbs! When can you start? Monday?"

"Uh, yes? I think?" He's squeezing me so tight I can't think straight.

"Okay. Get here Monday at ten and we'll fill out paperwork and I'll show you how to do everything. Sound good? Oh, and you can meet Sarah and Kiki then too. You're going to love them!"

He quickly walks me to the elevator and prattles on about Kiki and Sarah and how excited they will be when they meet me. As the doors close, part of me is excited and relieved that I have a job and the other part is wondering what the hell I just got myself into.

Chapter 5

Cameron

"YOU DID WHAT? TJ! We had a whole list of people we were going to interview next week!"

TJ absently looks over his shoulder as he shoves magazines off the new girl's desk into a cardboard box. "Kinky, she's perfect for the job. She answered all my questions exactly like I would have. You're going to love her. *Trust me.*"

Kiki growls and crosses her arms over her chest. "Does she have office experience?"

"Um...I dunno."

Sarah stifles a laugh as Kiki stomps around the room. I shove off the wall from where I was texting the real estate agent in charge of finding my next building. "She can't be that bad, Kiki" I chime in. "At least give her a try and if you don't like her, then find someone else. What's the big deal?"

"Exactly! *Thank you*, Cam. But you're going to love her. Even Oreo is fascinated by her."

"Oh great, so now my cat's deciding who to hire for our

new office manager position." Kiki gives TJ the stink eye. "The big *deal* is that we know nothing about this girl. She could be a total stalker. Have you forgotten that Sarah and I are married to celebrities? Not to mention that a majority of our clients are high-profile. Did she sign a non-disclosure? We can't just hire anyone off the street, TJ. We've tried that, it doesn't end well for us."

TJ chews thoughtfully on the end of a pen. "Um, I forgot about the non-disclosure. But I promise you, I can spot a looney a mile away. Shorts is *not* one of them."

Sarah snorts. "Remember the assistant TJ hired a few months ago when the guys went on tour?"

"Oh god, don't bring that guy up. He was awful," Connor mumbles as he leans back in the chair at the desk TJ is cleaning off.

"Would you say he was really that bad?" TJ's voice squeaks an octave too high.

"TJ, he went to the wrong house, left a ten-thousand-dollar gown on someone's front porch, and then cried and locked himself in our bathroom for four hours when I confronted him about it. Thankfully the dress was returned unharmed."

"He was always crying. It was weird." Sarah grimaces.

"I remember someone else that used to cry a lot," TJ mumbles.

Sarah whizzes a pen at TJ hitting him in the head. "Ow!"

"Or remember Carol?" Connor chuckles.

Everyone groans. "Oh god, don't bring her up."

I look up from my phone smiling. "Who's Carol?"

Kiki folds her arms over her chest. "TJ hired Carol after

Sarah had the twins to help run errands and scheduling. *Miz Human Resources* over there said she was perfect because she was into *Game of Thrones*. She was also into punk rock, which was fine, but she was *fully* invested. She had a spiked mohawk, excessive amounts of nose, eyebrow, lip piercings...you get the picture. She also played punk rock all day and was surly. If you asked her to change the music or do anything that required her to get off her phone, she would give you the middle finger."

"Remember the client we lost because Carol chained herself to the desk with that spiked dog collar she wore? She said she was wearing it because we worked her like a dog. She wasn't exactly the first impression we wanted people to see when they stepped off the elevator." Sarah giggles. "The final straw was when she lit a small fire in the center of the room and tried to burn some of Kiki's dresses. We had to call the police and obviously the fire department."

"You're shitting me. A fire? Why would she do that? And why am I just now finding out about this?" I narrow my eyes at Kiki.

"Apparently, she was an art major and she decided to do a live art exhibit for class. She was protestin' man's social imprisonment of twenty-somethings and the injustice of demanding them to work. Lovely las she was." Connor rolls his eyes.

"It was fine. Look no damages to the floors." Kiki quickly scooches a throw rug over a couple inches with her toe.

"I thought she looked like she was a go-getter. And she had a cool mohawk. She even let me touch it."

"TJ, Carol was crazy." Connor huffs out a laugh.

"Okay, okay, so Carol was…a bit fragile." TJ pretends to look through a magazine before throwing it in the trash. "She was artistic. Those artist types are temperamental."

"She was *mental* alright. She was a psychopath from Satan's lair that destroyed thousands of dollars' worth of merchandise. And she was only with us for four days!" Kiki exclaims incredulously.

"I was scared to bring the babies to the office that week."

"Okay, so maybe Vincent and Carol weren't the best…"

"And Delores the narcoleptic lady who used to soak her dentures at the desk."

"She made the best chocolate chip cookies when she wasn't sleeping…" TJ says wistfully.

"And Laura who would take selfies all day and post them with the hashtag #ImTatumReedsNewGirlfriend."

"She had great taste in men."

"Don't try and butter me up. Kimberly had to put several fires out over that one. And then there was creepy Edward who ate everyone's lunches every day."

TJ flaps his arms in exasperation. "He was hungry!"

Connor snorts and TJ playfully slaps his arm. "Okay, he was annoying, but I promise Shorts will knock your socks off. She even said I dance just like Prince."

Kiki rolls her eyes. "She obviously needs her eyes checked."

"I met her. TJ may be right about this one. I thought she was lovely. Apparently, Cam was an arsehole to her, but she wasn't sobbing after dealing with him, so that's a plus in my book." Connor flips through one of the magazines TJ discarded.

I hold up my hand, my attention now one hundred percent tuned in to this conversation. "Wait a minute, are we talking about that crazy lady who came into the bar yesterday?"

Kiki throws a wadded-up piece of paper at TJ's face. "Oh great, just fucking special, TJ. Crazy lady?"

"I don't know what Cam is talking about."

TJ ignores Kiki's minor tantrum as I think about the crazy woman who stood awkwardly in my bar clutching her purse. I haven't been able to stop thinking about her since she walked into my life yesterday. When I first came out from the storage room and saw her standing there in her jade-green silk blouse and black slacks, looking around nervously, my interest was definitely piqued. She was beautiful. Her honey-blonde hair curled softly down over her shoulders. Her light hazel eyes searched mine like she knew me from a different life. I'd be lying if I said she didn't have any kind of effect on me.

When I stepped into her personal space, the smell of her soft floral perfume made my blood pump faster. I had to get her out of the bar before I did something I would quickly regret. But that interest quickly fizzled when she refused to leave. She just stood there slightly shaking, coffee spilled all over her, looking vulnerable as fuck. It made me uncomfortable. The rational side of my brain wanted to escort her off the premises and lock the doors, while the irrational wanted to drag her down to the floor and make her scream my name.

I mentally shake myself, trying to clear her image out of my head.

"Earth to Cam...hello?"

I look up and everyone is staring at me. "What?"

"I asked you like three times why she was crazy. What did she do?"

I walk over to a chair by the elevator and sit down in it. "I don't know. Clearly, she was confused because she thought I was hiring. But she wouldn't leave when I asked her to. I had to physically walk her out."

"Oh great, we've got a stalker on our hands." Kiki throws her hands up in the air.

"I say we give her a try. I mean it would be kind of mean to hire her and then fire her before she's even started." Sarah shrugs as she works on her laptop on the ledge by the wall of windows.

"What kind of questions did you ask her?" Kiki asks TJ who pretends to ignore her. "Hellooo...Tammy Jean..."

"Ugh, I don't know." He opens the desk drawer and pulls out a paper with scribbled notes and pictures all over it. "Let's see...Her favorite color is purple. She'd rather have diarrhea in a pool than eat out in public naked, and she is totally on board with my creative new words." TJ gives Kiki a pointed look. "Oh, and she would handle a bitchy client with kid gloves. What's not to like?"

"She sounds awesome." Connor cheekily smiles as he flips a page.

TJ bends down and kisses him. "You're awesome."

"*Those* are the interview questions you asked her?" Kiki screeches. "What the fuck TJ, did you really ask her about sharting in the pool? Just because it happened to you—"

"We do *not* need to bring that up!"

I raise my eyebrow. "I think what's more concerning is that she said yes to the job after that interview."

"She must really need the job. I say we give her a try. Kiki, you and I can interview her again on Monday." Sarah smiles from over by the windows.

Great, now I'll have to run into her every day. No, no, no. I don't need that kind of distraction in my life right now. I don't *want* it. "What's her name?"

"Shorts."

I look around the room. "Her name is *Shorts*? What the hell kind of name is that?"

"Oh, sorry, that's what I call her." TJ refers to his notes again. "Her name is Anderson Daniels but she goes by Andie."

Kiki folds her arms over her chest and flings herself into the chair next to mine. "I don't even want to know why you call her Shorts." She sighs. "Well, Sarah is right. She must need this job more than we know to put up with the likes of you, TJ, but I agree with Cam, it worries me that she was totally cool with your interview. We'll see how Monday goes."

My heart starts to race faster at the thought of seeing her again. I'm not happy about it. I can't let distractions like this Shorts woman steer me off course.

Chapter 6

Andie

I WALK DOWN the concrete hallway to the elevator across from the doors of The Social Hour a little before ten on Monday morning. My blood is pumping with nervous energy as I feel uncertain and unprepared for what the day will bring.

I quickly glance over at the doors of the bar, but it's dark in there so I don't have to worry about running into the hot asshole that works there. The elevator ride to the second floor is quick, but the doors are slow to open. I wonder why they don't have stairs, seems like a waste to ride the elevator every time.

I step off, take one look at the man leaning against the desk, and hastily step back into the elevator. Oh my god, oh my god, I think I'm going to start hyperventilating. The elevator doors start to close as I clutch my purse to my chest. A hand prevents the door from closing and I want to reach out and bite it.

"Hey Shorts! Did you forget something?" TJ leans

against the elevator door and folds his arms, blocking me from the man in the main room.

"TJ!" I hiss. "Do you know who that *is*?" I widen my eyes as I lift my chin up.

"Do I know who who is?" he asks loudly. Too damn loud.

"Ssh!" I grab him and pull him into the elevator and jab at the close door button as I flatten myself against the side wall out of the man's view.

"Uh, I'm not sure what's going on, but if you're going to go get coffee, I'll have a venti non-fat mocha whip."

"TJ! Tatum Reed is standing in your office!" I cry out totally exasperated with him. "*The country singer?*"

"Oh, I know, isn't he fabulous? If I didn't have my own gorgeous sexiest man alive...grrr." He reaches over and presses the button and the door starts to creak back open.

Tatum Reed, *People Magazine's* sexiest man alive, mega country superstar is leaning against the desk with his boots crossed at his ankles and his muscular arms folded across his chest with a shit-eating grin on his face. He winks at me and I want to pass out. I quickly wave and press the close door button again.

TJ sighs. "Andie, seriously, I like elevator rides just as much as the next person, but I've got things to do, and if you're not off to get coffee then I'm quickly getting bored."

"TJ, *why* is Tatum Reed leaning against the front desk? Am I dreaming? This has got to be a fucking dream. I need to wake up," I mutter to myself as I pat my cheeks.

TJ takes a deep breath and props his chin on his fist as he leans against the elevator wall. "So I take it you don't know who Kiki and Sarah are."

"Uh, the other two girls that work…" It suddenly dawns on me as I connect the dots. I swallow and turn to TJ, my eyes wide. "Kiki is Kiki Reed? And Sarah is Sarah Ryan?"

TJ nods, his green eyes turning hard. "Is this going to be a problem? Because if it is, you need to tell me now."

I shake my head. "No, no problem, just a little surprised, that's all. Jesus, a dang heads-up would have been nice!" I swat my hand at his arm.

"Ow, you're a scary combo of the two of them. Sweet like Sarah and feisty like Kiki," he mumbles as he rubs his arm. "So listen, I might have told you an eency-weencie little lie when I hired you."

Dread fills my belly as I think of the daycare contract I signed this morning. "What kind of lie?"

"Kiki and Sarah want to do a formal interview with you. Mine was just preliminary. You know, weed out the crazies and all."

I nod. "Um, okay sure, no problem." I smile to reassure him, but now that I know who they are, I'm nervous as hell.

TJ claps and he's back to his happy-go-lucky self. He pushes the open button and I take a deep breath as the elevator door once again opens to Tatum as he bends down to kiss the beautiful brunette standing next to him. She immediately turns to me with a scowl on her face. Oh no, I hope that scowl isn't for me. I paste on a sickly smile and step off the elevator, my knuckles turning white as I clutch my bag.

I reach out my hand to Kiki first. "Hi, I'm Andie, thank you so much for giving me this opportunity." My eyes quickly flit to Tatum and back to Kiki when she doesn't respond.

Tatum nudges Kiki's side and she jumps into action. "Hi Andie, nice to meet you."

"Oh, Andie's here! Hi Andie, it's so nice to meet you!" A beautiful petite blonde comes rushing from the back room. She rushes up to me with a brilliant smile on her face. "Hi, I'm Sarah. Welcome!" Sarah immediately puts all my nerves at ease. She seems sweet and easy-going.

"Hi Andie, I'm Tatum. It's nice to meet you. Hope you can get this place organized and keep these three in line." Tatum extends his hand and winks at me.

Holy shit, Tatum Reed is seriously better looking in person than magazines, and he's wanting to shake my hand. I'm fangirling big time, but I can't let these four see that. I swallow and smile shakily as I clasp his strong hand.

"Nice to meet you, Tatum," I say breathily as I quickly drop my hand and step back.

"Okay, well, let's get her settled." TJ claps his hands before he guides me over to the desk. I put my purse down. "Andie, this is the front office and where you will be, obvi." He quickly steers me to the back of the room. "Back to the right is Kiki's space which often spills out into here, the breakroom, the bathroom, and then Sarah's room is to the left." He whirls me back around as we head back to my desk leaving me feeling dizzy.

"Great, now that you've gotten the tour, let's go grab a coffee and chat." Sarah smiles widely as Kiki kisses Tatum goodbye. The girls grab their coats and purses. TJ grabs his coat as well.

"Um, no, Tammy Jean. You have to stay back and answer the phone."

"What? Kinky, that's so unfair. Why can't Tatum do it?"

"Because I don't work here." He smirks. "Besides, I've got to pick up Chase from our house and take him to his doctor's appointment."

Kiki gives TJ a pointed look which immediately stops his whining.

"Fine. Get me a venti non-fat mocha whip, *por favor.*"

WITHIN FIVE MINUTES of sitting down at the coffee shop the three of us are laughing like old friends. I've been completely transparent with Kiki and Sarah about my personal life. I wasn't planning on telling them everything, but once Kiki warmed up to me a little, everything just spilled out. Enzo, Mason, my life back in Alabama, and why I decided to move to Nashville. I vomited it all out and they were both completely supportive.

"So, Andie, I've got to ask. What were you thinking during TJ's interview?" Sarah smiles and Kiki smirks.

"Oh, um, it was interesting for sure," I hedge, not wanting to throw TJ under the bus. He is the reason I have a job after all. I take a sip of my latte.

Kiki leans forward. "Andie, don't protect him. *Tell us.*"

I giggle and smile at their anxious faces. "Well, I was a little concerned when he asked me about having diarrhea at a pool party."

Kiki groans and Sarah grimaces.

"And then there was something about making up new words? I was kind of confused on that one. Actually, the whole interview confused me. And I was about to say the hell with it all, when he said I was hired." Kiki and Sarah both give me sympathetic smiles. "But to be honest, I accepted the offer because I need my life to start, and I need to pay my bills and start my photography—"

"Wait, you're a photographer?" Sarah asks excitedly.

"Yes...well, I mean I did it part-time back in Alabama. But you can only photograph so many families before you've done the whole town."

"I love photography! I like doing mostly landscape, and it's just a hobby, but maybe we can go out and do a shoot sometime."

"Sure, I'd love that!"

"And maybe you can start taking pictures for the blog and website since Sarah's workload has gotten so heavy."

"Oh, well I wouldn't want to take anything away from Sarah—"

"No! It would be so helpful! I feel so bad I don't have the time."

"That would be a huge opportunity for me, thank you! I'm trying to get my photography up and running."

"Ooh! We should talk to Tatum about hooking her up with photographer Ellen!" Sarah claps excitedly.

"Um, are you referring to Ellen Barr...?"

"Yeah, have you heard of her? She's super nice."

Had I heard of the famous photographer who captures the stars most intimate moments? Uh, yeah! I nod my head enthusiastically, trying not to pee in my pants with excitement.

Kiki smiles broadly. "Cool, I'll talk to Tatum. I think Sarah will agree with me when I say, Andie, you're officially hired! Besides, Oreo never was a bad judge of character." She winks at me, and I start to tear up. Even though I already thought I had the job, meeting these two women this morning has given me a confidence I didn't know I needed. I want to feel useful and wanted, and I want to help them in any way I can.

"Thank you both. This means so much to me and I promise, I won't let you down."

"Okay, but we can't let TJ know he made a good decision. Let's let him sweat this out a little. You okay with that, Andie?"

I shrug feeling kind of bad for TJ, but for some reason I can't describe, I trust these two. "Y'all are the bosses." I smile.

Sarah raises her coffee cup. "Cheers to finding Andie!"

"Cheers!" We smile as we clink our paper cups together.

Chapter 7

Cameron

I SLAM MY cell phone down on the bar and curse the realtor one more time. The building I wanted for our next Social Hour just fell through and now I'm back to square one. The realtor suggested I wait until spring, but the current location is doing so well I'd be foolish not to open another one. I refuse to throw the towel in at this point.

I'm irritable as hell and want to punch something. Maybe I should go by the Title Boxing Club and release some stress. My cell phone rings and I quickly pick it up hoping it's the realtor saying she's made a mistake. But it's not, it's Kiki. I sigh as I answer.

"Hey Kiki, what's up."

"Cam, it's an emergency! Are you downstairs?"

My problems are immediately forgotten. "Yes, what's wrong? I'm on my way up!"

I take our back stairs quickly up to the second floor and barge through the breakroom.

"Kiki!" I bellow. "Sarah! You guys okay?"

"Hey Cam! Thank goodness you're available. I just fed them so they should be good until I get back." Sarah smiles brightly at me as she passes her baby Wyatt over to me.

"Uh, what are you talking about? What am I supposed to do with this?" I hold the baby out from me at arm's length. "Not really a baby guy, Sare."

Sarah gives me a confused look as Kiki rushes by me. "Oh, Cam, thank goodness you're here. The babysitter had an emergency, TJ is who-knows-where, and Andie is out running errands for us. I need you to watch the babies until we get back from the photoshoot. Two hours max, I swear."

What?! "Kiki, no. I can't do this right now."

"Cam, it's an emergency!" she pleads with her puppy-dog eyes.

"So, take them with you!" I look down at Wyatt as he gums his fist, drool hitting the floor.

"Uh Cam, can you support his butt?" Sarah looks at me worriedly over her shoulder as she changes Lexi's diaper. I reach another hand out and put it under his butt, still keeping him suspended away from me in the air.

Kiki looks at me strangely. "Cam, you've held a baby before, why are you being weird? Hold him close to you."

"I'm wearing a silk tie." I eye Wyatt the drool monster dubiously and then look down at my favorite silk Hermès tie.

"Okay, whatever, we don't have time to worry about your clothes. Wrap a trash bag around your neck or something. Here's Chase's favorite snacks and I packed his lunch in the little containers in the fridge. Here's his diaper bag, oh and be careful, he's into everything now that he's mobile." She plunks a large bag down at my feet. "Here, put Wyatt in the playpen with Chase. I'll put a Baby Bjorn on for you." She straps a pink cloth-quilted carrier to my front before I can protest. "Wyatt and Lexi have some baby food and milk in the fridge. Sarah just gave them a bottle but I left instructions to reheat the ones in there.

"Kiki, I'm supposed to meet with the realtor in an hour!"

"Cam, can you please reschedule? We need you! Look, Sarah and I are doing makeup and styling for this pho-toshoot for the band and we're already running late. Please Cam, I'll owe you! Pretty please! Your nephew needs you. *I* need you."

I shake my head in frustration. "Kiki, I don't know the first thing about babies."

"Don't worry, it's a piece of cake. I texted TJ to come and help you. He should be back soon."

I sigh in defeat. "What do I need to do again?"

Relief floods Kiki's features as she gives me a big hug. "Don't worry, they'll probably nap the whole time. Alexis is a dreamboat."

"Whatever. Just hurry back."

Chapter 8

Andie

THE ELEVATOR DOORS slowly slide open and it's total chaos. What the hell is going on? I dump my purse and the dry cleaning on my desk and survey the damage. Toys are scattered everywhere, annoying Barney music is blaring from the speakers, somewhere from a back room a baby is screaming and there's a naked toddler sitting on the floor tearing pages out of a magazine like a wild man. I rush forward and pick up Kiki's son Chase who spits out his pacifier and gives me a gummy smile.

"What on earth is going on, Chase? Alexa, turn off the music!" I shout out.

The room is suddenly blanketed in quiet. A baby screams from Kiki's office followed by something crashing to the ground and a muffled curse. I quickly locate a diaper bag and put a diaper on Chase before he decides to pee on me.

"Dammit who turned off the music?" the hot asshole guy from downstairs grumbles as he steps out of the office. I almost burst out laughing but I keep it in, because the scowl on his face tells me this is not a good time to be smiling.

"Uh, hi." I wear my best poker face as I shift Chase to my hip. "Do you need help?"

"Do I look like I need help?" the hot asshole bites out irritably.

"Uh, yeah, you kinda do." I bite the inside of my cheek to keep the smile from forming. He's got one baby asleep in the pink Baby Bjorn he's wearing and another screaming baby he's tucked under his arm, like a football. He's got something orange splattered all over his white button-down, and something green smeared across his cheek. His hair is standing on end as if he's been yanking on it for days, and yet he looks...incredibly sexy.

I gently place Chase in a baby explore walker and stick his pacifier back in before turning back to the baby-holding hotness currently scowling at me. I reach out and gently extract Wyatt from him. "You can't hold him like that."

"He's colicky, I read on the internet to hold him like a football," he says irritably. "I've got this." He tries to hold on to poor Wyatt.

"Don't be an ass, just let me help you. We'll be a team, in this together." Wyatt screams harder and he relents. "Besides, I don't think he's colicky. He should be past that."

"Jesus that kid has some pipes on him. I don't know how his sister sleeps through it all. And that one"—he points at Chase who looks as innocent as a little lamb—"that one doesn't stop moving or trying to stick his finger in sockets or eating Oreo's cat food. He's a fucking terrorist."

I have to turn my back on him so that he doesn't see the smile I can no longer hide. I hold Wyatt to my chest so that his head can look over my shoulder and gently rub his back as I walk around the room bouncing and soothing him. He settles down within a minute. I turn back around to find the hot asshole studying me, his mouth slightly agape.

"I've been trying to stop his screaming for the last hour. How the hell did you do that?"

"Lucky I guess." I shrug. "He probably could pick up on your stress...and being held like a football caught by a tight end."

"I didn't sign up for this shit. Kiki and Sarah owe me big time," he mutters as he runs his fingers through his hair.

I take him in, in all his baby-holding glory, pink Baby Bjorn and all, and I'm not going to lie...he is fucking delectable. I'm pretty sure my ovaries just screamed out to my fallopian tubes to wake the hell up and get ready because this is the guy that I'm going to have babies with.

Wait, what? No Andie, no more babies. Jesus get a hold of yourself. Just because he's holding the most adorable baby girl on the front of his broad muscular chest, his shirt sleeves rolled up to showcase magnificent muscular forearms that wrap protectively around her, doesn't make him your next baby daddy. *Oh my god, heaven help me.* I tell myself to stop mooning over him and step forward.

"I'm Andie by the way. I know we met the other week, but not officially. This was the job I was interviewing for." I smirk as I hold out my hand for him to shake.

He hesitates a beat before he steps forward and clasps my hand, his scowl still in place. His strong warm hand envelops mine like a hug. His eyes reflect a myriad of emotions. Emotions I can't begin to try and decipher.

"Cameron Forbes," he says gruffly.

We stand there staring at each other, the electricity pulsing between us tangible...potent. I pull my hand out of his before it gets weird. "Are you the house babysitter?" I quirk my lips up into a smile. His eyes linger there for a beat before his frown deepens.

"No, I don't do kids." He scowls.

Aaand just like that my lust for him goes down the toilet. I can't get involved with a guy that doesn't like kids. *Get involved?* What the hell is wrong with my brain? This guy is making me think dangerous thoughts. Thoughts that I don't need in my life right now. Thoughts that got Mary Joe Berger pregnant with twins after she dared Michael Hunter to go skinny dipping with her the summer of our senior year. Sexy and dangerous thoughts. *No ma'am, you're not going there.*

"What do you mean you don't do kids? You're kind of watching three right now."

"Only as a favor to my sister. I have no idea what I'm doing."

"Your sister?"

"Yeah, Kiki's my little sister."

"Oh." How did I not see it before? They look a lot alike. Same dark brown hair, gray eyes and olive skin. Makes sense now that he would be watching her kids.

He scowls at me, so I scowl back. What's up this guy's butt anyway?

The elevator dings open and TJ steps off. "Well hello there Andie, kiddos...Cammy McPhee. No one told me we were having a party!"

"This is not a party," Cam says gruffly as he breaks eye contact with me. "Can you take over, TJ? I've got to get to a meeting."

What am I, chopped liver?

TJ picks Chase up out of the walker and gives him a raspberry on his belly making him squeal with delight. "No can do Camaroo. I need Andie to come help me."

"With what?" Cam flings his arms out. "This is an emergency, TJ!"

"You seem to be doing just fine." I grin.

"Says the girl that wouldn't leave my bar? Just a minute ago you insisted I needed your help."

My mouth drops open as TJ coughs in his hand swallowing a laugh. Wow, this guy is such an asshole! Is he always this rude?

The elevator dings again and Kiki and Sarah step off. "Sorry we're late Cam, oh good you've had help. Everyone survive?"

Cam stalks toward Kiki with a murderous look. "I'm late for my meeting. You're an hour later than you said."

"I know, I'm so sorry. I tried calling you. The photographer was being really picky and made the guys do one shot over and over. It was so annoying and exhausting."

"Well, I couldn't exactly answer my phone with the incessant screaming," he gripes.

"At least you managed to get your tie off."

Cameron actually growls as he runs his hand down his face. "Only because your little demon spawn threw some kind of green crap at it. My favorite tie is in the trash."

"No way my little angel could have done that to Uncle

Cam, could you booger butt?" Kiki swings Chase up onto her hip and kisses his smiling cherubic face.

"Don't let that charming smile and rosy cheeks fool you," Cam grunts as Kiki puts Chase back down to toddle around.

"How are my little monsters?" Sarah coos as she gently takes a sleeping Wyatt from my arms.

"I think Cam had trouble with this one," I whisper.

Sarah giggles. "Yeah, he's like his dad, he's a handful."

"Cam, you look a little...disheveled." Kiki smiles up at him as she unclasps a sleeping Alexis from the baby carrier.

Cam huffs as he takes off the pink quilted carrier. "She was the easy one, although she puts off heat like a furnace. Chase spit up baby food like the chick in *The Exorcist* and they all acted like animals when it came to feeding time. They threw half their food all over the floor." He looks around with disgust.

"Uh, yeah...you have a little something..." TJ points to his face. "Carrots...peas, or is that asparagus?"

Cam stalks off to the bathroom and we all burst out into laughter.

"It's not funny!" he yells from the bathroom which makes us laugh harder.

"I wish you guys could have seen it when I walked in." I giggle.

"Poor Cam, we did leave him with a lot." Sarah tucks Wyatt into the stroller and then takes Alexis from Kiki. "Hate to rush in and leave, but I've got to go pick up Jax from school."

"Andie and I are going to go to The White Dove to pick

up the dress for next week. I want to introduce her to the girls over there."

"Good idea. Thanks for your help, Andie. I'm sure Cam appreciated it."

Ha. I doubt that jerk appreciates anything. "No problem." I smile, keeping my thoughts to myself.

"Come on, Andie, grab your Skittles and let's go." TJ grabs his coat.

I look at him confused. "Uh, I don't have any Skittles."

Kiki sighs and rolls her eyes. "He means your purse. Skittles is *not* happening, Turd Juice!"

TJ loops his arm in mine and whispers, "See what I mean? No one appreciates me. I need new friends, like you."

I giggle because he makes me laugh, but my thoughts quickly wander back to the arrogant asshole who looked so deliciously hot holding a baby.

Chapter 9

Cameron

I EXIT THE bar leaving it in the capable hands of Connor before it starts to fill up. Once the regulars get there and start talking to me, I'll be stuck there until closing. It's been a long day and the last thing I want to do is go out on a date, but I've never canceled on a woman and I'm not about to start now. What I really want to do is enjoy a beer in the peace and quiet of my condo and watch the Niners game.

I pull the collar of my wool overcoat up around my neck. The temperature has dropped drastically throughout the day. I walk down the hallway and swing open the door leading out to the parking lot and practically run Andie over. Why is she standing out here in the freezing cold in a dark dangerous back lot? I look at her thin jacket and frown.

"Something wrong with your car?"

She looks away from me and quickly wipes her cheek. I think she's going to ignore me, but then she speaks. "My car is in the shop. I'm waiting for my Lyft ride."

"Why don't you wait inside? It's freezing out here."

"I don't want to miss it. He's ten minutes late as it is." Her teeth start to chatter and her beautiful lips look bluish in the dim street light. Shit.

"Come on Andie, cancel your ride, I'll drive you home."

"Oh no, I'm fine. I don't want to be a burden." She wipes her splotchy cheeks and I can tell she's been crying.

I sigh and look up at the starless night. I guess the date will have to wait. "You're not a burden, come on." I motion her with my head over to my car. She reluctantly trails behind me as I unlock it and open the door for her. She murmurs thank you as she ducks her head down getting into my car. Something floral wafts from her hair and it makes my pulse quicken. I take a deep breath of icy cold air as I try to bury my innate need to pin this woman to my car and devour her pouty lips.

I definitely don't need to be flirting with her while she's in a vulnerable state. Besides, she works for Kiki, I don't need to go messing that up. A relationship for me at this point in my life needs to be superficial. I can handle one-night stands and friends with benefits, hell I can even wine and dine with the best of them, but forevers, futures, and I-love-yous? Nah, not in my plan right now. And Andie definitely seems like a forevers kind of woman.

I saw the way she looked at me the other week when I was holding the babies, and I'd be lying to myself if my heartstrings didn't tug a little watching her soothe Wyatt as she swayed back and forth. But I need to stick to my plan. Maybe five to ten years from now I can start looking for something more serious.

I slide into my seat and glance over at her. "Ready?"

She sniffs and nods as she looks out her window. "Nice car."

"Thanks…you okay?"

"Yes, I'm sorry. Just going through a lot right now." She takes a tissue out of her purse and dabs under her eyes.

That's a loaded statement that I'm not sure I want to get involved in, but I can't just ignore it either. "Here, put your address in the nav system." I press a few buttons for her to get to the navigation map to help distract her. "Anything I can help you with?"

Her eyes flicker over to mine as her face glows in front of the screen. Her soft honey-blonde curls cascade down her shoulder. I want to pick up a lock, it looks so soft, and rub it against my skin like a total creeper. What the fuck is wrong with me?

She looks at the screen while she taps in her address. "You want to help me out? The crazy lady?"

Shit, did I call her that out loud?

"I'm sorry if I was rude."

She snorts and mumbles as she leans back. "For which time?"

My lips quirk up itching to spread into a full-blown smile. I like her sassiness. I pull out of the parking lot and turn left. "For all the times I was an asshole." I shift the gear as we speed up and her eyes watch my movement.

She folds her arms across her chest and sighs. "Apology accepted."

I give her a quick glance. "Really? You forgive that easily?"

She shrugs and bites her lip. "Generally, no, but you've

saved me from standing out in the icy cold weather and you're giving me a ride in this beautiful warm car." She drums her fingers on the soft leather seat directing my gaze to her thighs. She shrugs one shoulder up. "I'll give you another chance. We do work in the same building after all and you're the brother to my boss."

"Ah, so you're a pacifier."

"Did you really just refer to me as a rubber nipple?"

I swerve the car into the other lane and quickly correct myself. I glance over at her. "What? No! I meant someone that likes to calm people or situations."

She gently pats my thigh causing my quad muscles to automatically tighten under her touch. "I know, I was just messing with you." She smirks.

Her touch induces an electricity that goes straight to my dick. I shift in my seat and look over at her, briefly studying her profile as she texts something on her phone. She's oblivious to the current her hand just sent through my system. Her cheeks are no longer splotchy but a beautiful golden rose. Her eyelashes long, her cute little nose that has a slight little bump, her lips full and luscious. She's gorgeous and I suddenly can't breathe, her light floral scent enveloping me in our confined space. I want to pull her into my lap and kiss away whatever worries were making her cry earlier. I want to run my fingers up her silky thighs and…

I quickly dash those absurd thoughts out of my head. *Don't complicate your life, Forbes.*

"So how long have you lived in Nashville?"

She looks up from her phone and tucks it back into her purse. "Oh, about four months. I'm a transplant." She smiles weakly at me.

"Me too. Where are you from?"

"Have you ever heard of the movie *Fried Green Toma-toes*? The Whistle Stop Café?"

"Uh, vaguely..."

"Well, I live in a small town not even listed on a map about thirty minutes from that town. The book was based off of the Whistle Stop Café and that's their claim to fame. Small-town Alabama."

I nod my head. "Never been."

"You're not missing much. Where are you from?"

"San Francisco. Big-city California."

"Never been." She smiles. "What made you move here?"

"I opened The Social Hour here last year. My business partner and I are working on franchising the business. But lately I've been thinking about selling off my half of the California locations to him and just run Nashville and Chicago locations. But it's become a little more complicated than that."

"Sounds like a lot to deal with."

"I'm busy for sure, but I'm lucky I have Connor helping me run the Nashville location and I have an amazing manager running the Chicago location. I rarely have issues with her. I'm trying to open a second location here and convince Connor to partner with me on it. Sorry, I'm rambling and probably boring you to death."

She shifts in her seat toward me and smiles. "No, it's interesting!"

I glance at the navigation system and see that I have a few more minutes until I reach her house. I wish I had hours to spend with her. She's easy to talk to. Kind of crazy, since before tonight just the sight of her put me on edge.

"Connor and TJ seem like an odd combination, don't you think? Connor is so sweet and level-headed. Don't get me wrong, TJ is sweet too, but a little crazy."

"A little?" We both laugh. "I've known TJ a long time. He's been Kiki's best friend for years, and he's stuck by her side through thick and thin. He may be crazy, but he's a good guy. He's actually perfect with Connor. They balance each other."

"Hmm, opposites attract?"

The car suddenly becomes claustrophobic as the energy zings between us. I glance over at her quickly. "Exactly." My voice sounds rough like sandpaper. I wonder if she feels the electricity between us too, or if it's just me.

She takes a deep breath as we pull up in front of her bungalow-style house. It's small, but quaint. "Thank you so much for the ride..." her words trail off as she looks over at the people hanging out on her front porch. "What the heck?"

"Are you expecting company?"

"No..."

"I'll walk you up." I get out of the car before she can protest.

I place my hand on the small of her back as we walk up the stone steps to her wide front porch. People are sitting in her chairs or standing around chatting as they hold covered dishes. "Looks like you're having a potluck party?" I quirk my eyebrow at her.

"I have no clue who these people are. They must have the wrong house," she whispers back.

"Anderson Daniels? Paul Montgomery…thanks for hosting Vriendly Vegans."

"Uh…" Andie stands there with her mouth hanging open. A dog from inside the house starts to bark. I hide my grin as I cough into my hand.

"I um, I…it's nice to meet you Paul, but I think you have this all wrong. I never signed up to host a vegan potluck party."

"Tuesday night. Got it right here on my calendar, see?" He shifts his covered platter to his other hand as he shoves his phone into her face. "Right here, Anderson Daniels. Wait 'til you try my lemon quinoa risotto mushroom balls."

"Yeah, that's my name alright…lemon mushroom…wow that sounds…" The words die on Andie's tongue as she looks at the fifteen other people holding dishes. She gives a strangled little huff. "Do y'all like dogs?"

Andie unlocks the door to the house and lets them in. She turns back to me as I stand there with my hands shoved into my coat.

"Want to come in? Paul's balls apparently are amazing."

I laugh. "Hard to pass up, but I need to get going. Unless you feel uncomfortable with these people in your house?" *Ask me to stay and I will…in a heartbeat.*

Andie shrugs. "I'll be alright." She gives me a lopsided smile. "I mean their name is Vriendly Vegans. How crazy can they be?"

I arch an eyebrow at her which makes her giggle. "I'll pick you up in the morning. What time do you have to be at work?"

"Oh my gosh, no. I couldn't ask that of you. I don't

mind taking a Lyft. I'm sure you have a million other things you could be doing other than chauffeuring me around. Besides, my car should be ready by tomorrow afternoon. One more Lyft ride isn't going to kill me."

"Andie, ssh." I slide my hands up, cupping her face. Her eyes widen as her hands automatically circle my wrists. Her touch sears my skin there and I want to lean in and capture her beautiful full lips that are parted slightly in surprise. "I'm picking you up in the morning. I'll be here at eight."

"Nine," she breathily whispers.

I smile, winning this go-around. "Okay, nine. Have fun tonight. Call me if you need me." I quickly drop my hands and step away from her before I do something stupid. She turns from me and fumbles with taking her key out of the lock, the sound of lively chatter filtering out of the house. She looks at me over her shoulder. "Thanks again, Cam." She pushes open the door and slips inside.

I slowly walk back down the sidewalk and get into my car. I wait until my heartrate settles to a normal beat before I pull away from the curb.

Chapter 10

Andie

I LEAN AGAINST my front door after I slam it closed behind me. Holy hell, what was that? I get my breathing back under control as I peel off my scarf and throw it on the couch. I can hear the Vriendly Vegans chatting away, making themselves comfortable in my kitchen. Vader comes tearing around the corner from the kitchen and jumps on me, but I barely notice because I'm lost in a daze.

Who was that man and what the heck did he do with that asshole alter ego of his? The smell of ocean and woods still invades my nostrils as I try to breathe in and out. It took all my self-control to not keep touching him. Just patting his leg made my fingers itch to explore more hard muscle. I wanted to squeeze those muscular thighs and run my fingers up to his…nope, no…not even going there. I can't go there or I'll lose my sanity.

Vader jumps up again and whines, snapping me out of my fantasy.

"Okay, buddy, I know, so many new people in our

house. Let me text Mrs. Miller and see if she can keep Enzo for a little while longer."

I enter the kitchen and smile at all the strangers milling about chatting and unwrapping their vegan dishes. I let Vader out the back door and turn around to have Paul's balls shoved in my face. To say I'm a little unnerved is an understatement.

"Lemon quinoa risotto mushroom ball? It's my own secret recipe. The key ingredient is ancho and habanero chilis and lots of it. They are very moist." Paul winks at me.

"Erm, uh, I'm okay right now, thanks though." Paul looks deflated so I put on a bright smile. "But I'll be sure to try them before the night is over!"

"Good choice, Andie!" Some boisterous middle-aged lady sidles up next to me. "Paul's balls are spicy! Hi, I'm Helen. Here, try some of my peanut butter pumpkin seed bean dip." She pushes a pita chip with brown pasty gunk on it at me and I automatically take it so I don't look rude. I shove the chip in my mouth and immediately want to gag.

"Mmm, so good," I say around a mouthful of crap.

"Isn't it? I could eat a whole bowl in one sitting. My secret ingredient is pureed tofu and ricotta cheese."

Oh gross, I hate ricotta cheese. "Does everyone's dish have a secret ingredient?"

Mama would swack my behind right now if she were here to witness how rude I'm being. I quickly turn around and grab a bottle of water off the counter. At this point I don't give a shit whose it is, I need to wash this pasty sludge down my throat. I'm pretty positive Vader wouldn't even touch this.

"Woohee, Paul's balls are moist and spice-ee!" some guy with a beard yells out like he's a freaking cockadoodling rooster. I spit water out all over the counter. I quickly apologize to Helen who is still standing next to me as I grab a dish cloth and clean it up.

"Does anyone else here have my sixth-grade humor and find it hilarious that everyone keeps screaming about Paul's moist spicy balls?"

I look over my shoulder and bearded guy, Helen, and two other people give me awkward smiles.

"Guess not," I mutter as I throw the dishrag in the sink. Bearded guy starts talking about a new mountain bike he just purchased as he chews on a piece of broccoli and hummus and I quickly zone out. My thoughts immediately going to Cam.

I thought he was an arrogant asshole before tonight, but in the car I saw another side to him. Strong, devilishly handsome, capable Cam. That's the perfect adjective to describe him—capable. He's capable of bringing me to my knees and making me his. He's also capable of twisting my heart until it bends to his will...and capable of tearing it apart. I sigh deeply as bearded guy talks about gear shifting.

I can't get involved with Cam. Not only is he's Kiki's older brother, but he also works right below me. If it got messy, I'd have to quit my job and I don't have the luxury of doing that. Besides, I really like my job and I love working for Kiki, Sarah, and TJ. But the biggest reason why I can't get involved is Enzo. I have to be careful of who I let into my life now that I have him. His father is already a huge disappointment, I can't let another man let him down.

Besides, Cam made it clear he doesn't want kids, so that settles that.

I tune back in to bearded guy when he asks me a question. "I'm sorry, what?"

"Apparently she's still thinking about Paul's balls," Helen chides.

"I was asking if you like Voracious Vegans better than Vriendly Vegans?"

"Oh, um, yeah, that sounds nice," I say distractedly as I look around the room at the group that seems to have doubled since I let them in a half hour ago.

"Paul, it's settled!" bearded guy screams across the kitchen. Paul looks up mid conversation with a small group. "Andie thinks we should change the name to Voracious Vegans. You're now officially outvoted."

Paul's face turns red as his beady eyes flicker back and forth between me and bearded guy. *Oh shit.*

"No, I...I didn't know we were taking an official vote," I stammer as Paul makes his way over. "Vriendly Vegans is a lovely name."

"No, it's not, it's stupid," bearded guy says snidely.

So is mountain biking, but I'm not an asshole about it!

"Andie, did you really outvote me? You just killed my group name? The group *I* founded?" Paul looks like he's about to cry.

"No, no I mean, Voracious Vegans is catchy, but Vriendly Vegans is...very friendly. Both are great, I just can't choose!" I want to walk outside and scream right now.

"Or we could just call the group Paul's Balls. Andie has been saying that a lot tonight. I think she likes his balls and hasn't even tried one!" Helen chimes in as she winks at me.

Someone fucking kill me now.

"Now is not the time to try and be sassy, Helen," I grumble. She needs to shove her peanut butter bean crap in her damn mouth and pipe it. I feel my cheeks heat as Paul looks over at me. "I did not...I mean, everyone kept saying it, not just me. I'm sure your...balls are wonderful..." You could hear a pin drop in the room of now thirty people as I stammer. "Bless it." I snag a ball off the counter and shove it in my mouth in one bite.

"You get it, girlfriend." Helen's eyes are wide as she passes me a water bottle as I chew.

Paul clears his throat. "Andie, as the leader of *Vriendly Vegans*, I think you need to be a member for more than a few weeks for your vote to count." Paul dismisses me which slightly irks me for some odd reason since I didn't want to be a part of the group to begin with, but I don't give it too much thought because the heat from the habanero chilis start to burn my nose.

"Oh, come on, Paul, don't be a baby about this. No one likes the stupid name," some guy by the back door shouts over the now-quiet chatter.

Holy shit, I feel like I'm about to cry this thing is so fucking spicy. I grab the water bottle Helen handed me and start to chug it, but it doesn't diminish the fire in my mouth. How many goddamn chilis did he use? I start coughing as tears leak out of my eyes, but no one is paying attention to the fact that I'm slowly dying from the pepper that's eating away at the lining of my esophagus. I grab a paper towel because my nose has now turned into a faucet.

"Can someone hand me..."

Paul throws his plate into the trash can. "Fine! Change the goddamn name, see if I care! Voracious Vegans sounds like some kind of rabid dinosaur, but it's *your* group now, Mark. I'm officially stepping down."

Everyone groans and sighs. "Oh, Paul, don't be like that." Several members try to soothe him. "It's just a name."

"Nope, no! I'm *done*! Andie, thanks for hosting and for your *final* vote that killed my heart and soul." Paul picks up his platter of spicy balls.

"Wait, Paul, don't leave!" I wheeze out as I'm barely hanging on to the counter. Shit, how do I fix this? I just ruined this guy's *Let's Meet* group. I grab another paper towel and wipe my nose and down another bottle of water that Helen hands me. "Maybe we can officially take a vote now?" I'm desperately grasping at straws as I look around at everyone. Some people are smiling, some are glaring at me. *Is Paul crying?* "Y'all, I'm not even *vegan!*" I scream in frustration to the whole room.

I'm met with complete silence.

"Awk-ward," Helen says out of the side of her mouth. I glare at her and mouth, *Seriously?*

A throat clears in the silence, and someone giggles in the back by the kitchen.

I clap my hands. "Okay, well this was fun! Thank you everyone for coming! I hope you had a lovely time. Paul, I'm so sorry I ruined your group. Uh, man with the beard, congrats on being the new group leader." I paste on a big smile. "Okaeedoke, y'all, it's time to clear out! I've got to go get my son from the neighbors. I've had a lovely time, let's catch up soon."

Get the hell out, people.

"I'll leave you my dip. You sound like you could use a good cleanse." Some lady named Amy gently pats my arm as she leaves.

"Uh, thanks for hosting." Several people grab their dishes and head out.

Some guy looks back at me as he walks out with several members. "Who joins a vegan group and hosts a party and they're not even vegan?"

"She just *ruined* Paul's life," another lady named Cindy murmurs to Amy as they exit.

A wee bit dramatic don't you think, Cindy?

Paul and his spicy balls are long gone, without a goodbye or even a middle finger. I glare at bearded guy and Helen as they wave goodbye while they hustle out. I look at the mess around my kitchen and sigh. I'm too tired to clean up, but there's dip all over my counter and stupid Helen left her peanut butter crap. I put the bowl on the floor and Vader trots over to it. He takes one lick and then he paws at his mouth and runs into the family room.

"I knew it. That's some sick shit there, Helen."

I pour myself a glass of wine and lean back against the counter. What the hell just happened? I dip a carrot into Amy's cleanse and then think better of it and throw the carrot and dip in the trash. No clue what her secret ingredient is, but if it's a cleanse, I'm scared to even try it.

Note to self, leave the Voracious Vegans group asap, and hide the wine the next time I decide to go on the *Let's Meet* app.

Chapter 11

Cameron

I LOOK DISTRACTEDLY at my watch as the woman across from me drones on and on about her latest real estate find. I'm wondering what Andie is doing and how her vegan party is going. I smile thinking about the look of shock on her face when we pulled up to the group camped out on her porch tonight.

"Funny, right? I mean who puts a velvet ottoman in the middle of the master closet? Everyone would much rather have a valet table," she titters as she takes a sip of her martini. Great, Kendra thinks I'm smiling at her. I try to pull myself back into this date and this conversation, but I'm bored to tears.

"Yeah, that's crazy." I look at my phone.

I have to say as infuriating as Andie has made me, I find her strangely appealing. I'd much rather be watching her eat risotto tofu casserole with a bunch of strangers than listening to Kendra gab about the biggest closet she's ever seen. I sigh deeply as I reach for my beer and take a sip. I try to nonchalantly check the scores of the football game on the TV over by the bar. I'd give anything to be at home on my couch watching the game than sitting here trying to get through this godawful date. I feel Kendra's foot slide up my leg and I freeze.

"Maybe we should take this party back to my place like old times." She winks at me as she glides her finger along her wineglass. Old times...she's delusional. It was one forgettable time. I'd rather poke my eyes out than go anywhere with her. She's a beautiful woman, but there's a reason I couldn't remember her name when I ran into her at lunch with Kiki and TJ last month. She tracked me down through an old mutual friend after I never called her back and left a very lengthy voicemail recapping our whole history together, which was only one date. One date back in San Francisco I had gladly erased from my memory bank.

I agreed to this date because she said she was a realtor and when I mentioned I was looking for another spot for The Social Hour, she said she could help me out. Big fat lie. Fifteen minutes in I discover she doesn't have any contacts in commercial real estate and she just got her residential license a month ago. She's divorced and looking to get back into the game. My game in particular, but I'm not interested in playing.

"Look Kendra, I've got an early meeting in the morning, so I think we should just—"

"Oh! Yes, sure, we can go back to your place. I'm easy like that."

"No. I uh...no." I shake my head in frustration. "I mean I'll need a raincheck. I need to get a good night's sleep..."

"I get what you're hinting. I'd keep you up all night." She winks exaggeratedly at me. "I have to show a house at ten. Squee! Another possible sale!" She claps her hands giddily and I smile uncomfortably. I'm pretty positive Andie would ever say the word "squee." I tell myself to stop comparing Kendra to Andie, but I can't help it.

"Okay, thanks for understanding. Let me just pay the tab and I'll walk you out."

Kendra looks disappointed but nods her head enthusiastically. Thank god I asked her to meet me at the bar and I don't have to take her home, where she'd have undoubtedly asked me in and I'd have to be a dick and tell her straight-up no.

I walk over to the bartender and slip him my card as I watch the game overhead. I pull my phone out to see if Andie has sent an S.O.S text, but no such luck. Hands cover my eyes and I jump in surprise.

"Guess who?" Kendra giggles as she tries to kiss the shell of my ear. I reach up and grab her hands and pull them down. The bartender gives me a sympathetic look as I grimace at him.

"Hey Kendra, just give me a minute, okay?"

She slides her hands around my waist and I cringe. "I missed you. I was so lonely over there all by my wonesome," she pouts in my ear. Nothing grates more on my nerves than baby talk. The bartender quickly puts the slip down in front of me and I scrawl my name on the tab. "Wow, Mr. Forbes, that's quite a powerful signature for such a powerful man. Can I have your autograph?"

Everything that comes out of her mouth rubs me the

wrong way. I feel claustrophobic with her literally breathing down my neck. "Ha, uh, not tonight, Dollface." Women hate it when guys call them dollbaby or dollface. My sisters taught me that.

Kendra simpers next to me. "Oh my god, Cameron, I looove that nickname."

Of course she does. I guess it's time to bring out the big guns and be a dick. "Kendra, look…" My phone starts to buzz. I hold it to my ear and answer it without looking at who's calling, hoping upon all hopes that it's Andie or Kiki.

"Hello!"

"Ugh, you don't have to shout in the phone."

Crap, it's my sister Brooke. Guess anything's better than Kendra at this point.

"Hey Brooke, hold on one second, okay?" I pause for effect. "I know, I know, calm down, I realize it's an emergency, just give me one sec."

"What the fuck Cameron, don't use me to get out of a crappy date with one of your floozy skanks."

"Okay, don't cry, give me just a second, hold on."

"Cameron you're such an as—"

I cover the phone and look sadly at Kendra. "Sorry, Babycakes. I have to take this, it's an emergency. My sister just got dumped and she's bawling her eyes out. I'll call you later."

"Oh! Sure, no problem. Do you want me to talk to her? Maybe I can talk her off the ledge and then we can get back to our date." She tiptoes her fingers up my chest as she giggles.

Jesus, this woman. "No, she needs family right now."

"Oh, okay. I had fun tonight, Cam. Call me okay? Definitely a raincheck." She tries to kiss me on the mouth, but I turn my cheek to her. She blows kisses to me as she walks backward to her car. I sigh in relief and bring the phone back up to my ear when she finally gets into her car.

"Hey Brooke, thanks."

Brooke sighs loudly. "That was disgusting. You should be ashamed of yourself."

"Listen, you have no idea, she was awful. I was letting her down easy."

"Babycakes? So slimy. Seriously, I don't have time for your petty girlfriend problems."

"What do you want, Brooke?"

"As you know, Mom and Dad are coming out for Kiki's baby shower in March and I said to Graham Jesus would want us to go too. Although why she needs a second shower is beyond me. She should donate all her gifts to charity."

"You had two showers," I remind her. "And you kept all your gifts."

She sniffs. "Anyway, I need you to book us rooms at the Omni, a suite for us and a regular room for Mom and Dad. Near ours, but not too near, like maybe the floor below ours."

I sigh as I feel a headache coming on. "I'm not your goddamn travel agent, Brooke. Why can't you just call them in the morning and do it?"

"Cam, I don't have time for details like that. Please just do it. Oh, and make some dinner reservations while we're there too. We're not picky."

I roll my eyes. "Anything else, Princess?"

"You know I hate when you call me that. Gotta run, *ciao*."

Before I can utter another word she's hung up. I look down at my screen and I have four new text messages. My heartrate kicks up a beat when I think it's Andie, but it's not. It's Kendra.

Kendra: Miss you already, call me!

Kendra: I had such a great time tonight! Let's do it again real soon!

Kendra: I'm home, but I'm sad and lonely because you aren't here. Pouty face. Miss you!

Kendra: For your eyes only! ☺

Oh Jesus, she sent me a pic of her boobs. What the hell? I immediately delete her texts and picture and drive home wondering what fresh hell I just landed in.

Chapter 12

Andie

THE KNOCK ON the door makes me jump. I just dropped off Enzo at Mrs. Miller's house since she offered to watch him on the days I don't do daycare. Vader has been walked and fed, and I just got the puppy gate in place. I slip on my coat as I pull the door open. My breath is stolen by the incredibly handsome man filling my doorway.

"Hi," I say a little too breathlessly for my liking.

"Good morning. I brought you a latte. I don't know if you drink—"

"*Big* coffee fan." I grab the coffee and immediately take a drink. "Thanks!" He tries to look over my shoulder into my living room but I quickly step out closing the door behind me. I'm not ready for him to know about Enzo for some reason. It's like he's a secret I need to keep safe and close to my heart. I also don't want Vader to try and hurdle the gate, excited by a stranger and jump up on his nice suit. He arches an eyebrow at me.

"I have a puppy. He's sweet, but a little wild. I wouldn't

want him tackling you."

Speaking of his suit, I take in his charcoal dress pants, button-down, and tie. His wool coat is black and spotless. He looks like he belongs in a boardroom, not on my front porch. His hair is artfully mussed, but clean cut. His jaw freshly shaven, and he smells like leather, Christmas trees and fall all rolled into one. It makes me want to lean into him and nuzzle his neck.

"Ready?"

"Ready when you are."

I smile up at him as I take another drink of my coffee. I can't afford five-dollar lattes, so I wasn't about to turn this one down. I lock the door behind me. "So, do you ever not wear a suit, or were you born wearing one like in *Boss Baby*?"

"*Boss Baby*?"

I chuckle. "Oh, sorry, kids' movie. It's my godson's favorite. In the movie the baby was born wearing a three-piece suit." I smile as I glance over at him secretly wanting to rewind the last thirty seconds and take the foot out of my mouth. "Not that there's anything wrong with wearing a suit, you look damn fine in it, it's just…"

The words die on my lips as he looks up at me over the hood of his car and smirks, his eyes dancing. "Damn fine?"

"Fine. Good. You look just okay. I mean come on you know you look…okay." I shrug my shoulders, my cheeks heating as I fumble with my words.

He arches a sexy eyebrow. "So, I look just okay…"

I huff out a breath and take a sip. "You know you look good, now unlock the doors or else your ego is going to make us late, and whoever shows up last has to clean out the breakroom fridge on Wednesdays, and lordy, you do *not* want to get stuck on that duty."

He stands there smiling at me and I'm not going to lie, it takes my breath away.

"Cam."

"Yeah."

"I'm cold. Can you please unlock the door?"

"Oh shit, sorry," he mumbles as he quickly unlocks the doors by touching the door handle. I slide into the still-warm car, put my drink in the cup holder, and fasten my seat belt. It smells like rich leather, coffee, and Cameron. He slides in next to me and does the same. The engine purrs to life and he smoothly pulls away from the curb.

"Thank you again for driving me home last night and picking me up this morning."

"Do you need a ride to pick up your car?"

"No, thank you. TJ said he could take me, but I appreciate the offer."

"So, I'm dying to know. Are you an official vegan now?"

I cover my face with my hands. "Oh my god, you're not going to believe what happened."

I recap the story of Paul's balls which makes him laugh. It's the richest sound I've ever heard and it makes my blood hum with pleasure. It makes me want to make him laugh all the time.

"It's safe to say Paul and his balls will not be crossing your doorstep again?"

"I'd bet a winning lottery ticket on it." I smile wryly.

"What a travesty for Paul."

"I know! I ruined his life apparently."

He smiles amusingly at me. "That's not what I meant."

"Oh." *Oh!* "Can I ask you something?"

"Shoot."

"Miss Trudy Manners would probably tan my hide for asking you this," I mumble under my breath.

"I'm sorry?"

I take a deep breath and bite the bullet. "Why are you being so nice to me?"

He glances over at me and frowns, his focus returning to the road. "What do you mean?"

I look out the window at the scenery, too chickenshit to face him. "Well, you haven't exactly been Mr. Rogers welcoming me to the neighborhood and all."

He clears his throat. "I'm sorry I was a jerk to you before. That's not normally my nature. You just caught me off guard the first time we met."

"And the second?"

He shakes his head and smiles. "I thought you forgave me."

"And I have! I was just curious. Forget I asked."

"The second time, I was clobbered by three babies by myself for two hours and I'll admit, I lost my shit. And then you came in and just handled everything perfectly and I took my frustration out on you. I'm sorry."

"Fair enough. So…friends now?" My heart thuds heavy in my chest because I want to be more with this guy, hell I need to be more. I haven't had sex in over a year…but I can't. I need to keep my life simple. Mixing things up with Cameron Forbes seems complicated. So, friends will have to do.

His jaw ticks. "Sure, friends," he says gruffly as his phone rings with an incoming call. "I need to get this."

"Please, don't mind me." I smile as I take a sip of coffee and look out the window.

He speaks to the person on the other line and I can't help but listen to his smooth commanding tone. It makes my skin break out in goosebumps. He's speaking to a realtor I think and he's not happy. I glance over at him when he tersely asks her what the holdup is. I watch his jaw flex in irritation and it's hot as hell. He downshifts the Porsche as we turn on the street that leads to The Social Hour.

"I don't care what happened with the last property. This is the one I want, so figure out how I can obtain it. Renting is not an option."

I can hear the woman stutter, "Yes Mr. Forbes, I'll do what I can."

"Make it happen or I'll find someone else who can," he says curtly.

He hangs up on the woman as we pull into our work parking lot.

"Sorry about that, Andie. I didn't want to deal with that right now."

"It's okay. Things not going well with the new location?"

"No."

I glance over at him waiting for more, but he doesn't offer it up.

Suddenly TJ is knocking on his window scaring the shit out of us.

"Morning, Cam!" he yells through the glass.

"You better get out before he breaks my window." Cam

smiles.

"Aren't you coming in?"

"No, I have a meeting across town."

"Oh." He picked me up and dropped me off at work when he has a meeting across town? *Don't let him into your heart, Andie, don't you dare do it.* I swallow. "Cam, you didn't have to pick me up."

He turns to look at me. His eyes searching mine showing a raw vulnerability I've never seen from him before. "I wanted to," he says huskily.

And what do I want? I want to grab him by his tie and slam my lips to his. I want to straddle his lap and run my fingers through his thick chocolate-brown hair and make him beg for more. I lick my lips wanting nothing more than to take that leap as he leans slightly in, his eyes zeroed in on my parted lips. I think I'm panting. Am I panting? Oh god, Andie, don't pant, that makes you look out of shape and desperate. And I know Cam doesn't do out of shape and desperate. He looks like the type that only does Brazilian bikini models with zero percent body fat.

The windows in the car start to steam up probably from all my damn neurotic panting. Heat licks like fire along the fringes of his gray irises causing my blood to pump faster in my veins. Just one tiny little kiss as a thank-you. My heart can handle that, can't it? The electricity between us pulls us a fraction closer. A noise knocks against the window as TJ cups his hands and peers in.

"You okay in there, Cam? Oh, hey Andie! Didn't see you were in there too."

Cam and I spring apart. My heart is thundering in my

chest and I'm not sure if it's from the kiss that almost happened or TJ scaring the hell out of us again. I'm glad he stopped what was about to happen. Cam seems way out of my league in his fancy suits and fancy car. Not that I'm complaining, they are both beautiful, but I'm over here wearing last year's Target sale rack and currently don't have a car. Besides, we agreed to just be friends, I need to stick to that.

I smile shyly at him. "I better get out before he climbs in here with us. Thanks again, Cam. I appreciate it."

Cam rubs his jaw and huffs out a laugh. "No problem, Andie."

I get out and grab my pocketbook from the floorboard. I quickly wave to Cameron one last time as I shut the door. TJ is at my side in a flash as Cameron pulls away.

"Well, well, well. Cameron Forbes? Our little Andie has been a busy little bee. I never would have guessed that one!"

I wave my hand dismissing him. "Oh, pssh, nothing to guess, TJ. He just gave me a ride."

"Gurrl...I'm sure he did. I wanted to ride the Cam express train for years, until I met Connor."

"No...I meant a ride in his car." We get on the elevator and I press the button for the second floor.

"Whatever you want to call it—car, train, bicycle. Was he so amazing? I have no doubt in my mind he is. All that raw sexual power, those muscles," he groans. "Ugh, girl you are *so* lucky."

I look over at TJ with my mouth slightly agape as he prattles on because how on earth did catching a ride with Cam to work turn into a weekend fuckfest in his head? Then again, I don't want to dissect anything running through TJ's head.

"Wait until I tell Kiki about this turn of events." He starts doing the running man as the elevator door slides open.

"TJ, no! There's nothing to tell," I yell at him completely exasperated.

"Why does TJ look like he just won a lifetime supply of glow-in-the-dark lube?" Kiki asks as she stands by my desk sorting mail.

"No reason!" I yell slapping my hand over TJ's mouth.

Kiki quirks an eyebrow up. "Spill it, Turbo Jet."

TJ peels my hand away. "Cam and Andie are sleeping together!" He bounces excitedly on his feet as he happily claps his hands. "They had window steam!"

Goddamn panting.

Kiki's mouth forms an O as her eyes bounce back and forth between TJ and me.

"What?! No! Kiki, *no*, there is nothing going on between your brother and I. Absolutely not!" I cut the air with my hand driving the point home.

"Who's sleeping with whose brother?" Sarah asks as she walks out of the breakroom blowing on a cup of hot tea.

I growl in frustration and throw my pocketbook at TJ.

Kiki laughs. "Apparently TJ thinks Andie and Cam are sleeping together."

"Which is one hundred percent *not* true!"

"That's too bad, Cameron is a cutie patootie and a total catch." Sarah smiles as she takes a sip of her tea.

"And he's Kiki's brother!" I throw my hands up in exasperation. "He's bossy and rude and…just no, it's not going to happen. Sorry, Kiki, for calling your brother those things."

Kiki, TJ, and Sarah share a secret smile. "No worries, he can be bossy and rude."

"Cam gave Andie a ride to work this morning. I could have done window angels on the steamy windows." TJ winks at me like he's doing me a favor, which for the record, he is not.

Kiki and Sarah share another look.

"It's perfect." Kiki smiles.

"Yes! Agree." Sarah beams at me.

"Totes, so perfectly perfect."

"Y'all, stop talking and sharing googly eyes with each other like I'm not standing here!" I stomp my foot in frustration.

"Andie, what are you doing for Thanksgiving?"

"I have plans," I say hastily.

"Will you be here in town?" Sarah asks innocently.

"Listen, I appreciate what y'all are trying to do." I pick up my purse, walk over to my desk and sit down throwing my pocketbook in my bottom drawer. "But Cam and I are not going to happen. He doesn't know about Enzo, and I'm not sure I want him to." I look down at my desk and open my planner, unable to meet their eyes.

"I think it should be known to everyone in this room that I'm a professional matchmaker," TJ says casually as he picks up Oreo and kisses him on the head.

Kiki and Sarah both snort. "Says who?"

"Hello? If it weren't for me, Sarah would never have

gotten together with Lex. And if I hadn't pushed you back together with Tatum, you'd still be here sulking, dragging your broken heart around town."

Sarah and Kiki look at each other incredulously. "Are you *serious*? You weren't even living in Nashville when Tatum and I got back together."

"Yeah, and you were busy trying to make out with Connor during my issues with Lex."

TJ sighs heavily, putting Oreo back down. "The point *is* that I was there for your emotional baggage."

Kiki rolls her eyes. "That has nothing to do with matchmaking."

"Jesus Kiki, since when did you become so detail-oriented? Besides we're here to help Andie, not talk about *your* issues." Kiki throws her hands up in exasperation as Sarah and I giggle. "If anyone needs some penis in their lives it's you, Andie," TJ says solemnly as he takes his coat off.

"Ugh, gross, please don't use the word penis and any reference to my brother in the same sentence." Kiki sits on the corner of my desk.

"Andie, when was the last time you had the pickle in your dill?" TJ whispers loudly. He might as well have screamed it down the street for the way my face heats up.

I shrug and mutter, "A year."

"A year?!" he screeches. "Andie needs some dick with a capital D! Can we all agree on that?"

"Amen, sister." Sarah laughs as she sits on the window bench.

"Andie, just because you're a single mom doesn't mean you can't have fun," Kiki says softly.

"It's not that...it's just that Cam said he doesn't like or want kids, so why introduce him to mine? I'm pretty protective of Enzo and I don't want to get involved with someone who won't like him. Cam doesn't deserve that, Enzo definitely doesn't deserve that, and neither do I," I say resolutely, flipping through the appointment book.

Kiki sighs, "My brother is such an idiot sometimes. Maybe you can just have a little fun with him. Don't get Enzo involved, but get out there and mix it up with Cam. He's probably not looking for anything serious anyway. You need to get back in the dating pool. Use him to get your toes wet."

"Are you seriously pimping your brother out?" I huff out a laugh. Kiki gives me a devilish smile.

"Are you thinking what I'm thinking?" TJ singsongs.

"Nope, no one is thinking anything," I grumble.

"Yep! Operation Dill is in full effect." Kiki smiles triumphantly.

Sarah giggles. "No hair products this time, Kiki."

"Nope, this one is for the greater good." They all smile at me, making me uneasy.

"By the way, I stepped off the elevator first, so you're cleaning out the fridge, Andie."

I groan as I get up and grab a trash bag, but secretly I'm happy to escape their evil scheming.

Chapter 13

Cameron

THANKSGIVING CAME AND went with little fan fair. I spent it with Kiki, Tatum, Lex and Connor's family since I'll be heading out to San Francisco for Christmas. I've been an irritable bear because I still haven't been able to find a second location suitable for The Social Hour. Diana, my real estate agent, showed me an empty parking lot near the airport the other day and I fired her on the spot.

On a more positive note, my partner and I have come to an agreement on how we should split the business. I didn't want to sell him the name and start over from scratch and neither did he. We finally agreed that he would run the California-based bars, I would run the two I have, and we would split the franchising between us. I still own the buildings in California, so I feel like I came out on top. We've also agreed to bring in a third person to maintain branding between all the locations and handling the new franchises. Lots of lawyers, a mountain of paperwork, and a million headaches.

I haven't seen Andie since before Thanksgiving and I've caught myself a half-dozen times thinking up excuses to go upstairs just to catch a glimpse of her. I wondered what she was doing on Thanksgiving, who she was with. I thought about her when we all got together for the Alabama Auburn game at the bar and questioned why she wasn't there. Maybe she isn't a football fan? I don't know.

The truth is, I haven't allowed myself to find out much about Andie. I'm already annoyed that I feel a strong attraction to her and that she's gotten under my skin. That's all it can ever be.

A knock on the glass doors has me looking up from paperwork. Tatum and the rest of the guys in the band stand in front of the elevator. Tatum opens the door and waves. "Hey man, how's it going?"

"It's going. What are you guys doing here?"

"We were headed over to the studio, but Kiki wanted us to come by here first to iron out the details for my birthday party. Still good to have it here?"

"Of course. I'll come up in a minute."

"Cool. See you in a few." He lets the glass door go as he heads into the elevator.

I sign off on one more order and take the paperwork back to my office. I take the back stairs up to the breakroom. I saunter into the main room and see the guys standing around Andie's desk. She's beaming at Matt as he sits on the edge of her desk. He leans into her and whispers into her ear. Her cheeks bloom a beautiful rosy pink as Matt winks at her.

A fire fueled by jealousy I've never felt before ignites in my blood and I want to punch that smirk off of his face.

"What's going on?" I gruffly interrupt the chatter.

Kiki looks up. "Cam! Perfect timing. We were just talking about Tatum's party."

"Oh?" I arch an eyebrow as I size Matt up. I could take him down if I had to.

"We were just trying to figure out where we should set up the band. Any thoughts?" Connor's twin brother Lex asks me as he shoves Matt off the desk. "Get off her desk, you eejit."

I knew I liked Lex. "Probably the front room, don't you think, Connor? To the right of the bar."

Connor nods. "That's what I proposed."

"Good, then that's settled," Kiki says. "Guys, I'll need to finalize the guest list with you. Matt, did you ever get the phone number from that gir—"

"Never mind about that."

"But Matt, you were hounding me—"

"Coffee Girl, *it's cool.* Forget I asked. Besides, Andie here probably needs a date, right?"

I have never wanted to punch someone in the face more than I do in this moment. Andie worriedly looks around the group and her cheeks blush again.

"Oh, ah, I'm not going."

"What? Of course you are." Kiki slams her appointment book closed. "However, she'll be going with Cameron. Sorry, Matt, you will not be ruining Andie's night with your crappy come-ons and one-liners." Kiki winks at me.

"Actually—" Andie tries to interject.

"Crappy come-ons, oh please. Andie, tell me you weren't turned on by my love verbiage." He winks at her and she giggles.

"I mean, it did make me laugh…"

"Love verbiage? Jesus." Lex shakes his head in disgust.

"Which one did he use?" Tatum asks as he strolls in from the breakroom drinking a water and smiling.

Andie smiles up at Matt. "If I could rearrange the alphabet, I'd put 'u' and 'I' together."

Everyone groans except for Matt.

"Oh come on! That was good!"

"This gobshite doesn't even know how to sing the ABCs," Lex huffs out as he dodges Matt's punch and everyone laughs.

"What was that one he used the other night? Baby, if you were words on a page, you'd be fine print." Will says.

"Hey, she liked it and bought me a drink…among other things." Matt grins.

"I'm sure she was a real winner," Kiki deadpans.

"So, let's hear Cameron's pick-up line and we'll let Andie decide?" Matt challenges.

"Yes, I love this idea!" Kiki smiles at Andie who is squirming in her seat from all the attention.

I casually sit down on the edge of her desk and smile. "Andie, would you like to go to Tatum's birthday party with me?"

She smiles back at me as the rosy blush on her cheeks deepens. "Sure."

I wink at her and turn my attention to Matt who has a look of utter disbelief on his face.

"What? That's it? Andie, you're killing me." Matt pretends to look crestfallen.

"I don't need a pick-up line to ask a girl out." Everyone bursts out laughing as I smile at him. I stand back up, fist-bump Lex, and casually stroll out. *Amateur.*

"Cam, wait!"

I turn around on the back steps as Andie stands above me on the landing. The door shuts softly behind her. I look up at her expectantly.

"I…uh, you didn't have to…I mean…oh god, I'm horrible at this," she mutters as she wrings her hands.

I bound back up the steps until I'm standing just below her. I look up into her beautiful hazel eyes. "Yes, Andie?"

She sighs and closes her eyes. "I don't want you to feel like you have to take me with you to the party. Honestly, I'm not even sure I can go. My best friend might be coming into town, so…"

"So…bring her too. I'll pick you both up."

Her eyes pop open and she stares at me. "But…I'm sure there's someone else you'd rather take. I mean I'll probably be taking pictures the whole time anyway if I do go, I won't be much of a date, and then there's Mandy, my best friend. She's a handful, especially when she's had Fireball."

I chuckle as I take in her worried expression. "Well, perhaps we can shelve the Fireball for a night. Andie, there's no one else I'd rather take. To be honest, I'll be having to make sure everything runs smoothly, so feel free to wander the party and take pics."

"Oh, okay."

"Okay." I smile before I turn around and jog down the steps, not leaving her a chance to argue or back out.

What the hell am I doing?

Chapter 14

Andie

"AAH!!!! I'M SO excited to see you! I've missed you!"

I'm pulled into a barrel hug as soon as I open the door. Pure joy pulses through my veins as I hug my best friend who is more like a sister to me. Even though we're not blood related, she's my family.

"Let me look at you! Gosh you're a sight for sore eyes!" She roughly shoves me away from her and eyes me from head to toe. "You've lost weight, you bitch. I swear to god, I look at a marshmallow and I turn into one."

"You do not." I giggle as try to tug her into the house. "Get in so I can shut the door, it's freezing outside!"

"Mama!"

Mandy turns wide eyes to me. "Did he just say mama?" she shrieks causing my ear drums to explode as she practically throws me to the side, barging into my living room. "Mama's comin', my little Enzo maniac! Mama's here!"

"Uh, I think he's referring to me." I giggle as she swoops a stunned Enzo up against her bosom and twirls around the living room. Vader chooses this moment to burst through the doggy door from the backyard and starts barking and jumping on Mandy. It's total chaos, but I'm so happy, my heart could burst. Enzo starts to cry as Mandy shushes him, rocking him side to side.

"You don't remember me, do you? Don't you worry, Mister, you and I will be twinsies by the time I leave. Inseparable like peanut butter and jelly." She beams down at him and he immediately gives her a gummy smile back. "That's right, you and Auntie Mandy are going to be the bestest of buddies. I'm going to leave my kids with your uncle Deacon every weekend if that's what it takes."

I smother a laugh. "Is he really watching the kids all by himself this weekend?"

Mandy gives me a look over her shoulder. "Puh-lease, that man couldn't change his own underwear by himself much less watch three kids. He called his mother to come help him."

"Oh lordy, how do you feel about that?"

"Not great, but I really needed to get away. I mean they won't die eating ice cream for dinner every night, right?"

"I think she does it just to piss you off. Is she still claiming that watching QVC is more educational than *Sesame Street*?"

"Ugh yes. I just wear my *Ms. Trudy Manners' Etiquette School* sugary smile and say 'yes, ma'am' and 'thank you, ma'am' for this year supply of 'poo pourri' potpourri or whatever crap she's bought. I bat my eyelashes and say, whatever would I do without you, Delores?" She puts Enzo on her hip. "Whatever. I got in my minivan and peeled out of the driveway on two wheels before Deacon or Delores could trap me. Nothing was going to stop me."

"I've missed you."

"I've missed you more. Let's catch up!"

"Let me give Enzo a bath first and then we can have a glass of wine and you can tell me all the latest gossip without any interruptions. Are you hungry? I made a salad."

Mandy gives me a look of disgust and mutters, "No wonder you're so damn skinny."

She shifts her attention to Enzo. "What do you say Auntie Mandy gives you a bath while Mama relaxes and eats her gerbil food? Sound like a plan, little man? And then I'll tell her how Mary Kate got a job at *Leather and Lace*. Quite the scandal."

"No! What happened to the bakery job at Harris Teeter?"

"Guess she was buttering the wrong buns. She put her sugar on the wrong long john. She squeezed her jelly into the Boston cream...I could keep going." She smiles at me.

I hold my hand up. "I got the picture, thanks."

"Dah! Mmmbee!" Enzo shouts gleefully. He squeezes his fists open and closed and puts his fist to his mouth.

Mandy rolls her eyes. "Please tell me you haven't been doing that signing crap with him. I mean, it's so dang ridiculous. He'll never learn to speak if he's squeezing his fists and punching himself in the mouth all day long to ask for a god-dang cup of milk."

"Studies have shown—"

"Studies my ass," she grumbles as she walks down the hall. "Miiilk. Mmm-iiill-luh-*k*. That's how we learn to talk,

Enzo. Don't worry, Aunty Mandy's here now. I'll get you set straight."

I shake my head. I can't help but laugh. "Bathroom is on the right!"

"Not that big of a house! Would have found it!" she shouts back.

My smile widens as I head into the kitchen. I hadn't realized how much I missed having my best friend around. Even though Mandy can be loud and sassy, I know without a doubt she would do anything for me. It's hard to find people like that these days. I have Kiki, Sarah, and TJ in my life now, and they are supportive and wonderful, but it's not the same as having someone who knows every single detail of your life. Someone you can call at any hour of the night, who will drive to another state to come pick you up when your car breaks down and you're stuck. Mandy knows all my stories and helped me write most of them.

I pour two glasses of wine as I hear her singing "Itsy Bitsy Spider" and Enzo squealing in delight. I make a bottle of milk for Enzo and meet them in his bedroom where she's getting him in his jammies.

"Thank you for helping."

"Girl, this is nothing. He is the easiest, most adorable little hunky man I've ever met."

I laugh, and smile down at my baby. "He is pretty damn cute." I kiss him on his nose. "I'm just going to read him a bedtime story and then I'll be in. I poured you a glass of wine, and help yourself to whatever I have in the fridge."

She kisses Enzo and heads out of the room as I sit in the rocking chair and read him a story while he sucks down his milk.

I SIT ON one end of the couch while Mandy pours more wine into her glass.

"Okay, so I know you're only in town for the weekend, and you can say no…"

She eyes me over her glass. "What is it?"

"Would you want to go to Tatum—"

She jumps up off the couch. "Yes! Whatever it is, a thousand times yes!"

"Let me finish, you spaz. Would you like to go to—"

"Yes!"

"Oh my god, I give up. You have the patience of a gnat."

"Okay, okay, sorry. What is it? I promise I'll listen. Do I want to go to Tatum's concert? Uh, duh. Do I want to have a night of unbelievable sex with him? Hell yes, even though I'm a happily married woman. Do I want to feel Tatum's buns of steel? Double-down yes."

"Uh, maybe this is going to be a bad idea."

"Bad idea is my middle name."

I roll my eyes at her. "Do you want to go with me to Tatum's birthday party *under* one condition? No touching, flirting, breathing, fondling, or catcalling him."

"That's like five conditions." She pouts at me as I stare blankly back. "Wait…are you serious?"

I smile at her and nod knowing she's going to flip out. She's been a huge Tatum Reed fan since they started out. When she found out I was working for his wife, she had to put the phone down while she hyperventilated into a paper bag.

"Oh. My. Gawd! Seriously? Yes!" she screams as she jumps up and down on the couch.

"Ssh! You're going to wake up Enzo. And you're a dead woman if you spill wine on this couch Mama gave me."

"Oh, your mama and Enzo will understand. Auntie Mandy is about to meet her future husband!"

I giggle. "No, Auntie Mandy is not going to meet her future husband because she's already married *and* he is married to my friend and boss."

"Well, a girl can dream, can't she? And maybe pinch his tush and cop a feel…"

"No! No and no. Look, I'm not afraid to leave you here if you can't control yourself. And you know what that means."

She sighs and drinks her wine. "No Fireball," she mutters.

"Exactly. We can still have fun, but you will be under a strict no-touch, just-look policy. Think you can handle yourself, Amanda Reece Tillwater?"

"She folds her arms over her chest and sinks into the couch, pouting. "Fine."

"Okay then. Cameron will be picking us up tomorrow night. That's Kiki's brother, the one I was telling you about."

"The hot bar owner?"

"Yes, but we're just friends," I add hastily.

"Uh huh." She eyes me over the glass of wine. "Friends my ass. You just admitted you thought he was hot."

"*You* used that adjective to describe him. I just went along with it."

"Semantics, Anderson. Well, you know what this means?

We need to get shined up and purdy for tomorrow night! I gots to go shopping for some new cowboy boots! Yeehaw!"

I laugh. "Okay, we'll go shopping tomorrow. I'm so glad you're here, Mandy."

"Me too, Andie, me too."

Chapter 15

Cameron

I PULL UP to the curb in front of Andie's house a little earlier than expected. It actually wasn't very convenient for me to have to leave the bar and come get her and her friend Mandy, but I left strict orders for Connor and Kiki not to let TJ touch anything. He's like David Tutera on crack with this party. I get out of my car and take the steps two at a time up to her front porch. I ring the doorbell and pull out my phone that keeps vibrating as I wait.

> **Kiki:** Don't be mad.
>
> **Me:** You realize that immediately puts me on edge, right?
>
> **Kiki:** Technically, it's not a big deal.
>
> **Me:** I'm waiting...
>
> **Kiki:** TJ may or may not have brought in some glitter bombs.
>
> **Me:** What the fuck is a glitter bomb?

I hear commotion coming from the inside and the door

opens a sliver. A pretty heart-shape-faced brunette stares at me through the crack. Her eyes widen and the door shuts in my face. I hear muffled voices from behind the door and I lean in to listen better.

"Oh my god, Andie, you didn't tell me he was *that* hot. Smoking hot! What the hell is wrong with you? Why haven't you jumped his bones yet? How's my hair?"

"Shit, that's Cam? He's here already? Here, take Enzo and run him over to Mrs. Miller. Go out the back."

Enzo must be her puppy. I look at my watch as another text comes through.

Kiki: *Imagine a balloon filled with water, but instead it bursts open with glitter. Like a pinata.*

Me: *Okay I can handle one.*

Kiki: *So about that...*

The door opens and the breath wooshes out of me, my phone forgotten as it hangs limply in my hand at my side. Andie stands there in a red knit dress that hugs her curves in all the right places. Her hair naturally curls into soft waves and her lips are painted bright red. She looks like a movie star.

"Wow, Andie. You look...stunning."

Her smile widens. "Thanks, Cam, not so bad yourself."

Her tongue runs over her bottom lip and I want to capture her lips and kiss her breathless. I clear my throat as I take a step back. "Are you guys ready? I'm sorry I'm early, but I need to make sure everything runs smoothly for tonight. We'll have a lot of celebrities making appearances."

Andie chews her lip nervously as she looks over her

shoulder. "Uh, yeah. Give me a minute?"

I think it's kind of odd that she doesn't ask me in, but I don't dwell on it too much as my phone vibrates again.

Kiki: *Okay, you're not answering so I'll take that as a yes.*
Me: *What's a yes? I never received a question!*

I sit down on a rocking chair on Andie's front porch waiting impatiently, but hop up immediately as the front door opens again and Andie and her friend Mandy walk out.

"Well butter my butt and call me a biscuit, you're more handsome in person! You must be Cameron, I'm Mandy." A busty brunette practically picks me up off the ground as she barrel hugs me.

"Okay, he's met you." Andie fidgets beside us after what feels like a full-minute hug, but Mandy isn't letting me go.

"Whatever you're selling, I'm buying it." She inhales deeply. "You smell so nice," she purrs as she squeezes tighter. I now know what an anaconda's prey feels like.

"Mandy, let him go."

"You're so tall, and well built." She leaves an inch between us as she leans back to squeeze my arms.

"Mandy, stop touching him!"

I look over at Andie for help but she has her face buried in her hands. I look down at Mandy's cute heart-shaped face.

"I could seriously leave my husband for you." She smiles impishly up at me.

"Mandy Tillwater! You are not leaving Deacon. Seriously, hands off, woman, or I'll make you stay at home. We've gone over this!"

Mandy releases her tiger claws and I take a step back and

smile as I run a hand through my hair. "Nice to meet you, Mandy."

"No, sir, the pleasure is *all* mine." She fluffs her hair as Andie rolls her eyes.

"Oh Jesus, this night is going to be a disaster. We better get a move on." She stops as I unlock the doors of a black Range Rover. "Wait, where's your car?"

I catch Mandy mouth *a Range Rover* to Andie which makes me smile as I open the doors for both of them. Andie slides into the front and Mandy takes the back seat.

"So, what happened to the Porsche you were driving the other night?" She looks around the car.

"The other night?" Mandy peeps up from the back as she caresses the leather seat next to her.

"I have an SUV too," I say.

"What happened the other night?" Mandy asks. "Bless it, this leather seat is softer than Michael's baby butt. My kids would grind Cheez-Its and apple sauce into this leather faster than a hot knife through butter."

I put the car in gear and pull away from the curb. I chance a quick glance over at Andie's profile. She's stunning in red and if Mandy weren't in the back yammering on about leather seats and meeting Tatum Reed I'd pull this new SUV over and make good use of the back seat. I want to kiss that red lipstick right off her lips and make her beg to have me inside her.

I shift uncomfortably in my seat as I adjust my hard-on. I look in my rearview mirror at Mandy because I swear she hasn't taken a breath in the last five minutes and I'm worried she might combust.

"So, Mandy, I take it you are a big Tatum Reed fan?"

Mandy guffaws. "Only *the* biggest. He's so sinfully sexy. And that voice. Ugh! I could lic—"

"Mandy, remember what we talked about," Andie abruptly cuts her off.

"I don't remember. What did we talk about?"

Andie sighs and folds her arms over her chest as she stares at the roof of the car. "About how all the guys in the band are off limits and you will not do anything embarrassing tonight. Remember you promised?"

Mandy huffs, "I did no such thing."

"I knew this was a bad idea," Andie mutters. I reach over and grab her hand, threading her fingers with mine. I feel her stiffen next to me, but she doesn't pull away.

"Hey, us Southerners are proud of our crazy. We don't hide it up in the attic, we bring it right down into the living room and show it off." Mandy smiles a big shit-eating grin which makes me laugh and Andie groan.

"No one is more embarrassing than TJ." I squeeze Andie's hand as she smiles at me. "So, Mandy, how long have you guys known each other?"

"Me and Anderson? Since we were babies. Our moms were in jazzercise class together. Andie couldn't get rid of me if she tried. We didn't bond right away; it took until about the ninth grade for little Miss Prim and Proper up there to realize how cool I really was. But I'm like Gorilla Glue. Our friendship started out slow and kind of runny, but once that shit cemented our bond was unbreakable."

I smile over at Andie who giggles and rolls her eyes. She's fucking adorable.

"But once you get to know Andie, she's a lifer. A friend 'til the end, ride or die...I'll be there for you—" Mandy starts to sing the *Friends* opening song.

"Okay, I think he gets the point." Andie sends daggers over her shoulder at her friend, effectively shutting her up.

"I guess I'm lucky Andie just wants to be friends with me then, huh?" I wink at her and squeeze her hand. Her cheeks blush and she pulls her hand away.

"Well that shit won't last. You'll be dry-humping each other by the end of the night," Mandy mutters and laughs from the back.

"What was that?" I look at her in the rearview mirror.

"I said, that shit—"

"Oh good, we're here!" Andie shouts as I pull into The Social Hour parking lot. Andie gets out and I can hear her grumbling to Mandy as they get her photography equipment out of the back. I try not to eavesdrop, but it's hard not to with how loud Mandy is.

"Oh my god, are you trying to embarrass me?!" Andie whispers angrily.

"Who me? No! I'm trying to *help* you. That man is sinfully sexy, like sex on a stick, how many licks does it take to get to—"

"Ugh! Shush! He'll hear you. Just pinky swear you'll behave tonight."

"I'll behave," Mandy says miserably as they come around to the front of the car. "But I'm getting my dance on! I didn't buy these new boots for nothin'."

I look down at her turquoise cowboy boots. "Perfect, you can dance with TJ." I smile as I take the camera bag from

Andie as we walk toward the front door. This evening will either go terribly good or terribly bad.

Mandy might just be the flame that ignites TJ's glitter bomb.

Chapter 16

Andie

MANDY'S TALONS ARE digging into my arm as we enter the party. We spot the band guys chatting with some guy that looks vaguely familiar onstage. Cameron takes our coats and heads to his back office leaving me to deal with the hot mess at my side.

"Ohmagod, ohmagod, ohmagod..."

"Do you need a paper bag or something?" I rummage through my purse for a brown bag. I've thought of every scenario that might occur tonight. I even brought my taser. You never can be too sure with Mandy and I wouldn't hesitate to use it on her. I know she'd thank me later, once she regained her muscle control.

She starts doing her Lamaze breathing as I steer her off to a dark corner. "Get it under control, sister."

Mandy starts fanning herself. "Okay, sorry, I'm good. I just can't believe this is really happening. I'm in the same room with Tatum Reed, Lex Ryan, Matt Greer, and Will Ford and there aren't any security guards to keep me off of them. I mean, what are the chances? *Who are you* and how do you know these people?!"

I laugh. "I know, I freaked out a little too when I first found out, but they are just regular, super nice guys. And don't forget they are taken and so are you." I hold up her ring finger in front of her face and waggle it around.

"Pfft, I know, but a girl can still dream. Besides, Matt and Will are single."

I smile. "Yeah, I'm well aware of that little fact."

"Something happened. What happened? Tell me!" She shakes me, rattling my teeth in my head.

"Stop! Nothing happened."

"Andie! Yay, you made it!" Sarah and Kiki come up to us and they both hug me. "Hi, you must be Mandy! I'm Sarah."

"Hi Mandy, I'm Kiki. So glad you could come!"

Mandy straightens her shoulders back and tries to smile but ends up baring her teeth and looking constipated. "Hello. The pleasure is mine." She curtsies.

"She's a little star struck." I laugh nervously and pinch Mandy's arm.

"Oh my god, did I just curtsy?" she whispers in horror next to me.

"You did."

"Shit."

Sarah laughs. "Girl, I get it. I think we all were at one point when we first met the guys."

"*The guys.* She called them the guys. Can I call them the guys too?"

Kiki laughs and puts her arm in Mandy's. "Come on,

Sarah and I will introduce you to them. Andie, I think Cam is looking for you." She winks at me as the three of them walk away. I'm onto her and her dill-pickle plan even if she thinks she's being sly.

"Mandy, I'm watching you!" I shout as she waves her hand in the air.

I LOOK AROUND the crowded room and pick the camera up that's hanging around my neck. I asked Kiki if she would mind me taking pictures as a thank-you for hiring me and lifting me out of the depressing state I was in. She was more than excited to let me have a crack at it.

I immediately start clicking the shutter, capturing people mingling and laughing. Country stars I've only seen in magazines or on TV mill about hugging each other and thumping each other on their backs, celebrating Tatum. I hide behind my lens and capture every smile, every smirk, every...nose picker? Eew gross, bet that guy didn't think anyone was watching him. Never would have suspected him as a nose picker, but hey, I guess even celebrities get the boogies. I can't wait to share who it was with Mandy.

I get a few of Tatum and Lex with Sarah and Kiki dancing and laughing. I get one of Matt hitting on some girl over by the bar. I take some of Will slow-dancing with a cute redhead. I'm in my element capturing moments that will last forever and it makes me completely at ease and happy. I don't need to be the one mingling with A-list celebrities and musicians. I don't need to know the latest gossip or who's dating who. I just want to capture the real moments, the shared smiles, the love.

I look up from my camera and scan the room looking for Mandy. I spot her over by the bar chatting animatedly with TJ and Cam. I lift my camera, zoom in, and take a few of them. She swings her head back and belly-laughs at something TJ is saying. I snap a few more. I'm so glad they are getting along.

I watch Cameron through my lens under the pretense of taking pictures. His sharp chiseled jaw, his straight nose and sexy smirk make me want to trace every angle of his beautiful face with my fingertips.

He laughs at something Mandy says and my panties immediately disintegrate in this tight-ass dress. Even with all the star power in this room—the gorgeous faces of talented men and women—the only one I can't keep my eyes off of is Cameron Forbes. I've been watching him all night, as he works the room effortlessly while I hide behind my camera. He's like a politician, shaking hands and smiling, probably saying something perfect and profound, charming the pants off of everyone around him.

I tug on my tight dress wishing I could have worn something loose-fitting, but Mandy insisted I wear this to wow my new hot boyfriend. Ha. *Not* my boyfriend. Not even close. I groan because my feet are killing me. I wanted to wear my cowboy boots, but Mandy wouldn't let me. She said I needed to show off my sexy legs. It's so unfair that she gets to wear her cute new ones and I'm stuck in these stiletto death traps.

I wonder what it would be like to be his girlfriend though…could I mingle with all these fancy people, making up clever conversation? Stand at his side like pretty arm candy with a smile pasted on my face? Mandy and I barely passed Ms. Trudy Manners' etiquette school our moms made us take one summer…heck, the last party I was at I ended up ruining Paul's vegan group.

The answer is no, I can't be Cameron Forbes' girlfriend. He's way out of my league with his posh polished suits, his tousled hair and his drop-dead-sexy smile. The truth is I'm an introvert at heart. I'm better off just laying low, living a simple life and raising my son. Even if all my friends are right, that I need to get back out into the dating world, it just doesn't seem possible right now, at least not with Cameron. I need to date a mediocre guy to get my feet wet again. Not someone who knocks me on my ass with his devasting smile, smoky gray eyes, muscular arms that could hold me tight, and lips that would probably make me orgasm on the spot.

An arm wraps around my waist and I lower my camera when words are whispered into my ear. "You're freakin' hot in this dress."

I look over my shoulder and ease away from Matt's hold. His words rub me the wrong way. I know most girls would be creaming in their panties to have his arm around them, but not this one.

"Oh, hey Matt, how's it going?"

"Andie, you're killing me. I want to peel this dress off of you with my teeth."

I snort. "Do women really find that appealing?"

He runs his finger from my shoulder to my elbow and he might as well drag sandpaper down my arm. I roll my shoulder away from him and take a step back. "Aw, come on, Andie, are you telling me I don't have any effect on you?"

I smirk. "Zero, Romeo."

He thumps his heart, a pained expression on his face. "There are a ton of girls in here that would love to have me in between the sheets."

Eew. "I'm sure."

"There you are, Matt! We've been looking for you everywhere!" Sarah grabs Matt's arm and swings him around.

"What the…"

"Hey, look who we found! Cameron was looking for you, Andie." Kiki shoves Cam forward as TJ grabs the camera from my hands. "Okay, and we're off!" Kiki bumps me into him with her hip as Sarah shoves Matt away from us. The three of them are like a whirlwind microburst leaving me feeling dazed but still somewhat intact.

Cameron steadies me as I teeter in my stupid five-inch heels. I grab on to his muscular forearms and smile, embarrassment heating my skin. Holy hell it's like grabbing on to a piece of granite. I want to press my hands to his chest, but I quickly drop them.

"Sorry about those three. They can be a lot to handle." He smiles wryly at me as he shoves his hands into his pockets.

"Ha, yes. I'm quickly finding that out."

"Great party, Cam! I'm definitely booking my next event here!" some guy from behind me shouts, but Cam doesn't take his eyes off of me as he nods his chin in acknowledgment. I'm drowning in his gray irises, unsure of what to do or say.

"Want to dance?" He doesn't wait for an answer as he guides me over to an area of the bar that's been converted to a dancefloor. Other couples are swaying to the Christmas music. He pulls me into his arms and I can't help but giggle.

Cam dips his chin and murmurs. "What's so funny?"

I point up at the ceiling. There must be close to two hundred mistletoe balls hanging from the ceiling all around the bar. "Someone got a little mistletoe happy." I smile.

"You mean TJ."

I grin as I mirror his teasing smile. "He's been playing Dave Barnes' Christmas album for the last two weeks. When the mistletoe song comes on, he blares it. We all want to kill him."

As if on cue, Hillary Scott from Lady A and some guy start singing Dave Barnes' "Christmas Tonight."

"Oh my god, that's him! That's Dave Barnes in person! I knew he looked familiar."

"Sounds like you're a fan." Cam smirks as he effortlessly moves me around.

I laugh. "No, yes. I mean, he's great, but TJ has probably scarred me for life when it comes to Christmas music."

"He has that effect on people." His hands slide up and cup my face. "Andie, may I kiss you? You know, mistletoe and all."

Butterflies thump like crazy in the pit of my stomach as I look into his mesmerizing eyes. Is this really happening? I'm scared to kiss Cameron, scared I'll want more, but I tuck those feelings deep down because who can say no to this guy?

"I guess it's bad luck if we don't?" I want to kick myself for sounding so breathless.

"Damn right it is," he murmurs as he swoops down and captures my lips in a dizzying kiss before I can change my mind. My hands grip his shoulders as I cling to him for dear life. He coaxes my lips apart as he angles his head taking the kiss deeper. His tongue gently sweeps over mine. But before I can get down and dirty with his tongue, he ends it. He releases my lips and I slowly open my eyes to find his smoldering stormy gray ones searching mine. My brain is short-circuiting because I can't form any thoughts or sentences. You know that scene at the end of *Dirty Dancing* when Baby's eyes are lusting after Johnny after he just kissed her and she looks like she could melt into him? Yep, that's how I feel in this very minute. This guy just Patrick Swayzed me.

I want to turn the bar lights on and shout 'It's closing time!' and drag him out of this bar cavewoman-style and beat anyone with my purse who tries to get in my way. I want to shove him up against the outside brick wall and have my dirty way with him. My glazed eyes refocus and I look over his shoulder to see TJ high-fiving Kiki and Mandy then giving me two thumbs up. Heat crawls up my neck and blossoms on my cheeks.

I straighten my dress and step out of Cameron's arms, but he's not having it. *Did he just growl?* He pulls me back flush against his rock-hard body and smashes his lips to mine. My fingers curl up into his silky hair. The world around us drops away as I get lost in the kiss, his tongue tangling with mine. I can't breathe, but I don't care because

Cameron is breathing for the both of us.

"Connor, now!"

"No, TJ, it's too early!" I hear Kiki shout just as Cameron breaks away from my lips. All of a sudden there's a loud poof and all I can see is glitter. Some people start screaming, most are cheering. It's like I'm in a human-sized snow globe as glitter rains down all around us.

"What the fuck?" Cameron growls as he looks around at his once-pristine industrial-chic bar that now resembles Candyland on crack. "Kiki!" he shouts, but I start cracking up. I can't help myself as I look at him covered in white iridescent and silver glitter. It floats all around us, it's absolutely magical. Hillary, Lex, and Dave start to sing "Happy Birthday" and the whole bar joins in as Kiki pulls Tatum onto the stage.

I twirl around and take in the whole scene. Everyone is completely covered in glitter as they sing "Happy Birthday." My eyes end up back on Cam who is scowling as he searches the crowd.

What the hell...toes have been dipped, so I might as well take the plunge, because I was right, I do want more. I pull his hand toward me, getting his attention and smile up at him as I unsuccessfully wipe glitter off his cheek. His stormy eyes search mine. He quirks an eyebrow in question as I take in his devastatingly handsome face.

"You've got a little glitter on you."

He snorts and shakes his head. "I think I have glitter in places no one should ever have glitter."

"Yikes." I grin up at him. My hand moves into his hair and I tug him down to my lips as he chuckles. I gently press my lips to his, kissing him slowly as I memorize the texture and shape of them. Goddamn, he's a good kisser. The people, the noise, the music, it all falls away as Cameron Forbes claims my lips and my heart. I hear a whimper and I'm astonished that it's coming from me as Cameron groans and deepens the kiss.

"I've been wanting to kiss your red lips all night," he says huskily as he kisses down my neck.

I let out a strangled noise as I pant, closing my eyes as I cling to his rock-hard body.

A throat clears to my left. "Hey Andie, I hate to break up this insanely hot moment, but we've got to get home." I spring apart from Cam feeling like I just got caught in the back seat of the car by my mama.

"Oh, yes, uh…gosh is it ten already?"

"Yup. Sorry Cam, we turn into pumpkins at ten. Got to go!"

Cam smiles, confusion clearly written on his face. "Oh, okay. I'll take you home."

"Oh, no, I wouldn't want you to leave the party early. It's really okay!"

"Andie, I brought you here, I'm not letting you find a ride home. Let me just tell Connor and we'll go." He holds up a hand as a protest is about to leave my mouth. "This is happening, so no arguing."

"Okay."

"Grab your coats from my office and I'll meet you at the front door."

Mandy loops her arm through mine. "Ohmygod, ohmygod, ohmygod!" She shakes my arm as we steer through the crowd to fetch our coats and my camera. "You made out with the hot hunky bar owner!"

I smile at her crookedly. "I know, I was there."

"Andie! You guys were on fire! I mean there was smoke coming off you! Even I wanted to get in on that."

I giggle. "It was pretty hot. The scary thing is, I want to do it again."

"Who wouldn't?"

I laugh. "But I can't. That was just a one-time thing. There was mistletoe, glitter...I was just dipping my toes."

"Guuurl, I'd dip a whole lot more than my toes. I'd strip naked and skinny dip in that shit."

I shake my head trying to clear it. "I can't fall for him. He doesn't know about Enzo and I'm not sure I want him to." I give her a stern look. "Okay, shush, here he comes."

"Ready, ladies?" He tries to wipe some of the glitter off his shirt, but it's useless. "I'm so pissed at my sister and TJ."

"Go easy on TJ. It really was a spectacular glitter wonderland."

He wraps his arm around me as we head out into the cold and all I want to do is turn into him and bury my nose into his warmth. I may have told Mandy I didn't want my heart to get involved, but I'm afraid it already is.

Chapter 17

Cameron

I WAS WORRIED the ride home would be quiet and awkward, but there was no chance of that with motormouth Mandy telling us about everyone she met. She really is hilarious, but Jesus the woman can talk. I couldn't get a word in even if I tried.

"Did y'all see that one woman in the leather dress with her boobs and cooch hanging out? She got pissed because guys were practically panting and their eyes were popping out of their heads. But my memaw always said, *'If you don't want people touching your critters, don't make your barn look like a petting zoo.'* I mean don't get me wrong…you go girl, live your best life, but don't get mad when I can see your cooch and call ya out on it."

Andie gasps, "You didn't."

"I did. I don't care who you are, don't dress like you lost half your clothes in a tornado and then complain when you get attention."

I rub my hand across my jaw and try to smother a laugh.

"Oh Jesus," Andie whispers next to me.

I step out and open the car door for them. I grab Andie's hand and tug her to me before she can bolt up to her porch. "I had a really good time tonight."

Her hazel eyes burn into mine as she smiles. "Yeah, I did too."

"Listen, I know Mandy is here for a short while, but I'm leaving town Monday, and I'd like to see you again before I leave. Can I take you out tomorrow night?"

"Oh, um—"

"Yes! She says *yes!*" Mandy shouts from the porch.

I smile down at Andie as her cheeks blush. "So, that's a yes? Mom said yes."

"I don't think I have a choice." She chuckles. "Yes."

I tuck a loose curl behind her ear. "Goodnight, Andie." I softly kiss her lips and then I step back before I take it further knowing Mandy is probably filming us live on social media.

Andie sighs, "Goodnight Cam, and thank you for the ride home." She quickly walks up to the porch and then gives me a last wave as she enters her house.

I speed back to the bar afraid of what damage might be done. Erratic thoughts zip all around my brain, my senses bamboozled. I can't get the taste or smell of Andie out of my head. The feel of her skin, the softness of her lips. Shit, I wanted to keep this light and easy, but this woman has managed to burrow herself under my skin with just a kiss.

BACK AT THE bar the party is still in full swing. I survey the damage done by the glitter and cringe. I'm going to have to shut the bar down for a few days and get an industrial cleaning service to come in here and hose the place down. I look around and locate Sarah, TJ, and Kiki giggling in a corner booth, and march over to them.

"You three are in so much trouble."

Kiki rolls her eyes. "Oh Dad, it's not that bad, besides Tatum is having the time of his life."

"Not that bad? Kiki, my bar looks like a fucking platoon of unicorns went on a bender in here."

Sarah giggles as TJ sighs. "I know, isn't it amazing?"

"No, it's not fucking amazing, it's going to cost a fortune to clean this up!"

"Cam, sit down, have a hot toddy and relax." TJ pushes Kiki over so there's room next to him. I sit down next to Sarah across from them.

"Ow, scootch over, Turd Jam." Kiki shoves him back. "Don't worry, Cam, we'll foot the bill."

"Are there any other surprises I need to know about for tonight?"

"No, but I was delighted to see you and our lovely Miss Andie gettin' it on on the dancefloor."

I clear my throat. "We were not 'gettin' it on'."

"Ooh! Can I plan your wedding? I promise, there won't be glitter. But I have this amazing idea—"

"No!" I bark out. I look at TJ as if he's crazy, because let's face the facts, he is. "No weddings. It was just a kiss. There was mistletoe…and stuff. I would have been a jerk if I didn't kiss her. I'm not getting married, so don't get any ideas."

"Oh, that was more than just a kiss, Cam." Sarah sighs dreamily next to me. "That was two people who were meant to be together."

"We're just friends," I say gruffly. "You know I don't want anything serious right now."

"I don't kiss *my* friends like that. You guys were on fire." TJ fans himself.

"You guys, drop it," I growl.

"Well, that's too bad. She's a keeper." Sarah winks at TJ and Kiki.

Kiki nods. "She is, but you're right, Cam. You should play the field right now. Besides, it looks like Matt is really into Andie. They would make a cute couple, don't you guys think?"

"Totes agree, Kinky. I mean even though he has his tongue down some boar's throat right now, it doesn't mean that he doesn't have feelings for Shorts."

"What the hell is a boar?" I spy Matt at the bar who is kissing some woman. The thought of Matt touching Andie makes my blood boil.

Kiki flicks TJ's ear. "Boar is not catching on."

"Kinky, don't be jealous that I came up with it."

"So not jealous."

Sarah giggles as I groan in annoyance. "What the fuck is a boar? Like a pig with tusks?"

"No Camaroo, a boar is a band whore…boar."

"I mean I see the logic…" Sarah shrugs.

"Thanks, Sare Bear." TJ high-fives her across the table as Kiki gives Sarah the stink eye.

"Don't encourage him."

I look around at the crowd. "Andie's too smart to hook up with someone like Matt."

"Hmm…" Kiki shrugs innocently. "Maybe, but you're an idiot if you let him try."

I grumble in annoyance as I sip my beer and look back over at Matt. Over my dead body will he be trying anything with her, but I don't have to let these three buffoons know that. The truth is I don't know what the hell I'm going to do when it comes to Andie, and that worries me the most.

Chapter 18

Andie

CAM IS PICKING me up in an hour for our date and I'm so nervous I feel like I'm going to throw up. I'm trying to play it cool in front of Mandy, but she sees right through me.

"Are you sure you don't want me to cancel? I feel terrible going on a date while you're in town visiting."

"Don't feel bad, I want you to go. You're not getting out of this, so no more excuses! What are you scared of anyway?"

"I don't know. I feel like a teenager going out with a boy for the first time. It's crazy! He's just so...so Cam. I can't explain it."

"Be excited, not scared. He is delicious, that one. He exudes confidence, sex appeal, and he's just an all-around nice, cool guy." She rolls a pair of socks and throws them in the laundry basket, smirking. "You two would make some beautiful babies..." Mandy holds up her hands in defense as I narrow my eyes at her. "I'm just sayin'!"

"No, no more babies. Ugh, I guess if it goes well tonight I'm going to have to tell him about Enzo."

"I don't know what you're so worried about. How could you not fall in love with this hunky little chunky monkey?" Mandy gets down on the floor next to me and tickles Enzo causing him to giggle.

"Ma Ba!" He reaches for Mandy.

"Shut the front door! Did you just call me by my name?" She squeals loudly which makes Enzo's face crumple into tears. "Oh no! Don't cry, Auntie Mandy's so sorry! She just got excited! No crying little man, I got you," she coos as he settles back down.

I just smile at the two of them as I fold the laundry from the basket next to me. "I'm so glad you're here."

"Me too." She smiles back at me. "Why don't you guys come back with me for Christmas? I just know my buddy will be devastated when I leave."

"You know I want to but it's a really busy time at work right now."

"It's not like it's that far. You came home for Thanksgiving and were back by the weekend."

"You're right. Okay, I'll see if I can get off for work."

"I'm sure Sarah and Kiki will let you have a few days."

I nod. "No promises, but I'll try, okay?"

"Good enough."

The doorbell rings and I hop up and spin in a circle. "Oh Jesus, he's here! How's my hair? Are you sure about jeans, or should I have put on a cute dress? Oh god, I'm dressed all wrong aren't I? I don't even know what we're doing! Shit, stall him! Tell him Enzo's yours. I'm not ready!"

Mandy stares at me like I've lost my mind, which I feel like I have. She gets up from the couch and comes over and gently shakes me. "I'd like to slap you right now, but I don't want to leave a mark on your pretty cheek. Get it together, sister. You look damn fine. Your hair and makeup are perfect. Grab your coat and gloves. I've got Enzo and Vader and we're going to have a par-tay!" She hugs me as I smile tremulously at her. "Go. Have. Fun. You deserve a little Cameron Forbes in your life right now." She not-so-gently pushes me toward the front door. "Besides, I won't be your best friend anymore if you don't go on this date."

I open the door and immediately suck in a breath of sharp cold air. Cameron is dressed in a crewneck sweater with jeans and jacket. He looks like he just walked off a photoshoot for one of those sexy winter men's fashion magazines they have at the office. Gah, he's so incredibly gorgeous as he smiles at me.

"Ready?"

"Yes, what are we doing?" I quickly close the door behind me before Mandy decides to burst through it. I look back over my shoulder as we head down the steps and see her waving excitedly from the front living room window. She gives me two thumbs up as she fans herself and then falls off the couch. I giggle as I turn back around.

"What's so funny?"

"Oh, nothing, just Mandy being Mandy."

"I don't think I want to know." He grins as he grabs my hand.

I smile. "Probably not."

He opens the door to his Porsche and I slide in.

"Not the Range Rover?"

"It has glitter all over it."

I smirk as I look over at him. "You still have some in your hair."

"I took three showers today. I can't get rid of it."

"So where are we going?"

"I thought we'd head to Glow over at First Horizon Park."

"Oh! Okay...what is that?"

"It's like a winter wonderland park with lights, ice skating and snow tubing...well, fake snow."

"Okay, I'm game." I smile at him as he pulls away from the curb. "So how is the bar today?"

"A mess," Cam groans. "I've hired professional cleaners to make it presentable again, but I'm still pissed at Kiki and TJ." He rubs a hand across his jaw. "I'm sure they will do something else and I'll forget about this and move on to the next disaster."

I giggle. "You're a good big brother, Cam."

"Hmm. What did you and Mandy do today?"

"Uh, just hung out and had girl time."

"Does girl time include Cheerios?"

"Huh?"

He smiles at me as he pulls a soggy Cheerio out of my hair. Oh my god, Enzo must have had them on his sticky fingers when I went to kiss him goodbye and he grabbed my hair.

"Oh, ha ha, you know Mandy, she's always throwing something at my head." I grab the Cheerio from his fingers and toss it out the window.

He gives me a quizzical look so I quickly change the topic. "So! Did you ever find a place for your second location?"

"Not yet, I had to fire my realtor. I've started with a new one, but we haven't gone to look at anything yet."

"That has to be frustrating. I'm sorry."

He smiles over at me before returning his attention to the road. "Nothing to be sorry about. It's just business, and my current location has been doing well, so I'm very fortunate."

I nod and look out the window. Cody Webb's song "Gettin' Somewhere" plays on the radio and I smile as I hum along feeling like I'd like to slide over next to him and get somewhere. My mind goes to last night's kiss and I shift in my seat in anticipation of getting a repeat performance tonight. My stomach fizzles with nerves and excitement. I like Cameron. A lot. It's hard to believe the surly guy I met a couple months ago is the same sexy smiling devil looking over at me.

"What?" I smile.

"Nothing. I'm just happy you're here. You're cute when you sing under your breath with the music."

"Oh no, was I singing?" I have the worst voice ever. "Was I off-key?"

"His grin widens as his eyes flick over to me and then back to the road. "I mean, I wouldn't ask Tatum if you could duet with him."

"Yeah, no that would never happen. I would just be a backup singer."

Cam rubs his hand along his jaw again. I notice he does it when he's conflicted about something. "Yeah, no I don't think that would happen either. Maybe in the shower. By yourself. And put the dog out back so he doesn't howl."

I playfully slap his arm. "Hey! That's not nice. I'm not *that* bad." He looks over at me and his beautiful grin widens. "Okay, I'm pretty bad. Let me guess, you're just an amazing singer."

"I haven't had any complaints."

"Of course you haven't. Well, you're *my* first complaint and I wasn't even singing that loud." Cam eyes me suspiciously. "Okay, fine, Mandy may have mentioned I sing like Oscar the Grouch."

Cam busts out laughing as we pull into Glow. "Come on Oscar, let's do this."

My exasperation with him quickly dissipates as I see thousands of beautiful twinkling lights. "It's so beautiful," I whisper as we walk into the park under the lights. Cam takes my hand and guides me over to the snow tubing. "Are we really going to do this?" I laugh, kind of nervous that I'll go flying off the tube. A five-year-old runs screaming by us in delight to get in line.

Cam arches an eyebrow. "You scared, Andie?"

"No!" *Yes, terrified. God, please don't let me pee in my pants.* "Let's do this. I'm not letting that kid show me up."

Cam laughs as he throws his arm around my shoulders and guides me toward the line. "That's my girl, in this together."

"In this together." I smile at his word choice he scoffed at when I said it to him that day he was babysitting. Goosebumps break out on my skin. I like the sound of being his girl.

"Do you have good insurance?"

"Uh…what? Why?"

"No reason." He grins. "You know, just need to know in case you break an arm or leg."

I elbow him in the ribs causing him to grunt. "Ha, very funny." I nervously wipe my hands down my jeans as we step up to get on the tubes. I sit down awkwardly and practically fall out on the other side as Cam deftly jumps into his.

"On three, Andie." He looks over and winks as I try to right myself in the tube. "Last one at the bottom has to buy hot chocolate."

"Oh, bring it on!"

"One, tw—"

I shove off before he gets to two and I hear Cam yell 'cheater!' from behind me. I smile gleefully as the wind wooshes against my face, exhilarated by the sloping ride. Suddenly Cam appears in my peripheral vision as he grabs my tube.

"No! Get off!" I laugh and shriek as I shove back. But I guess I shove a little too hard because he loses control, careening his tube off of mine. His tube flips as he lands hard on the ground at the bottom, splayed out like a snow angel as I gently come to a stop. I'm doubled over laughing as the guy at the bottom of the ride helps me get out.

"Oh my god, Cam, are you okay?" Tears are leaking out of my eyes. He side-eyes me as he gets up and brushes off his jeans. He grunts as he bends over. I suddenly sober up, oh my god he really is hurt.

"Shit Cam, are you okay?"

He looks up and gives me a devastating smile. "Besides my ego being terribly bruised and the wind knocked out of me, I'm good."

Oh, thank god. "I'm so sorry." I start laughing again.

"You sound it," he grumbles as he straightens up and hugs me to his side and limps a little as we walk away. "Okay, so check that off the list. Want to go ice skating?"

"I'm not very good."

"Just like snow tubing huh?"

I throw my head back and laugh. "I mean, what did you expect when you grabbed my tube? I don't like to lose."

"I'll remember that next time. Let's go skate, I'll get you one of those skate walkers those kids are using over there."

I huff. "I'm not that bad!"

He grins at me. "That's what you said about singing."

I want to kiss that smug smirk right off his face. He rents our skates and we quickly lace them up and walk awkwardly toward the ice. Let me tell you, there's nothing more unsexy then trudging on rubber mats in ice skates, and then getting on slick ice and falling right on your butt. Cam's black skates stop right in front of me as he helps me up. I laugh in embarrassment.

"You weren't kidding. You're terrible." He grins down at me.

I playfully shove him while still clinging tightly to him. "I grew up in Alabama, not Canada. Not exactly a hot bed for ice skating facilities or frozen ponds."

Cam starts to skate backward as he pulls me forward. I nervously grip him harder. "You're pretty good at this, how did you learn to skate?"

"I grew up playing ice hockey. Still play pick-up games with some guys on the weekends."

"Why am I not surprised," I murmur as I watch our feet. "Is there anything you can't do?"

"Snow tubing apparently." He chuckles.

I finally start to get the rhythm as he swings around to my side and holds my hand. "What other kinds of things do you like to do besides running your bar?"

He smiles. "I like to box, rock climb, run, swim, football, read, watch movies…"

"He does it all." I smile shyly at him.

"What do you like to do besides photography and not being a vegan?"

It's on the tip of my tongue to tell him about Enzo, but something keeps me from blurting it out. "I like to run, read, and go to movies. I really want to travel more. That's on my list. I want to see the world."

"So, what's holding you back?"

I smile wryly at him. "Oh…I don't know, work, money, responsibilities." I shrug. "Someday I'll be able to go off into the unknown."

"What's the one place you'd like to go, the top of your list?"

"Hmm, I've always wanted to go to Italy. It just seems so exotic…the food, the wine, the scenery."

"Italy is beautiful for all the reasons you mentioned."

"You've been? I'm so jealous. What's one place you'd like to go?"

"I'd like to see New Zealand. Some friends of mine went last year and their pictures were incredible."

"Seems really faaa-agh!" My arms spin like propellers as a kid speed skates by me and bumps into me. I go down hard on my butt. "Ow. Did you see that little punk?"

"Want me to go skate him down and shove his nose in the ice?"

I smile as he helps me back up. "Yes."

"Okay, give me a second. He'll be easy to catch up to, I think it was that eight-year-old over there."

He starts to pull away from me and I giggle pulling him back. "No, no, don't go pound on the little second-grader." I look into his eyes and can't wipe the smile off my face even though my butt is throbbing. "But thanks for offering."

Cam laughs as he reaches over and tucks an errant curl behind my ear. "You ready for some hot chocolate there, Gretzky?"

"Yes! You're buying...remember *you* lost." I nonchalantly try to rub the soreness out of my butt without Cam noticing. Dang I went down hard.

"How could I forget...You sure you're okay?"

My cheeks heat up as I nod. So embarrassing, I probably looked like I was trying to get a wedgie out. "Come on, superstar, let's get my sore butt out of these skates before I really do break an arm."

Chapter 19

Cameron

I CAN'T REMEMBER the last time I've had this much fun on a date before. Andie is just so refreshing. She's not constantly checking her phone or her hair and makeup. She's just being herself. She's goofy and silly and beautiful. She's not afraid to laugh at herself which I love. I return our skates to the guy behind the counter while Andie puts her boots back on. We head to the hot chocolate stand when she points to the sign.

"Oh look! They have gailauto! I love gailauto."

"What on earth is gailauto?" I look over at the counter puzzled by what she sees.

She rolls her beautiful hazel eyes. "How do you not know what gailauto is? You've been to Italy."

I look between the ice cream and her as a huge grin spreads across my face. "Do you mean gelato?"

"Huh? No, it's gail-auto."

"No sweets, it's gel-ato."

"Oh Jesus, I'm going to kill Mandy. She's always told me it's pronounced gailauto. Chocolate is my favorite so I ask for it every time we see it somewhere. It's gel-at-o? Are you sure?"

"Um, about one hundred percent sure." I chuckle as her cheeks bloom pink. She's so fucking adorable.

"I sound like the biggest hick right about now, don't I?"

"You sound perfect." I pull her to me and softly kiss her lips. I've been struggling all night to keep my hands off of her.

"Eh hem, can I help you?" The lady behind the counter glares at us, clearly irritated with our PDA.

"Can I have two hot chocolates and a scoop of chocolate gailauto?"

Andie buries her face in her hands. "I'm never going to live this down."

"No." I grin as I kiss her neck right under her ear. Damn she smells so fucking good.

"That will be ten dollars." I hand her the cash. The clerk rolls her eyes at us as she slams the hot chocolate and ice cream down on the counter. "Next!"

"Well, she's in the Christmas spirit." Andie giggles as we walk away toward the lights. "Where do you have to go tomorrow?"

"California. Working out the details of what's going to happen with the California locations with my business partner Josh."

"How long will you be gone for?"

"I'm not sure. Could be a few days, could be longer." I shrug.

"I'm glad we got to do this before you left."

I smile. "Me too."

"This is so good. I wish it would snow here, then we could make snow cream."

"What is snow cream?"

"What? How have you never had snow cream?"

"I'm not sure?"

"It rarely snows in Inkdale, but when it does we make snow cream out of the snow. It's like ice cream, but it's the Southern version."

"You take snow and make it into ice cream? Why not just buy ice cream from the store?"

"Because that's not the point."

"What if there's dog pee in your snow cream?"

She wrinkles up her nose. "That's disgusting! You don't scoop up dirty old snow."

"I don't know, I'd only accept snow cream from someone I trusted. You never know."

Andie snorts as she eats her gelato. "You're crazy. Who would do that?"

"Have you met my sister and TJ? They would."

She laughs. "Good to know. We will not teach them about snow cream."

"You're learning fast."

We walk under several archways of lights and it really is a winter wonderland. I watch Andie as she laughs and eats her ice cream, telling me some story about something TJ did the other day. I'm smiling at her, but I'm not really listening because all I can see is her. She's so beautiful and funny. It slams into me hard as she smiles over at me with a smudge of gelato on her upper lip. I'm fucking falling for this girl, going full speed and I can't stop.

I pause at a bench and set the two hot chocolates down on it. I take her ice cream from her and wipe her lip with a napkin and her eyes grow wide as she grabs another napkin and harshly wipes her lips. "I got it all." I smile down at her. "You look like a goddess standing here." I swoop down and claim her lips before she can protest. But I don't have to worry about her pushing me away because she tugs me closer so that our bodies are aligned perfectly.

I thread my fingers through her hair and angle my head so that my lips fit perfectly over hers. She tastes sweet like the chocolate and I groan wanting more. I deepen the kiss and our tongues clash as I claim her mouth. I've never felt so turned on and attracted to a woman before Andie. She pushes all my buttons to go.

I break the kiss and her eyes flutter open. I stare down into her greens and browns as they swirl together. The lights all around make her look ethereal, her hair curling softly over her shoulder. I know she can feel how hard I am for her. I need to get her out of this jacket, sweater, and jeans and see her beautiful skin against mine.

But it's not going to happen tonight. And I need to slow this train down before we get kicked out for indecent acts and public nudity.

"Let's go. I should get you back to your girls' weekend." I kiss my way from her earlobe down her neck.

"Yes. No…okay. Go." She looks dazed as I hand her the hot chocolate and take her other hand tugging her along toward the exit.

We get into my car and head back to her place. What I wouldn't give to take her back to mine. I slip her hand in mine as we talk about insignificant stuff. We pull onto her street. "Can I call you when I get back into town?"

She turns to me and smiles softly. "I'd really like that."

I pull up to her curb and hop out and come around to her side. I hold out my hand and help her out. I run my hand through her hair and kiss her lips softly. "Thank you for tonight, I had a really good time."

She smiles up at me, her eyes shining bright. "Me too, Cam."

I look up at her front door and smile when I see her friend watching us through the glass. I look back down at Andie and kiss her nose. "I'd walk you to your door, but I'm a little scared Mandy might attack me. I can't tell who's more excited to see you, her or your dog…they're both foaming at the mouth."

Andie giggles and I'll never get tired of hearing it. "Probably a good idea. Once she gets a hold of you, she won't let go."

I smile wryly as I draw my index finger down her cheek. I can't seem to stop touching her. "I figured. I'll call you when I land tomorrow if it's not too late."

"Okay," she breathes out.

I dip my head and gently kiss her lips. "Goodnight, Andie."

"Night, Cam. Thank you for a wonderful night." She rushes up her front steps to a vibrating Mandy standing on the other side of her storm door as I get back in my car. I can't say I'm disappointed that she didn't ask me in, but it might have been a little awkward with Mandy watching us make out. I'm finding myself feeling disappointed I have to leave town tomorrow because I'd like to see her again, but I'm not in any rush with her. Besides, something tells me if I try to move things too fast, I might spook her.

Chapter 20

Andie

MANDY PULLS ME inside with a big grin on her face. "Oh my god, how was it? He's so freakin' hot! Did you touch him? Did y'all do the nasty? Your lipstick is wiped off, you definitely kissed him. Oh my god can I name the baby? Was that a Porsche? Deacon will shit a brick when I tell him."

"Do I need to get my taser out of my purse? Geez, take a breath. Was Enzo okay?"

"Like you have to ask. The perfect Saturday night gentleman," she huffs as she plops down on the sofa and props her legs on my coffee table. She reaches for her glass of wine. "So, you think this guy is a keeper?"

I sigh, "Just dipping my toes, remember?"

"I'd dip my vajayjay."

"I'm aware." I laugh as I whiz my throw pillow at her head.

"Hey! You almost made me spill my wine."

"Thanks a lot by the way for making me look like an ass!"

"Erm…which time?"

"For telling me that Italian ice cream is pronounced gailauto."

"What are you talking about?"

"It's gelato, not gailauto."

Mandy bursts out laughing. "For real? I swear I thought it was pronounced gailauto, honest to God. That's what Deacon calls it."

"God, I felt so dumb."

"I'm sure Cameron thought it was charming."

"Yeah, about as charming as when Aunt Purdy removes her teeth at the dinner table and puts them in her water glass."

Mandy grimaces.

I sigh. "I don't know, Mandy. He's so perfect. Too perfect. He's got to have some hidden flaw or a skeleton in the closet…"

She props her elbow on the couch arm and rests her head on her hand. "Hmm, like Mason?"

"Exactly! Mason the rodeo clown."

Mandy eyes me over her glass as she takes a sip. "You know, not every guy is going to turn out to be a total turdbox like Mason Mahoney. Not every guy will up and leave you. Look at Deacon, I mean yeah, he drives me bananas with his incompetence with the kids and throwing socks on the floor by the bed, and his mom is a total cow, but I know he loves me and the boys. I know he is in it through thick and thin to the very end. I never have to question that love, it just is."

I remove an imaginary piece of lint off of my jeans. "I

know...it's just...when I'm with Cam it feels too good to be true. I don't know, I keep waiting for the other shoe to drop."

"Well, quit it. Just enjoy the ride and he might surprise you."

I smile. "He is a pretty fantastic kisser."

Mandy sighs, "He is."

I give her the side-eye. "And you would know that how?"

"Oh, well, I might have video'd you two the other night at the party and watched it five times."

I smirk. "Five or five hundred?"

"I'd do him."

"You seriously need help." I laugh as I pour more wine into her glass. "Hey Mandy? Thanks."

"For what?"

"For being here, for being my support...for videoing the hottest kiss of my life." I smirk. "I'll need that deleted off your phone by the way."

Mandy takes a large gulp of wine as she avoids my gaze. "What's your opinion on YouTube videos? Yay or nay? Asking for a friend."

"I swear to god, Mandy Tillwater, if that video is on YouTube I will show the photo of you pinching Lex Ryan's ass to Deacon."

"Deacon wouldn't care. He knows how delish that tush is. In fact, can you ask Sarah to get Lex to autograph it?" Mandy groans. "God, that accent. I think he might be more delish than Tatum...I don't know, I just can't choose! And then there's your total babe on a stick. What's a girl to do? Do you think Sarah can record Lex saying sexy things and send it to me?" She throws herself across the sofa.

I laugh. "Um…no. You are seriously sick in the head."

"Only for best friends, hot kisses, Irish accents, and squeezable asses. Oh, and my new cowboy boots of course."

"Of course. I guess I'll give Cameron a try. The real test will be when I tell him about Enzo."

Mandy sits up suddenly. "You're going to tell him? Yes!" She fist-pumps the air making me giggle.

"I'm scared to, but he needs to know about him, I can't keep him a secret."

"You should never keep that handsome little stink a secret."

"It's just a lot to spring on someone you like. Especially someone who said he doesn't want kids."

"Aah, so you admit you *like* him. Now we're gettin' somewhere."

I roll my eyes as I hug a pillow. I do like Cam. I like him a lot. Now I just have to find the courage to introduce him to Enzo.

Chapter 21

Andie

CHRISTMAS WENT BY in a flash. I was really glad to be home and spend it with my parents, Mandy, and her family. Kiki and Sarah told me to spend New Year's down there too if I needed the time, which I did. I missed my parents a lot, and it was nice to be home. I felt terrible leaving them high and dry for New Year's, but TJ stepped in for me and made it clear that I needed 'me' time. Something about self-care, waxing and making my nails look decent. I wasn't sure what he was blabbing on about so I just ran with it.

I hadn't heard one word from Cameron except for a text letting me know he made it to California the day after our date. It's been weeks now and I'm left wondering *what the hell?* I left him a voicemail on Christmas and New Year's wishing him a happy one, and both times I got a generic "Merry Christmas!" and a "Happy New Year friends" in return…on a group text. To say my heart didn't sink a little down in my chest would be an understatement. I feel stupid and confused. I thought we had so much fun on our date, but it's been crickets since then.

New Year's Eve was spent trying to dislodge two peas that Mandy's son Michael stuck up his nose. That was loads of fun. It finally fell out after Michael started sobbing while Mandy and Deacon argued over how to take it out. That kid can produce a lot of snot. We played games with some other friends they had over but there's no doubt that holidays make you feel lonely when you're single. I kept wondering what Cameron was doing or who he was spending his New Year's Eve with. It didn't matter, it's not like we were a couple. We went on one date, for God's sake. One incredible date where he made my heart fall head over heels for him.

Mandy said I needed a New Year's word of the year. I told her hers should be self-control. She just winked at me, laughed, and said 'nah'. But she's right. My New Year's resolution is to focus on me. Men come and go. I need to get my photography business up and running because that's what brings me joy. That is what I need in my life right now—Joy.

Chapter 22

Cameron

"HEY, IT'S ANDIE, Merry Christmas Cam, hope you have a great day with your family. Just wanted…to wish you a merry Christmas."

"Cam? It's Lisa. Just wanted to wish you…" *Sob.* "I'm sorry, I just miss you and thought we'd be spending Christmas in Vail together." *Sob.* "I love you. Merry Christmas."

"Hey Cam, it's Andie…again. Just calling to wish you a happy New Year's!"

"Cam, it's Lisa. Why haven't you called me back? You're such an asshole, you know that? At least have the decency to call or text on Christmas even though we are broken up. I thought we were friends at least. God, you're such a cocksucker, why did I ever get involved with you? Ugh!"

"It's Lisa." *Sob.* "I'm sorry Cam, I didn't mean it." *Sob.* "I just miss you. Happy New Year."

"Hey Cam, it's Andie…um, just checking in to see how you are. I haven't heard from you in a few weeks and

I…anyway, hope you're doing okay." Pause. "Crap, how do I erase this?"

"Hi Cameron, it's Kendra. I haven't heard from you since before Thanksgiving. I've left you a couple messages, but maybe they got erased. I hate when that happens. Here's my number in case you lost it. 776-6632. I miss you! Let's go out next week, 'kay?"

"Cameron, it's Josh. We're having some issues with Charles. Remember what we talked about over Christmas? It's bad, man. Gonna need you to come out here ASAP and help me with this. Let me know when you book your flight."

"Cameron, it's Kendra. Duh, of course you have my number. I called you, so you automatically have it. Anyhoo, haven't heard from you. Call me! I've got you in my calendar for next Tuesday night! Same time, same place!"

"Cam, it's Kendra. I'm at our special table. Did you get my message? Your mailbox isn't full…Anyway, I'm going to wait another hour for you. Then I'll take this party back to my place if you know what I mean. Can't wait to see you."

I LOOK UP just in time to see Tatum, Lex, Matt and Will get on the elevator and head upstairs.

"Where are they going?" I bark at Connor.

He looks at the empty lobby and shrugs as he dries some mugs. "Didn't see them, Boss, but there's only one place upstairs."

I grind my teeth in annoyance. Poor Connor, I've been a

bear to be around these past couple of weeks because there have been some issues with the franchising development, a mess with my manager Charles, and with my realtor not being able to find a location.

I push away from the bar and head upstairs. I haven't had a chance to see Andie in a couple weeks since I've been in Chicago and San Francisco, but I'm not about to let Matt hang around her, and even though she's not officially mine, for some inane reason a hot streak of jealousy slaps me in the face as I take the steps two at a time. I walk into the kitchen to find Kiki grabbing a water.

"Hey, Cam! What are you doing up here?"

"Can't I just come to check on my little sister and say hi?"

"Uh, I guess, it's just that you've been gon—"

"So how are you feeling?" I cut her off as I look over her shoulder into the main room. "Where are the guys? I saw them come up here."

"Oh, yeah, um I think they're talking to Andie. I'm feeling goo—"

"Oh great glad to hear it. Okay, I'll just say hi to them."

Kiki arches an eyebrow as she trails behind me.

Andie's looking at Matt like she'd like to lick him like a melting ice cream cone. I immediately bristle at the attention she's giving him. I only catch the back end of the conversation so I'm not sure what they're talking about, but I don't like the way he's looking at her either.

"Tomorrow night. Unless you're bringing a date, then I'll have to get you an extra ticket." Matt winks at her.

Tatum rolls his eyes as he hugs Kiki to him.

"No, no, not seeing anyone." She shakes her head, her eyes dilated as if Matt has put her in a trance. The thought of Andie and Matt together makes me want to rip his head off. "I'd lov—"

"*No*," I say a little too sharply, the word leaving my mouth before I catch myself. Everyone looks up at me in surprise. Shit, shit—*think fast, Cam*. I clear my throat as Andie's eyes narrow at me. "No…way…that sounds like fun. Count me in…"

"Oh yeah, good idea. Give the extra ticket to Cam. He always has a girl in his back pocket." Kiki smiles widely at me.

I give Kiki a scathing glare, catching Andie rolling her eyes as my gaze falls back on her. "I won't need it," I say through my teeth. I know what Kiki's doing and it's pissing me off.

"Ah, yeah, that's cool Cam, you coming too? I didn't think it would be your thing." Matt eyes me suspiciously.

"Mate, trust me, it's not your thing," Lex whispers to me, but I ignore him. My jealousy over Andie sweeping dangerously fast through my bloodstream like a wildfire.

"It's my thing," I say with gruff finality. I have no clue what I just accepted a ticket to, but by the confused look on Matt's face and Andie's wide eyes, I know I've got this in the bag. Tatum smirks as Kiki coughs into her hand, but I ignore them. "So, what are you guys doing here?"

"We're heading over to a photoshoot that Ellen Barr is doing for our next album cover. I've set it up for Andie to join her and get some tips." Tatum kisses Kiki on top of her head. "You girls ready? Is Sarah coming?"

"She's meeting us down there." Kiki smiles as she rubs a hand over her rounded belly. "Ready, Andie? You nervous?"

She smiles shakily. "A little. This is a big opportunity and I don't want to screw it up." She stands up and Matt throws an arm around her.

"Ah, you'll be fine. The pictures from Tatum's birthday were fantastic."

I'm five seconds from ripping his arm off when Andie steps away from him. "I'll meet you guys downstairs, I just have to talk to Cam for a second."

Matt snaps his fingers. "Hey Cam, you'd be perfect for the charity event. You in?"

"Of course. Anything for charity."

Lex shakes his head as he walks by me. "Fucking eejit. Don' say I didn't warn ye."

The guys and Kiki get on the elevator as Andie and I linger by her desk. Kiki gives me a look. I'm not quite sure what she's trying to convey. It's either if I screw this up she'll slash my tires, or I better back the fuck off and she's still going to slash my tires. I can't tell so I just give her a flat stare in return. After the doors shut I turn my attention to Andie.

"Andie—"

"Cameron—"

We smile at each other. "Ladies first." I sit down on the edge of her desk.

She folds her arms over her chest. "I was going to ask you what's been going on? I mean, we talked after our date and then nothing. Crickets. I haven't heard from you in over three weeks. I know you've been in town for a few days because I saw your car. I mean, I'm not stalking you or anything, I just..." She sighs and sits on the other side of her desk. "I feel so stupid, like I've been ghosted. Did you ghost me, Cam?" She shakes her head. "No, wait, please don't answer that. Look, I like you. I thought you felt the same, but if you don't then that's okay. I just...need to know where I stand with you."

I shake my head feeling bad for having ignored her, but also feeling frustrated because this is exactly why I can't have a girlfriend. My last girlfriend Lisa said I was more in love with my job than I was with her. Unfortunately for her, she was correct.

"I'm sorry. It's my business...I've been distracted with it. I like you too, I just..." I run my hand across my jaw. "I'm a busy guy. I have a lot going on with work. I don't want you to think I'm ignoring you, because I'm not. I haven't stopped thinking about you since our date, but I have to be real with you. I'm not going to be the type of guy who will always be available at the drop of a hat. I've got too much going on and if you need that kind of attention, then I'm sorry, I'm just not in the position to give it to you right now. I need simple."

She looks down at the floor and nods. Her eyes meet mine and they look shiny. She looks incredibly vulnerable. I want to reach for her, but I don't.

"I get it. It's okay. I'm not looking for anything serious right now either. I just wanted to make sure I didn't do anything wrong."

Giving in to my urge, I get up and pull her up from the desk. I tip her chin up so her eyes meet mine. "Don't ever think you did something wrong. It's all on me when I'm being a dick and I don't call or text, okay? Look. I have to head out of town tonight for an emergency, but I'll see you at this charity event."

"Is everything okay?"

"I don't know. I'll call you."

She exhales and looks up at me. "Don't make promises you can't keep." She pulls out of my arms and I can feel her retreat physically and emotionally. "They're waiting for me. I better get going."

"Andie…"

"Wish me luck, Cam." She smiles at me over her shoulder as she gets on the elevator.

"Good luck," I murmur as the elevator doors close. I can still smell her lingering floral perfume and I miss her already. "Fuck."

"Well *that* was pathetic."

I jump out of my skin as I look up in the direction of the voice. "Jesus Christ TJ, how long have you been sitting over there and how on earth did you manage to stay silent through that?"

He's lounging in the window seat that Oreo usually occupies. "Long enough to hear how you just mucked that all up."

I run my fingers through my hair willing my heartrate to calm down. "I don't know what you're talking about. I didn't muck anything up."

TJ sighs as he stands. "You did, my little urban cowboy. This is going to take more work than I thought." He stares at me with his hands on his hips as if I'm one of his clients that needs a head-to-toe revamp. He throws his arms in the air, disgust clearly written across his face. "Ugh, Cam, I'll just have to do it all myself. You just sit there and look pretty." He storms out of the room.

I look off into space wondering what the hell just happened and how I managed to piss off three people in less than hour.

Chapter 23

Cameron

"I CAN'T BELIEVE I let you talk me into this shit."

She straightens the collar of my shirt. "Uh, big brother, I didn't talk you into anything. You stepped into your own pile of doo when you were trying to be all macho around Andie. In fact, I tried getting you to give the ticket to one of your flavors of the month."

I scowl as I tuck my shirt into the tight-ass jeans she has me in. "I thought you were trying to make Andie jealous."

Kiki chuckles. "Ah Cam, I love you and would do anything for you, but turning one of my girlfriends into Cambait isn't in my wheelhouse."

I huff out a laugh. "You're such a liar."

She shrugs as Sarah steps in and puts something in my hair and starts mussing it up. "Want some makeup, Cam?"

"Do I need makeup?" Sarah and Kiki step back and survey their work. Sarah smiles. "Nah, I like you *au natural*. You have a nice deep tan. How is that anyway? It's January."

"Kiki, these jeans are way too tight."

"Even better," she appraises. "Maybe undo some more buttons on your shirt. Get that Rico Suave vibe going."

"No."

TJ walks in and starts a slow whistle. "Huminah huminah. Where are we off to, Cam Bam?"

I sigh and look up to the ceiling. "If you two so much as utter a single word to him about this I will never talk to you again."

Kiki and Sarah stand silently as they smile at TJ.

"No!" He starts to laugh. "No way!"

"I don't know what just happened or how weird it is that the three of you can communicate on another wavelength, but I hate you all."

"Oh Cam, don't be such a sourpuss, I think it's cute." TJ flings himself onto Sarah's couch. "You're super hot when you're pouty though."

"Going to the Romance Writers Sexiest Cover Model convention where women will be fondling all sorts of body parts does not sound like fun in my book, no pun intended."

"SHUT. THE. FRONT. DOOR." TJ slaps his leg and howls. "That's not what crazy-eyes Kiki was conveying." He wipes tears from his eyes. "Oh my god, this is too good. You have to let me tag along."

"No! Absolutely not."

Kiki digs around in her purse. "Crazy-eyes already has you covered. What are best friends for, Tammy Jean?" Kiki hands him an extra ticket.

"You have officially been written out of my will," I grumble.

"The best part is, Matt signed Cam up to be in the silent

auction where one lucky lady will get to go out on a date with him."

"It's for charity," I snap as I put on a belt. "And for the record, I didn't know what I was saying yes to."

"Don't worry, Cameo, I'll make sure I win your date. How did you not know you were signing up to be Romance Cover Boy of the Year? Ooh, I think they have a yummy calendar too. Are you going to be in that?"

I look at him as panic starts to stir my blood.

"Oh, that would be fun!" Sarah smiles at me.

"Wouldn't it be funsies if they had a life-sized book cover and you could pose as the cover model in one of them? We are so doing that if they have one." TJ claps his hands giddily.

"Great," I gripe. "So, did you all know Matt was going to be a celebrity MC at this thing? And why him? It's kind of random."

Sarah shrugs. "He might have mentioned it about five hundred times. He was asking all of us girls if we wanted to go. And we thought it would be good for Andie to meet some professional photographers, so we're going to support the two of them. I'm not sure how he got involved. I think he dated one of the organizers for a bit."

"Yeah and Cam couldn't contain himself. He just *had* to go too." Kiki smirks. "Said it was his *thing*."

"Hey y'all ready?" Andie knocks on the door saving me from any more harassment as she steps into the room. Her eyes dilate when they see me. "Wow Cam, you look...different."

"Super hot, right, Shorts?" TJ winks at her as he sashays

out of the office. "Meet you all downstairs. I'm just going to let Connor know I'm going. Don't forget your Skittles!"

I look at the girls quizzically. "The candy?"

Kiki shakes her head. "Don't ask."

I turn back to Andie. "Do I look stupid?" I look down at the tight jeans and dark navy button-down Kiki has me dressed in.

Andie bites her lip and her eyes get dreamy. "Stupid, um…no…"

"You look really pretty," I say as I step closer to her. Her hair is pulled up into a topknot with loose tendrils framing her face. She smells really good too. I want to run my nose along her neck.

She steps back, putting some space in between us. I look around the room but we're alone. "So, you ready for this?" She gives me a bemused smile.

"If you mean am I ready to get auctioned off on a date with a romance reading enthusiast…no."

"Ah yes, the date. She'll be a lucky lady." She bites down on her lip as she swings her purse onto her shoulder. I step back into her space and place my hands on her hips.

"I swear I had no idea Matt was signing me up for this, he said it was for charity. Honestly, I just wanted to go because you were going. I didn't even know what it was. And when I'm up on that stage tonight, the only woman I'll be wishing was taking me on a date will be you."

"Cam…" She sighs. "It doesn't matter. Keep it simple, remember? That's what you wanted."

"Andie—" I know what I said, but I don't want this indifference from her. I want what we had on our first date. I want more.

"Okay you two, it's time! We have to go!" Kiki shouts from the other room.

"Can we talk after this whole thing is over? Maybe go to dinner?"

Her eyes nervously dart around the room. "I guess...but just as friends, okay?"

I grab her waist and pull her in for a quick kiss. Her hazel eyes light up with surprise before I release her and stride out of the room.

THOUSANDS OF WOMEN mill about the arena-sized conference center going from booth to booth of photographers and romance writers. Male models are signing books and taking pictures with groups of women. Some women are crying they can't believe they finally get to meet the man of their dreams. I uncomfortably tug at my collar as I stay with TJ and Andie while Sarah and Kiki go off to look for Matt. The women next to us eye me brazenly as I avoid eye contact. *I should have listened to Lex, dammit.*

I think of all the things that I could be doing at the moment, all the thing I need to be doing, and then I look over at the reason I'm here. She's talking animatedly to a photographer and I think to myself it's worth every butt-pinch I've received since I walked in. She's so beautiful as she throws her head back and laughs. The photographer introduces her to one of his models and I immediately tense as the guy gives her a once-over and smiles genuinely at her.

"Don't worry, Mancam, he's gay. Trust me I've got good 'dar. A lot of these beefy baes are."

"I wasn't worried," I say gruffly as I turn my attention away from Andie.

"He who denies it, cries it," TJ singsongs.

I side-eye him. "That doesn't even make sense."

TJ sighs. "On the outside you're denying your love for her, but on the inside you're just a little lost boy crying for his mommy."

"Uh, this conversation is making me seriously uncomfortable, and that's pretty fucking hard to do considering we are in a room with over a thousand women who want to get in my pants."

"Your macho-cheese-mo makes me swoon." TJ sighs next to me. "Fine, suit your sizzles, but I know the truth."

"Did you forget to take your medication today?" I breathe in relief as Andie walks back over just as Kiki comes up behind us. "I found Matt. He's over by the stage, so let's head that way."

I lace my fingers with Andie and she smiles at me. "You nervous?"

"Nah, just want this over with."

"Don't worry, I'm betting your bid will go pretty high the way all these women are drooling over you."

"Luckily I'll have TJ outbidding everyone."

We reach the stage and spot Matt standing with a group of other people. We shake hands after he gives the girls and TJ a hug. "Ready for this, man?"

"I can't believe you entered me in this."

"All for charity." Matt winks at me.

"Yeah, yeah, just tell me what I've got to do."

"Donna here will get you all set. Have fun, man." He smiles as he thumps my back and then gets swallowed up by people wanting his attention.

"Mr. Forbes? Hi, I'm Donna." Donna adjusts her reading glasses that are hanging from a chain around her neck. "Well, aren't you yummy." She giggles as she checks off something on her clipboard. "Okay, if you'll just follow me, we'll get you changed."

"Changed?"

She arches an eyebrow. "We can't have you fully dressed, now can we!"

Huh? "Donna, pardon me for asking, but I thought this was a date auction for charity."

Donna peers at me over her leopard-print readers. "Prince Charming wasn't afraid to take his shirt off to win over Cinderella, was he?"

"I'm pretty sure Prince Charming won over Cinderella with his 'charming' smile and stellar dance moves, not with his biceps."

Donna smirks. "Well, Mr. Forbes, this is the modern-day version. Now quit yapping and follow me."

She bustles through the crowd and I have to quicken my pace to keep up with her, wishing I could have about twelve shots of whiskey in my system right about now. There's no getting out of this and Donna seems like a woman who isn't about to be easily swayed by my smile or some sweet-talking.

I'm about to be fed to the sharks and I'm scared shitless.

Chapter 24

Andie

"POOR CAMERON," SARAH murmurs next to me. Women are screaming all around us as the men make their way down the catwalk. "Um, Kiki, will he be the only ones in jeans?"

Kiki looks at us with wide eyes. "He's going to kill us if they make him wear a mankini."

So far, the guys have come out wearing Speedos or Sungas. Kiki, Sarah, and I look at each other and start laughing so hard we all have tears in our eyes. "Oh my god he's going to be sooo pissed! Where's TJ by the way?"

Kiki looks around the crowd but doesn't spot him. She just shrugs and our attention returns to the parade of eligible bachelors. Cam comes out last and I feel like the wind has been knocked out of me because he is the most gorgeous man my eyes have ever feasted upon. He struts down the runway like a trained model with all of his glorious muscles and ten-pack abs. Is ten even a thing? I don't know and I don't care. I'll count them later when I'm licking them one by one.

Whoa, I must be channeling Mandy at the moment. Quite presumptuous of me to think I'll ever be intimate with Cameron Forbes. But damn, he's smoking and he knows it by the smirk he's sporting, and by the women going nuts.

Kiki laughs. "Where the hell did he dig those up and why is he the only one that gets to where fitted swim trunks?"

TJ suddenly appears, panting and waving a white sheet in front of us. "Go Cam!" he screams like a tween at a Taylor Swift concert. "Oh, I love his shorts. Nice!"

"Where have you been?"

"Oh bejeeze wax, ladies, let me tell you, these women in here are *nutcray*! I was in a bidding war over Cam with a ghastly lady from Omaha named Marsha, another woman named Mary Joe from Kentucky who is a recent divorcée and enjoys margaritas on the patio and sunset cruises. And finally, there's Lenoir, a grandmother of six who likes to bake her world-famous chocolate chip cookies and knit scarves for dogs in her local shelter."

"That's crazy." Sarah watches the guys on stage.

"I know, right? That's a lot of scarf knitting."

"What? No." Sarah hits him in the chest. "That guy just made his bicep move in different directions."

Matt introduces each of the candidates and the ladies around us scream so loud I have to hold my fingers in my ears to keep from going deaf. He finally reaches Cameron and the noise in the room is deafening.

"At last, ladies, meet Cameron Forbes, owner of The Social Hour bar here in Nashville, with locations also in Chicago and California. That's right, ladies, he will jet you off to the location of your choice for an intimate evening alone where he will wine and dine you and maybe read you a few steamy passages from one of your favorite books. A romantic night with your own personal millionaire business mogul Mr. Forbes." Cameron gives Matt a panicked look as ladies go wild around us. "Dude, are those turtles on your shorts?" Matt says.

Cameron looks like a deer in headlights as Matt sticks the microphone in his face. "Uh, yeah. Save the turtles and all that."

"Oh my god, I didn't know Cam was a VSCO girl!" TJ claps as he hops up and down.

"What the hell is a VSCO girl?" Sarah asks.

"You know, the teenage girls who want to save the turtles, wear some kind of backpack, scrunchies, and carry a Hydro Flask water bottle."

"Never heard of it. How do you even know what teenage girls…you know what, never mind." She shakes her head.

"Oh my gosh, girl, let me tell you, it's—"

"TJ, focus!" Kiki shakes his arm to get his attention. "Aren't you supposed to be over at the table outbidding the highest bidder?"

"Oh totes. So…about that. Connor gave me a cap on how much I can spend. So…yeah. That's come and gone."

"What? TJ! Oh my god, Cam is going to kill us!" Kiki cries. "We have to get over there and be the last." Kiki grabs TJ's hand as she busts through the crowd with her pregnant belly pushing women out of the way. "Coming through! Move it! My water just broke!"

"Oh Kiki, you are so bad." Sarah laughs as she and I

apologize to the women left in our wake.

We reach the bidding table and find Cameron's number. A formidable-looking woman is standing in front of his bidding sheet with her arms crossed.

"That's Marsha, she's super scary," TJ whispers as the four of us approach her.

"TJ, you distract her while I grab his bidding sheet."

"What? Kinky, no! She growled at me earlier and I may or may not have peed in my pants." TJ squirms uncomfortably as he whines. "She could snap me like a twig."

Kiki rolls her eyes and squeezes herself in between Marsha and another woman. "Oh hey, Marsha, I'm one of the judges. I just need to check all the bidding sheets and make sure everyone has a bid."

Marsha looks irritably at Kiki but doesn't budge.

"Hi Marsha, I'm Sarah. Wow, did you get your visor signed? By who?"

"Mr. December," she growls.

"Oh, I love Mr. January. Which one is Mr. December up there?"

Marsha turns and points to the stage allowing for Kiki and me to grab his sheet.

"Oh wow, hmm…"

"What is it?" I arch my neck to see.

"It's kind of high. I'm not so sure Tatum—"

"Kiki! This is your brother we're talking about. Do you really want Marsha to kidnap him and tie him to her bed? Because she's seriously putting off vibes from the lady in the movie *Misery*…" I look around to make sure Marsha is still distracted. She's showing Sarah something on her phone. TJ is animatedly talking to some older woman who's digging through her purse.

"You're right, you're right." She scribbles as a woman rushes by and picks up all the papers. "Hey! I was writing on that!"

"Bidding is over!" the lady shouts and then she does a double-take at Kiki's belly. "Some people, I swear. Disgusting! Bidding on a date with a man while pregnant with twins. Shame on you," she mutters as she scoots past us.

"Hey! He's my *brother* and it's *not* twins!" Kiki looks around as the women close by give her strange looks. "Well that didn't come out quite right." She smiles as her cheeks bloom pink. "It's for charity, right?"

Matt starts to speak into the microphone as we make our way back to the stage.

"You guys owe me for that one," Sarah grumbles. "Marsha had to show me her all of her pictures. She took a lot. Poor Mr. December. By the fifth picture he looked like he wanted to lose it."

"I promise I'll make it up to you." Kiki squeezes her into a side hug.

"Alright, alright! Who's ready to find out who their next book boyfriend will be in real life?"

The women once again go bananas as I hold my ears. "I think I feel a headache coming on," I grumble to Sarah. She nods in agreement as Matt starts reading the names off. Winners try to climb up on stage to reach their dates but security holds them back.

"Boy I hope Cam doesn't get Marsha. She looks like she could bench press Cam in her sleep." TJ grimaces as we watch Marsha elbow her way through the crowd to get to the front. She's holding two bags of books, a signed hat, and several posters. I swallow nervously for Cam.

"She certainly seems very enthusiastic." I hope Kiki was able to outbid her.

"And our last date for a night at The Social Hour bar with Mr. Cameron Forbes goes to...huh, should have known...Anderson Daniels."

"No!" Marsha shouts as she looks around at who could have stolen her date. I shrink back behind TJ in case somehow she knows it's me. All of a sudden it dawns on me that I owe a substantial amount of money for this so called "date."

"Wait, what?" I look at my three friends who are high-fiving each other. "Kiki, how much was that bid? I can't afford that!" I start to panic as I look back up at the stage. Matt smiles at Cameron and shakes his hand.

"Don't worry about it, Andie. Tatum and I bought the date. It's our gift, and it's for charity, right?" She smiles cheekily at TJ and Sarah.

"You guys planned this all along, didn't you." I eye them warily.

"Um, well kind of. TJ not following through was real." Kiki elbows him in the ribs.

"Ow, you hooker. You know good and well Connor would kill me if I won a date with Cam."

"It's not like you'd actually go on a date with him!" Kiki looks over at him with exasperation as we clap the men off the stage. "Uh, TJ? Where the hell did you get all the scarves from?"

"Oh these? Adorbs right? Lenoir had a few extra in her bag. Although, I'm sweating a little, and they kind of smell like dog pee." TJ wrinkles his nose as he sniffs a scarf. "But I did manage to get her to give up her chocolate chip recipe, so totes worth it."

Sarah grabs his arm as we head toward Matt. He has a blonde bombshell hanging on him as he signs autographs for some women and takes pictures. "Where are we supposed to meet Cam?"

"I don't know, I'll text him." Kiki quickly types in her phone. I'm anxious to get back home to Enzo. I left him with Becky and I'm always nervous if I leave her in charge for more than two hours. Mrs. Miller is home, but I hate to have to depend on her even if she told me she was always available. I don't want to take advantage of her kindness.

"Well, if we can't find him soon, I'll just take an Uber home. I've got to get home to Enzo."

"Have you told Cam about Enzo yet?" Sarah asks me.

"I'll take you home."

A deep voice behind me has us spinning around.

"Oh, hey, Cam! You looked great up there!" Sarah smiles widely at him as she squeezes my hand.

He crosses his arms over his chest. "Thanks," he grunts. He turns his attention to Kiki and TJ. "You and me? We're gonna have words."

"*Me?*" Kiki points to herself incredulously. "I *saved* your ass! TJ was the one that walked away from the bidding."

"What? Kinky! Only because Connor would have had my balls if I won a date with Cam! I like them just the way they are thank you very much. They're like cute little nug—"

"No one wants to hear about your nasty puny little hairy dates, Tammy Jean."

"Puny?" TJ gasps.

Cam sighs. "Are you two done yet?" he bites out and they immediately quiet down. "I was accosted outside the dressing room by a woman named…Marsha? She mentioned she knows my pal TJ." His eyes narrow on TJ. "She wanted to know how much the final bid went for so that she could top it. Apparently, she's been saving up for this event for two years and she had her eye on Mr. December, but when she saw me, she changed her mind. She wants to lay naked in satin sheets and whisper sweet nothings in my ear as we listen to the Piña Colada song in front of a fire, sipping on appletinis."

"Well, that sounds—"

"Psychotic?"

"I was going to say detailed…down to the appletinis on satin sheets…" Kiki tries without success to wipe the smile off her face.

"Marsha sounds like she knows what she wants." Sarah giggles. "A take-charge kind of woman."

"Oh, she'll take charge alright. Cam might have just met his match. Two alphas fighting like tigers in satin sheets. Grrr." TJ claws the air.

Cam shakes his head in annoyance as I bite down on my lip to keep from laughing. "You three are annoying assholes. Thanks for the heads-up on the swimsuit competition by the way." He grabs my hand.

"You're acting like I set this whole thing up. If I might remind you, *you* volunteered for this." Kiki arches an eyebrow at him.

"Come on, Andie, I need to get out of here before Marsha finds me. Right now she's over by Matt arguing with the charity committee." Cam tugs me behind him.

"Bye, guys! It was fun!" I shout to them over my shoulder.

"Cam! Cam!" TJ shouts.

We turn around to see what he wants, along with several women around us.

"Do you like piña coladas and getting caught in the rain? We're *dying* to know!"

Cam gives him the middle finger as the three of them fall into fits of laughter. "Assholes."

WE'RE DRIVING BACK to my house in silence. It's not exactly a tension-filled silence, but it's not exactly comfortable either. I try making small talk because it's making me nervous.

"Well, you survived it."

"Yeah." His jaw ticks and I try to figure out if he's mad at me for something or still ticked off at being thrown to the wolves at the auction.

"I liked your swimsuit."

"Hmm."

"Is something wrong?"

He looks at me for a brief second and then downshifts the Porsche as we turn onto my street. "Who's Enzo?"

I swallow past the sudden lump that fills my throat. I wasn't ready to share Enzo with him yet, especially after he completely left me hanging after our last date. Nerves sizzle in my stomach as I try to figure out what to say. I could make something up, but what would be the point of that? He'll find out eventually whether we are together or not. He pulls up to the curb in front of my house.

"Come in and I'll show you." I quickly get out of the car and wait for him by my steps. He eyes me warily as we walk up the wide stone steps to my front porch. I open the door and Darth Vader greets us enthusiastically. "This is my puppy, Darth Vader." I smile at him over my shoulder. "Are you okay with dogs?"

"Of course. *Star Wars* fan, huh?" He smiles as he bends down to pet Vader who is whining and whipping his tail against us.

"Mandy's foster dog had puppies and her kids named them. Hi, Becky!" I call out to my teenage babysitter who is lounging on the couch. I spy my little man playing with blocks over by his toy corner. I walk over to him and pick him up. I take a deep breath and turn around to face Cam. "Cam, meet my son, Enzo." I smile shakily as I kiss Enzo's cheek. I sneak a peek at Cam, but he looks like a stone statue, his expression indiscernible.

I turn my attention to the teenager who is snapping her gum and staring all googly-eyed at Cam. The sooner I get her out of here, the quicker I can explain things to him. "Uh, so thanks, Becky. Everything go okay?" I hand her twenty-five dollars from my purse.

"Sure thing, Ms. Daniels." She blows a bubble with her

gum as she eyes Cameron up and down. "What's up with him?"

"Oh, Cameron, this is my babysitter and neighbor Becky. Becky, this is Cameron."

Becky waves as she stuffs her water bottle, money, and phone into her backpack. "Cool."

Cameron gives her a stiff smile but doesn't say a word. Becky looks at me and scrunches her nose up. "Is he deaf?"

"Uh…"

"He's H.O.T., Ms. Daniels, but kinda weird, but maybe because he's deaf he doesn't want to talk. There's a kid in my biology class that's deaf, but he talks and signs, so yeah, that's cool. Should I try signing to him? I know a couple of words."

"Um, Becky, he's not deaf." I smile nervously between Becky and Cam. This seems to break Cam out of whatever trance he's been in. He smiles as he looks down at the floor. He reaches out a hand to Becky.

"It's nice to meet you, Becky."

"O.M.G, I die." Becky's face turns bright red as she tosses her backpack over her shoulder and scurries to the front door, ignoring Cam's outstretched hand.

"Well, she's…interesting." Cam smirks.

I wipe my hands nervously on my jeans. "Let me get him ready for bed and then maybe we can talk?"

Cameron nods stiffly as he sits down on my couch.

I hustle into the kitchen as I snuggle with Enzo. I breathe in his baby powder and lavender scent and it calms my nerves. "Did you have a good night, my little love bug?"

"Mama baba mo!" He jumps excitedly in my arms. I

warm up some milk in his bottle and head back down the hall to his room. I change his diaper and put him in his pajamas before I sit in his rocker and softly sing him a lullaby. His eyes start to droop as he gets to the end of his bottle and then they close as I continue to rock. The door creaks causing me to look up and I see Cam leaning against the doorjamb.

"Hi," I whisper as I stand up and gently place Enzo in his crib. I turn his under-the-sea lamp on and his white noise lamb and cover him with a blanket. I quietly walk out of the room and Cam follows me back to the living room. We sit down on the couch and the silence gets to be too much for me. "Do you want a beer?"

"No, I'm good."

I find my nails suddenly super interesting to look at. "He's eighteen months."

"Are you married?"

I look over at him. "No! I mean, I was with my ex Mason when he was born, but he left us back in Alabama when Enzo was just three months old. Enzo wasn't planned, and his father couldn't handle the pressure of having a baby. But no, we were never married."

Cam shakes his head. "I'm not going to lie, Andie, I'm surprised you never brought him up before."

"I know, I'm kind of protective over him."

Cam nods. "I—"

I turn to him on the couch. "Look, Cam, I get it. It's a lot to take. I understand if you don't want anything to do with me knowing I have a kid."

"That's not what I'm thinking. Where's his dad?"

I bite my lip. "I'm not sure. He's on the rodeo circuit. He hasn't seen Enzo since he up and left."

"Jesus." He sits back on the couch and runs his fingers through his hair. "Are you still in love with him? Do you think there's a chance the two of you will get back together?"

"No. I'm not sure I was ever in love with him, and no, we will never be getting back together."

"You've been raising Enzo all by yourself?" A look of tenderness crosses his face.

I swallow past the lump in my throat. "Yeah."

He stands up and extends his hand to me. I place my hand in his and he lifts me off the couch. He places his hands on my hips as he gazes down into my eyes. He tucks an errant curl behind my ear. "Why would you think I wouldn't want anything to do with you?"

"It's just…I mean, it's not just me I have to think about. I have responsibilities."

"Yeah…so do I, so?"

"Mine depends on me to live and breathe."

He chuckles quietly. "Yes, mine does too. My business is my baby, I take it very seriously. If I ignore it, it will die a slow death."

I nod as I stare at his broad chest. "Can I be honest with you?" I peer up at him.

"I'd appreciate it."

I lick my lips nervously, his eyes tracking my movement. "I'm kind of scared to get involved with you. Casual or not, I…I'm not sure my heart and head will survive it. It's not just me I have to think about."

He's silent a beat. "I'm scared too. I don't want to let

you down. Can we just see where this goes? I want to get to know you. And I realize we're both busy people who have responsibilities, but I like you a lot, Andie. I can't seem to get you out of my head."

"Can you promise me one thing?"

"I'll try my hardest."

"Not good enough."

He quirks a smile. "Okay, yes, whatever it is, I promise."

"Can you not leave me high and dry like you did after our last date? It messes with my head and I don't need any man-drama in my life right now. I'm on board with seeing where this goes, but if this doesn't work, then so be it...but don't leave me wondering. When Enzo's baby daddy up and left it was the biggest kick in the gut."

"I'm so sorry. I promise I will never leave you hanging again." He tilts my chin up and I get lost in his smoky grays. "Can I kiss you?"

I weigh my options. Being this close to him fogs my brain. I can't think, I can't breathe...I just want him.

"Yes," I whisper as he dips his head and gently kisses my lips.

I wrap my arms around his neck and push all my worries away. *So much for just dipping my toes*, I think, as I let myself completely fall in.

Chapter 25

Cameron

HER LIPS COLLIDE with mine and I'm momentarily surprised because I thought I was going to have to slowly coax her into kissing me, but she dives in head first. I part her lips with my tongue and eagerly taste her sweetness. She moans and the kiss intensifies. I run my hands over her perfect ass and then grab the backs of her thighs, lifting her up. She wraps her legs around me as I start to move backward down the hallway, careful not to make too much noise and wake the baby.

Baby…I can't believe she never told me about him. To say I was shocked is an understatement. At first I thought Enzo was her dog, then tonight when I overheard Sarah talking about him I thought it was Andie's boyfriend. So, to see her holding a toddler knocked me on my ass. It doesn't change how I feel about her though. If anything, it makes me respect her more for being a hard-working mom. But it does make it harder to keep this casual. I've never dated a single mom before and it scares me a little. I don't want to screw this up or hurt her.

She reaches her hand out as we're still lip-locked and shoves a door on the left at the end of the hallway open. I walk her through and gently set her down on the bed.

I place my knee on the bed. "Is this okay?"

"Wait, I need to turn music on or something." She pulls her phone out and turns on a music station.

"Are you worried your parents will hear us?" I tease.

"No, just Enzo."

I nod as she sits up and fists my shirt as she pulls me toward her. I capture her mouth in a dizzying kiss and she moans which makes my blood pump into overdrive. She starts to unbutton my shirt as my fingers lift hers up and pull it off. I reach over and turn the bedside lamp on because I want to see her beautiful body.

She makes a distressed noise as she reaches over and turns the lamp back off. I chuckle and stop touching her. "Andie, what are you doing?"

"What do you mean?" she pants as she pushes my shirt off.

"I want to see you."

"Cam…" she whines.

"What? You're beautiful. I want to be able to see all of you." I switch the light back on and she looks around nervously. I start to undo the buttons on her jeans and hook my fingers into the waistband to slide them off when she clasps her hands over mine.

"Wait! Cam, I'm…I don't have the same body like I used to. My hips are wider, I have stretch marks, my boobs are—"

"Perfect. You're perfect." I kiss her stomach and then move to her pert nipple as I suck it into my mouth. God, she tastes so sweet, just like I knew she would. She threads her fingers through my hair and I hum in pleasure as I kiss my way down, pulling her jeans off with me. I tug them off and stand up looking down at her beautiful body. "You're gorgeous, Andie, every inch of you."

"I'm not a Brazilian bikini model." Her lip curves up into a nervous smile.

I raise my eyebrow and huff out a laugh, baffled by her comment. "I like you just the way you are." I bend down and kiss her panties. I'm so hard I'm aching to be inside her. I know we said we were going to take it slow, but I'm not sure I can.

"Cam—"

"Andie, I want to fuck you. With the lights on. Will that be alright?" I move the silky fabric aside and run a finger back and forth over her slit. She's so wet.

She looks at me with wide eyes and closes her mouth. She nods yes and scoots back on the bed. I smile to myself as I pull her panties off. I run my hands over her hips and rest them on her thighs as I spread her legs. She's fucking gorgeous and for right now, in this moment, she's all mine. I groan in anticipation as I smell her sweet scent. I lick her slowly and she arches into my mouth as she pants my name.

"Yes Cam, oh my god, yes."

I look up at her as she arches into me wanting more. I grab her hips hard and suck her sweetness, licking and stroking her to a frenzy. Her fingers pull my hair which makes me groan against her. I want her to come hard into

Chapter 26

Andie

"HE'S IN THE shower," I whisper. "So, I can only talk for a second."

"Give it to me!" Mandy shouts in my ear.

"Ssh, you're so loud. The neighbors can hear you through the phone."

"Anderson Daniels you are wasting precious seconds of details! And wait a second, why is he showering alone?"

I giggle. "I have a little human being named Enzo that woke us up at the crack of dawn. I think I got about three hours of sleep last night." I take a big gulp of coffee.

Mandy groans, "I'm seriously so jealous right now. I was up at the crack of dawn because the cat came into the bedroom and puked up a hairball. No one, and I mean no one, can sleep through that wretched noise, except Deacon, of course."

"Oh, I just heard the shower turn off, I'll call you later."

"Nooo! You are the worst best friend ever!"

"No one asked you to share your cat-puking story." I

shift Enzo on my hip as he tries to grab the phone. "I'll call you later."

I hang up on her just as Cam comes walking down the hall with a small white towel wrapped around his waist, his wet hair slicked back. Droplets on his shoulders beg to be licked off. He is so sinfully delicious. I blink a couple times to make sure he's real and not an illusion. He smiles at me as my eyes travel down his gorgeous toned physique. He has an eight pack, I counted last night, and it is freakin' delightful to run my fingers over the ridges and hard muscle. His V dips down into the towel and I swallow past the nerves that have suddenly constricted my throat.

"Good morning, beautiful." He steps up into my personal space and kisses my swollen lips. He steps back and takes a hold of one of Enzo's hands. "Hi little man, you're an early riser, huh?"

Enzo grabs his index finger and gives Cameron a gummy smile. "Baba na na!"

Cam smiles back at him and my heart melts. "Nice to meet you too, bud." His eyes return to mine. "I'm going to get dressed and then I'll hang out with this guy so you can shower if you want. I have to head over to The Social Hour because we're trying out a Sunday brunch thing. You guys could come along if you want."

I smile. "I'd like that. Are you sure it's okay to bring Enzo?"

"Of course. I think Kiki and Sarah are bringing the kids."

I breathe out a sigh of relief and nod my head. "Yes, we'd love to, wouldn't we buddy?" Cam smiles at the both of us and my heart swells to ten times its size. I look at his naked chest. "Won't you need a change of clothes?"

"Yeah, I'll run over to my condo first. Do you mind meeting me there?"

"No, that works." I smile back at him as I put Enzo into his highchair.

Cameron tugs me around into his arms. "If Enzo weren't sitting here watching us, I'd have my wicked way with you against this counter." He kisses me again as my heartrate spikes. My hands slide up into his hair causing him to groan. He gently bites my bottom lip as he releases me and saunters back to the bedroom.

"Oh buddy, I'm in so much trouble." I turn to Enzo as I take a big gulp of coffee and sink into the kitchen chair.

"CAM, THIS BRUNCH is unbelievable!" Sarah gushes as she exchanges a crying Wyatt over to Lex for her sweet sleeping Alexis. "I swear this baby sleeps through anything."

"Ugh, I'm so jealous. Chase was up three times last night. I don't know what's going on with him. Growth spurt or teething."

"Just wait until you have two!" TJ waggles his eyebrows excitedly.

"I guess we got off easy then with the six a.m. wakeup call, huh?" Cam whispers to me, but the smile slides off my face as I look up at the rest of the table and they are all zeroed in on us. "Ah shit." Cam slides a hand down his face.

"Shit!" Chase shouts at the table.

"No! Chase Cameron Reed that is a bad no-no word!" Kiki admonishes the toddler as Tatum chuckles. "Cam, seriously? Try to use words like snickers or shucks. This is not funny!" She thwacks Tatum's shoulder. "Chase has the memory of an elephant. He'll be repeating that word for the next year!"

Cameron tries to wipe the smile off his face. "I'm sorry, Chase. Uncle Cam shouldn't have said that." He gets up from the table and lifts Chase into his arms. "Come on buddy, let's go restock the Bloody Mary bar."

Everyone's head swivels in my direction. I start to sweat under their questioning stares. TJ starts to slow clap and I wince. "I guess Marsha didn't get to roll around in the satin sheets with Cambam, because Andie was the one making the appletinis."

I roll my eyes and try to deflect. "So how about that new account we got yesterday morning." I smile brightly.

"Operation Dill I'd say is successful." TJ high-fives Kiki and Sarah.

"What's Operation Dill?" Tatum asks suspiciously. He arches a brow at Kiki. "Kiki, what now?"

"Nothing, nothing I swear. Just a friendly little wager between the four of us. Don't worry, Tater Tot, it's all good." She gets up and kisses his cheek as she heads over to my side of the table. She leans down and whispers in my ear, "Thank you for making him so happy, Andie. I haven't seen my brother this relaxed in a long time." She kisses my cheek. "I'm so glad you told him about Enzo."

Normally all this attention would embarrass me, but I

feel elated by her revelation.

"He makes me happy too," I whisper back as I squeeze her hand.

She looks up and her smile grows. "There's my little nugget!"

Cam passes Chase over to her and she takes him back to her seat.

"Everything okay?" Cam leans in and nuzzles my ear.

I smile at him and nod. "Everything is perfect." He leans over and kisses me on the lips before he turns his attention to the rest of the table. Kiki is right, this is the most relaxed I've ever seen him. TJ winks at me and I feel my cheeks heat as I smile at him. Enzo bangs the table next to me and TJ hands him a spoon which he immediately grabs onto. I place some blueberries on his plastic mat to distract him.

"Shit."

I look up as Cameron tenses next to me. "What's wrong?"

"Well, well, well, Cameron Forbes. What a *surprise*."

I look up to see a tall thin brunette woman dressed in a French floral blouse with pale pink slacks and a matching purse. She doesn't sound surprised, she sounds pissed. The table goes silent except for the babies gabbing, because they have no idea they are about to witness a shitshow. Cam's arm is around the back of my chair and he doesn't move a muscle.

"That's 'that's not Lisa'," TJ whispers loudly to Kiki who pantomimes him to zip it. I'm trying to process everything around me, but I'm having a hard time getting my brain to reboot. Who is Lisa and who is *this* woman? Cam sighs heavily and starts to get up.

"No, no, please don't let *me* interrupt. I mean, you'd expect him to invite his *girlfriend* to brunch with friends, am I right?" She laughs a little off-pitch.

Voices around me sound tinny as I try to grasp what she's saying. *Girlfriend?* You would have thought him having a girlfriend would have been brought up in our "honesty" conversation last night. My heart feels like it's beating too fast in my chest, like a trapped hummingbird thumping its wings against my ribcage.

Cameron stands up and strides over to her. "Jesus Christ, Kendra, we went on *one* date. That doesn't make you my girlfriend for fuck's sake. You're embarrassing yourself right now in front of my family." He takes her elbow but she wrenches her arm free.

"You bastard! So you fuck me and then you move on just like that?" She snaps her fingers in his face. Sarah covers her eleven-year-old son Jax's ears as she looks at us with wide eyes.

Cam makes a distraught noise. "That was forever ago!"

"And what about December, huh?"

December? Didn't *we* go on a date in December? I look around the table, but everyone's attention is on Cam.

"What the hell are you talking about?" Cam seethes as he tries to steer her out of the bar, but she digs her heels in. "I only met you for drinks, and it was because I needed a real estate agent."

"Call it what you want, Cameron Forbes, but you used me...you...you bastard!" She picks up the closest drink from the table which happens to be Lex's Bloody Mary and dumps it over Cam's head. We all gasp in disbelief. Kendra slams the glass back down on the table waking up Wyatt and causing him to cry, but she doesn't even notice or care. "Don't ever call me again!" She sobs as she stomps out of the bar.

"Mate, wow...I thought Matt was bad with women." Lex hands him a napkin as he gets up and walks away to soothe Wyatt.

"Jesus Christ," Cam mutters as he wipes tomato juice off his face. His dress shirt and slacks are completely ruined. "I'm sorry about that, everyone."

"Cam, you look like you got skunked."

"I think he just did. Geez Cam, that was...insane. Are you okay?" Kiki hands Chase over to Tatum and grabs some napkins, but I'm completely frozen in my seat. I feel like I've just watched an intense movie and I'm still trying to interpret my feelings over it. Enzo fusses next to me and I turn my attention to him. I lift him out of his seat and hold him close to me, but he continues to fuss. I try to put a pacifier in his mouth, but he takes it out and throws it down. I smile apologetically at TJ.

"It's almost naptime, so I better get him home."

"Do you need a ride?" TJ looks sympathetically at me and I know it's not because Enzo is acting fussy.

"No, I'm good, I drove."

"Okay Shorts, I'll call you later." He gets up to hug me and whispers in my ear, "Don't worry, that crazy Kendra was *not* his girlfriend."

I look past him over to Cam. "It's okay. I'm fine. I'm not his girlfriend either, so..." I shrug as I reach for my diaper bag shifting Enzo to my other hip. "Thanks for brunch, y'all. I have to get Enzo home for his nap."

"Yeah, we need to get going too." Tatum stands and gathers up Chase's toys. I hug Sarah and Kiki and kiss them goodbye.

"Andie, can I walk you out?" Cam asks gruffly as he runs a towel through his hair.

I look him over, but it's hard to take him seriously when he has tomato juice poured over his crisp clean white button-down. "Ah, it's okay. I'll call you later, okay? You need to clean up and I need to get this fussy guy home."

Cam nods and doesn't push me. "I'll call you." He leans in to kiss me, but I rear back, barely holding myself together.

"No offense, but you're covered in tomato juice."

He nods and takes a step back. "You're right, I'm sorry."

I wave goodbye to everyone and hightail it out of there.

Chapter 27

Andie

THE DRIVE HOME happens in a blur. Tears leak out of my eyes because I have no idea what just happened. I'm mad, I'm sad, I'm confused. I can't seem to get a grasp on my feelings and it's pissing me off. I need to call Mandy and go through the last hour with her. Who was that woman? And if Cam hadn't jilted her, then why was she so pissed? I need to calm down and think this through rationally before I can talk to Cameron.

I find a spot down the street from my house and gather my diaper bag and Enzo. I wipe the tears from my wet cheeks and stop short as I notice someone sitting on my front porch. *What the hell?*

"Andie." Mason stands up, his familiar eyes glint under his large cowboy hat.

"Mason?" No, no, no…this can't be happening. Mason is the last person I want to deal with right now. "What are you doing here?"

"I was in town, you know, for the rodeo."

"Of course," I say dryly as I fumble with my key in the lock.

"Can I come in?"

"It's not really a good time for me right now, Mason." I sigh in relief as the key turns.

"Please, Andie. I want to talk to you and see my son."

I growl irritably as I turn around. "How did you even find me?"

"Mary Kate got your address for me from your mama."

Ugh, fucking Mary Kate. Mama must not have known she was going to use it to give to Mason. "So, you show up here out of the blue on a Sunday afternoon to see *my* son who you abandoned a year ago?"

"Aw, come on Andie, don't be so dramatic. You make it sound like I don't give a shit about him."

I want to punch him in the face so badly in this moment, it takes all my self-control not to. "Get the fuck off my porch."

"I'm not leaving until I see my son. Is that him?"

Not the brightest crayon in the box. I roll my eyes in annoyance. "Of course this is him, what other baby would I have?"

Mason bends down and peers at Enzo. "Hey dude. You gonna be a cow-roper like your old man?"

"Not if I can help it," I gripe as I open the door. I was hoping he would leave before I got my key out of the lock. Mason follows in behind me. "Oh please, come on in."

Vader comes rushing up to him. "Oh hey doggy, when did you get a dog?"

"A while ago." *You would have known that if you ever*

I'M SITTING IN my chair watching Mason snore and ignoring texts from Cam, Kiki, and TJ. I just can't deal with them at the moment.

Mason snores so loudly he wakes himself up. He looks around the room in a panic.

"You're in my house, Mason."

"Oh, hey. I must have fallen asleep." He smiles devilishly at me as he wipes a hand across his mouth and then stretches. "Want to join me over here like old times?"

Ugh. "No thanks."

He sits up and yawns. It's disorienting having him in my house when Cameron was just here this morning walking around in a towel. Mason doesn't belong here.

"Hey, do you mind if I grab a quick shower? I'm feeling kind of grubby."

"What? No, you can't use my shower."

"Oh come on, Andie, just a five-minute one. Then Enzo will be up, I'll spend some time with him and be out of your hair."

I groan in frustration. "What are you doing here, Mason?"

"I told you. Shower? Please? Come on. I'll be quick."

"Ugh, just go take a fucking shower!" The sooner I give in to him the sooner he'll be out of here. My phone buzzes again.

Cam: *Andie, please call me.*

Cam: *I'm worried about you.*

I grab a throw pillow and scream into it. Why can't everyone just leave me the fuck alone? I type out a quick text.

Me: *I'm fine Cam. I'm not really in the mood to talk right now. Please just give me some space and I'll call you later.*

Mason walks out, freshly showered and sits down on my couch, stretching his long legs out. I tuck my phone behind me. I once found this man incredibly attractive. He was such a catch for our small town. But now, I can't find one attractive quality about him. He clasps his hands together.

"So…" He watches the game on the television.

"So? It's been a year and all you have to say is so?"

He looks over at me. "I came to see Enzo, and you."

I roll my eyes. "Why now?"

"I'm sorry about the way I left things." He looks down at his feet. "I just wanted a life, you know?" He smiles at me and I want to knock all his teeth out one by one.

"Oh, and I didn't? And since when does having a child make your life suddenly end? If anything, it makes the world brighter…more vibrant, better."

Mason's smile slides off his face. "You were better suited at taking care of him. I had dreams, Andie. I'm sorry, but I needed to follow them."

I scoff, "Since when were your dreams to run away with the rodeo?"

Mason stands up and starts pacing. "Mary Kate never gives me shit over this."

I see red at the mention of that skank's name. "Are you two *together*?"

"Hey, I'm sorry you're jealous of my dreams, but I'm not

the one who got pregnant."

I hold up a hand. *Dear God, please give me the strength not to murder this dipshit right now.* "Uh, last I checked it takes *your* sperm to meet my egg and do the tango. Enzo was not immaculate conception, you fucking idiot."

"How do I know he's even mine? Mary Kate said—"

"Seriously?" I stand up, rational anger making every bone in my body vibrate. "I don't give a *fuck* what Mary Kate said, you know I never cheated on you! She's hellbent on making me miserable for some unknown reason, spreading rumors that Enzo wasn't yours. She's one of the main reasons I had to leave Inkdale. Unfortunately, he *is* half yours. Hopefully he got all of my brain cells."

Mason glares at me, but I give it right back to him. "When did you become such a bitch? Jesus, Andie, I came here to see Enzo. Are you going to let me or not?"

Forget his teeth, I want Darth Vader to rip his balls off. "I'm not going to keep you from Enzo, but I'm also not going to have you float in and out of his life when it pleases you. That's not fair to him. He's going to need his dad."

"No shit, Sherlock," he mumbles. "That's why I'm here."

"Excuse me? Where have you been for the past year?" I cross my arms over my chest, restraining myself from shoving him.

"I got it, Andie, stop busting my balls about this. You're talking to me like I'm a deadbeat dipshit."

God, I so wished I had my phone recording this so I could go back and replay it when I'm feeling lonely.

I start to pace around the living room to burn off some of this adrenaline coursing through my system. "Fine, then we should talk about visitation rights, what weekends you will have him, if you want him during the week, that kind of thing. Or we can go to a mediator if you'd rather."

Mason sits back down on the couch. "Whoa, whoa, I can't take him on the weekends. I'm still bull riding. I go where the wind takes me, Andie."

"So…what? You just want to pop on over whenever the wind blows you through Nashville?"

"Yeah."

I rub a hand down my face. I'm going to hunt Mary Kate down and strangle her for giving him my address. "And what if it's not a good time for us?"

"Who? Are you seeing someone?"

"No, you idiot, me and Enzo!" I flop my arms at my side in exasperation.

"If you have a boyfriend, I don't want him around Enzo."

"If it were up to me, I wouldn't want *you* around Enzo."

Mason shakes his head and looks at me seriously. "Don't make me get lawyers involved, Andie."

I'm vibrating with anger. "Ha! That's rich, Mason. Don't fucking sit there on *my* couch in *my* house and fucking threaten me!" I clench the chair in front of me so tightly my knuckles turn white. "We haven't even discussed backpay for child support."

Mason grunts. "I don't like this new side of you. What happened to the sweet Southern girl who thought I hung the moon?"

I fold my arms and look away from him. "She died a quick death when you left me with a hundred bucks and a baby to raise by myself."

He's silent a beat. "Listen, I've got to go. I'll come around tomorrow."

"I have to work, Mason."

"Well who the fuck watches Enzo while you're at work?"

"Uh, it's called daycare."

"Are they decent?"

I snort. "I don't think you really get a say in where I send Enzo."

"He's mine too, Andie."

"Could have fooled me."

He ignores me as he pulls his boots back on. "I'll stop by in the morning before you head out. Can I just peek my head in?"

I shrug, suddenly bone-tired by this conversation and this man-child in front of me. "I guess."

I lead him down the hallway and quietly open the door to my sweet sleeping angel. Mason quietly walks in and peers into the crib. "He looks like you." He smiles as he kisses his two fingers and places them on Enzo's head.

As much as I hate this asshole, my heart clenches for Enzo. I know he'll need his dad in his life. Mason smiles at me as he heads out of the room. I walk him to the front door. He walks through it, then turns around as I'm about to close the door.

"He's a cute kid, Andie. I'm sorry we argued. I don't want to fight with you."

I sigh, wishing things could be different. "I don't either, Mason."

"So hey, do you have forty bucks? You know, since I left

that hundred for you with the note?"

I roll my eyes. *How on earth did I ever think I loved this asswipe?*

"Nope." I slam the door in his face.

I grab my phone and text Mandy.

Me: *Turn your car around. There's been a change of plans. I'm coming home tonight.*

Chapter 28

Cameron

I CHECK MY watch, hoping I'm not too late and that she hasn't already left for work. I guess I could always swing by there before I leave for the airport if she's not home. I'm worried because she never returned my phone calls yesterday. It took all my self-control not to come over to her house last night. She wanted space and I wasn't going to crowd her, but I needed to explain Kendra to her.

What a shitshow that was yesterday. I can't even begin to explain how embarrassed I was in front of not just my friends and family, but the crowded patrons that were there for a nice Sunday brunch. Instead they got *Jerry Springer*. That crazy woman came into my place of business and shit on it.

I'm not sure how I'm going to explain her to Andie, except for the truth, that she's totally delusional. I can only hope Andie will forgive me for making her feel like a fool, because by the hurt look in her eyes yesterday when she left, that has to be how she felt. I let my guard down with Andie. She took my heart and made it her own, and now I'm at her mercy.

I pull up in front of her house and lock my car as I get out. I walk up her stone steps and pause when I see a guy in a cowboy hat sitting in a porch chair. I look around and then proceed. Who the hell is this person hanging out on her porch at eight a.m.? Is he homeless?

"Can I help you?" I ask.

"Who the fuck are you?"

"Cameron Forbes. I think you might have the wrong house, man."

"Is this your house?"

"No."

"Then I don't have the wrong fucking house," he snarls as he slowly stands up. He's wiry, but shorter than me. He cracks his knuckles in a show of intimidation. "I'm going to count to ten and then you can get the fuck off my girlfriend's front porch."

"Your girlfriend?"

"Did I stutter, dickmunch? Get back in your fancy car and get the fuck out of here."

I eye him over and smirk. This must be Andie's ex. "Is Andie home?"

He steps forward and tries to take a swing at me, but my reflexes are better and I easily manage to duck out of the way. He leaves his face exposed and I return his advance with a right uppercut and land squarely on his jaw. His face flings back and I step back as he stumbles. He tries to recover but I jab him in the left eye and he howls.

"Tell Andie I stopped by, cowboy."

I get back in my Porsche as her ex holds his hands to his

face, slouched against her porch railing. Fuck, my knuckles are already starting to swell. I try Andie's number again but it goes straight to voicemail. I speed over to The Social Hour to see if she's upstairs.

Chapter 29

Andie

"WHAT ARE YOU going to do?" Mandy sits down on the couch with a steaming mug of coffee as I sit on the floor stacking blocks with Enzo in my parents' living room.

"I don't know. I can't believe he had the nerve to show up on my doorstep."

"I can't believe Mary Kate had the nerve to ask your mama for your address."

"Please," I scoff, "you know she'd go to whatever lengths possible to get in Mason's pants."

"He's such a jerk face. I'll kung fu his ass if he ever tries to pull the lawyer crap again."

I sigh and run my hand through Enzo's soft golden curls. "No need to pull a groin muscle over that idiot. I mean the truth of the matter is, he is his dad and he does have the right to see him. I honestly don't want Enzo to grow up without a dad, but what the hell was he thinking just showing up out of the blue?" I place a block on top and Enzo stands up and knocks it down, giggling. "You little monster, did you just knock down my blocks?" I tickle him until he wiggles away from me. I sigh deeply. "I don't know what to do, I'm kind of at his mercy. I feel helpless."

"Well, as Mama always says, you're only helpless when your nail polish is wet, but even then, you could still pull a trigger if you had to."

I smile ruefully at my friend. "You're crazy."

"You know I'd help you bury the body." She smiles and sits back sipping her coffee, mulling over the situation. "Okay let's talk game plan if he shows up again. Ooh! I know, we can roleplay. I saw this on Dr. Phil."

I look at her dubiously as she puts her coffee on one of Mama's macramé coasters.

"Okay, it totally didn't work, but let's give it a go anyway. It will help prepare you. I'll start. I'm Mason, obviously." She gets up and goes to my parents' kitchen. Vader jumps up and follows her, wagging his tail. "Pretend this is the front door!" she shouts across the room.

"Okay."

"Yo woman, sup? What's the sitch?" She swaggers into the room.

"He doesn't talk like a cast member from *Jersey Shore*." I laugh and roll my eyes at my idiotic friend as she does gangster arm movements.

"Okay, okay, starting over." She leans up against the hallway entrance wall and nods her head. "Hello, Babycakes. I've missed you. Can I take a shower?"

I giggle because she has it all wrong except for the shower part, but I play along to appease her. "I can't say I feel the same, and no on the shower."

"Yes! Good answer!" She fist-pumps.

"Uh, aren't you supposed to be in character?"

"Dammit, yes, 'kay, let's keep going. Sorry, I got excited." She walks into the room and sits down across from me. "I want to see Enzo."

"Here he is."

"Oh my gosh he's so adorable with his little curls and those dimples." Mandy grabs him and tickles him. "My squishy wishy wittle gremlin." Enzo squeals in delight as he stands up and grabs a handful of her hair and tugs. "Ow! Dang Mister, I think you just took a chunk of my hair out." She looks up at me as she tries to wrangle her hair out of Enzo's slobbery fist. "This is not part of the acting, because Mason doesn't have long hair."

"Obviously," I deadpan as I try not to laugh. "Look, this has been super helpful, but we can stop the…uh, roleplaying. To be honest, I don't know if I'll ever see him again. He's not exactly Mr. Dependable."

"What if he wants to get back together?" Her eyes widen as she shakes her head no.

"I don't care how lonely I am or how long I've gone without sex, that's not happening. As much as I once wished for a whole family, he's proven to me that he can't be trusted. And I don't know, since meeting Cam, I feel different. Cam is so sweet, smart, funny, and…" I sigh.

"And what? Sexy as sin?" She grabs my shoulders and shakes me when I don't answer her. "What is that sexy beast to you, Andie?!"

"He's over is what he is," I say sadly as I start to put the blocks back in their bin.

"No, he is not over, you just need to process." She lays on her back and puts Enzo on her legs as she lifts them up in the air swinging him around. "He said that wasn't his girlfriend."

"Mandy, she said he had sex with her and dumped her. What if that's how it's going to be with me? Will I be showing up at The Social Hour all crazed out, pouring beers in his lap? Is that what he'll turn me into?"

"Only if you're cockadoodle crazycakes." She smirks.

"I left him a voicemail the other day telling him I think it would be best if we were just friends. It's just...easier that way." I haven't heard back from him, so I'm assuming he's cool with that decision.

"Sometimes I want to slap that pretty little head of yours silly."

"He wants simple, so that's what I'll be." I shrug my shoulders, ignoring her.

She throws a pillow and it hits me square in the head. "You're so full of shit. You couldn't do casual if it smacked you in the butt. And from what it sounds like, neither can Cam. You both are delusional."

"Face it, Mandy, it's over."

She sits up and puts Enzo down on the floor. "It ain't over 'til the fat lady sings and this lady hasn't even warmed up her vocal chords yet."

I laugh. "Quit calling yourself fat, you're beautiful."

She waves my comment away. "You may have said fuh-geddaboudit, but *we* have not."

"We?"

"TJ, Kiki, Sarah, and I are just as invested in this as you

are."

I groan. "Y'all need to butt out."

"I mean, I have to live vicariously through someone, and since you have that sex-on-a-stick pining after you, might as well be you! I'd rather think of my fantasy Cameron Forbes than my reality...Deacon Tillwater, while making hot passionate love."

"Ugh, I'd rather you not. I think I just vomited in my mouth." I get up and let Vader out back. "And I hate to break it to you, but he was never pining. In fact, he's probably moved on already."

"Damn that stupid-head Mason Mahoney and crazy brunch lady. I'll talk to TJ, we'll fix this. Soon enough we'll have Cameron Forbes running to you, not away from you."

"Oh Jesus, since when are y'all in cahoots?"

"We have a common goal in mind, Babycakes."

"Which is?"

"To help our loved ones find their happily-ever-after."

I roll my eyes. "Ha, no such thing. Remember? I don't believe in happily-ever-afters."

"God you're depressing when you're mopey."

I drop the block bin back in its place and pick up Enzo. "That's all we need, Enzo, Mandy and TJ as fairy godmothers."

"Bippity-boppity-boo, bitches!" she cackles as she gets up to go home.

Chapter 30

Cameron

I SLAM MY file drawer closed as I finish putting things in order. I lay my head in my hands as I lean my elbows on my desk. I can feel a headache creeping up the back of my skull. Soon it will wrap itself around the front of my forehead and start pounding if I don't take ibuprofen.

"So...what happened?"

I look up to see Kiki leaning in my doorjamb with her arms folded over her chest.

"What do you mean?"

"Don't play stupid with me, Cameron. My office manager has requested time off for the past week."

The thought of Andie makes my head pound harder. Part of me wants to go find her and the other part wants to just forget about her. I look up at my sister as she taps her foot in impatience. "I didn't do a thing. Maybe you should ask her."

"Cam, don't mess with me. I'm pregnant and moody."

"Kiki," I sigh, "I have a headache coming on and I have

to catch a flight to San Francisco in two hours. I really don't have time for this."

"So that's it? You're just going to give up on her? It's Valentine's Day, Cam!"

"What does Valentine's Day have anything to do with it?"

"Sometimes I just want to strangle you. Look, you're lucky it was me who came down to speak to you. TJ is wearing down a path in the wood walking back and forth across our office as we speak."

"Well you can tell TJ to stay out of it."

Kiki throws her hands up in exasperation. "Just tell me what happened and we'll leave you alone." She plants herself down in the chair across from my desk. I groan in defeat because she won't leave until I talk. "Please, Cam?"

I sit back in my chair and rub my forehead with my thumbs as I stare up at the ceiling. "Andie is the first girl I've felt something for in as long as I can remember."

"More than Lisa?"

"A hundred times more than her."

"That's amazing!"

I drop my hands and give her a flat stare. "Yeah. So I thought. I think it spooked her when Kendra came to brunch, and then when I went to her house the next morning her ex was there. On top of that, I also just found out she has a kid. It's a lot to process, Kiki...whatever. It doesn't matter now."

Kiki scrunches up her nose. "Her ex? Enzo's baby daddy?"

"Yeah, and back to Enzo...you knew she had a kid and didn't think to mention it to me?"

"Yes..." she says tentatively as she squirms in her chair. "But would it have made a difference in how you feel about her? I don't fault her for not telling you, Cam. She's a single mom—"

"With her ex back in the picture."

"Well, you don't know that for sure, do you? Since I've known her she's been a struggling single mom. I'd be really surprised if she was back together with him, especially right after you two got together."

The thought of Andie struggling hurts my heart, and Kiki's right, there's no way she'd be with him the night after we slept together, but now...I'm not sure of anything. I pack my laptop away in its case and look at my watch. "She called me and left a voicemail saying she just wanted to be friends. So that's it, whatever there may have been between us is over."

"That's bullshit." Kiki leans forward in her seat. "Look, she was afraid to tell you about Enzo because you said you didn't like kids."

"I never said that," I scoff.

"Uh, yeah, you said something to that effect when you were babysitting our little monsters back in October."

"I was outnumbered and grumpy. I hated everyone that day."

"Well, when you're a single mom and you hear a guy you're interested in say he doesn't like kids, that's kind of a no-brainer. Mama bears like to protect their little ones."

"She still lied to me."

"Mmm, more like omit, and I know she's sorry about that, but if you truly feel something for her, and you think you could accept her and Enzo, then maybe you could give her another chance?"

I sigh. "You don't get it, Kiki. She made it clear she just wants to be friends. Face it, we're not going to be more than that." I rub my temples as the pounding increases. "It's messy. We keep missing each other's phone calls. We're like two ships in the night passing silently by. Whatever her ex is to her, I'm not sure I want to get involved in that right now. I have a lot going on with work. Charles has fucked up big time."

"Oh, I knew this would be coming. I tried to warn you about him. What happened?"

I scrub my hands down my face. "Sexual harassment. A couple of female servers who no longer work there have filed a claim."

"Oh no."

"Yeah, and Josh wants to get out. He's starting a family, and he's done with the whole business. He wants to move out of California to Portland and take over his father-in-law's business. It's a mess." I move some things around my desk in agitation. Talking about this makes my blood boil.

"I told you Charles was skeezy." She sighs. "I mean Josh just can't walk away and leave you hanging. What are you going to do?"

"I think Josh is going to give me full ownership of The Social Hour. He doesn't want to be involved in a scandal. He wants to settle out of court with Charles."

"That asshole deserves jail time." She slowly gets up out of her chair.

"Probably so, but unfortunately, there's no hard evidence. He could just spin it that they dated and now she's a scorned lover." I sigh and rub my jaw. "Honestly, I just want to walk away from the whole thing, but I can't."

"I'm sorry, Cameron. Let me know if there's anything I can do." She rubs her belly and arches her back. "Back to the reason I'm here. If Andie called you again, would you take the call?"

"Yeah, of course I would. But she hasn't, and now I've got work to worry about. I can't handle girl drama right now. Between crazy Kendra, Lisa leaving me random crying voicemails, and Andie's ex trying to swing a punch at me, it's too much."

"Whoa, there's a lot you haven't been sharing with me."

"Look, I've got to run by my condo to grab my bag before I go." I come around my desk and pull my sister into a hug. "I'll give Mom and Dad a hug from you."

"I wish you didn't have to go back to California again." Kiki sighs.

"Trust me, I wish I didn't either."

"Always working. Happy Valentine's Day, Cam. Love you."

"Happy Valentine's Day. Love you too. Stay out of trouble." I grab my car keys and laptop. I quickly exit my office before she can convince me to stop what I'm doing and go find Andie.

I'm not sure what to think about Andie, her ex, or her just wanting to be friends and not taking my calls, especially after she gave me grief when I didn't call her back over the holidays. My heart feels burned, but maybe it's for the best. I've got too much going on with the business to worry about a girlfriend right now. I just want my life to be simple.

"Don't give up, Cam!" Kiki shouts down the hall. I wave to her and head out into the cold night.

Chapter 31

Andie

I TOLD MY mom all about Mason and she felt awful for giving Mary Kate my address. Mama thought she had something important to send me and it was something I needed right away. What on earth would Mary Kate need to send me? A new pair of see-through stripper heels? Mama frowned upon that retort. I told Mama I'd be sure to write her a thank-you note for that one-hundred-and-ninety-pound bag of trash she sent my way. Mama didn't appreciate my sarcasm either.

I'm a little scared that when I'm back home Mason will show up again unannounced again. Mr. Miller said he would keep an eye on my place while I was at work. I have no idea if there is anything legal I can do especially when I have no way of contacting Mason. I worry this is how it will always be, always wondering if Mason will just pop up out of the blue. I don't want Enzo to have a sometimes, half-ass, I'll-be-there-if-I-can kind of dad. Mason is the definition of disappointment. My parents and Mandy think so too. Hell, half the state of Alabama would probably agree with me.

I've been back in Nashville after my weeklong hiatus for two weeks now, but knock on wood, he hasn't shown back up on my doorstep. I haven't seen Cameron either. The first week I got back I'd find an excuse to go down to the bar for something in hopes that I'd catch him, but he'd either be out of town or in a meeting. Connor's sympathetic looks started making me feel like maybe he was trying to avoid me, so I stopped looking for him.

I've kept myself busy working overtime since I took the week off but I really just want to curl up and sleep. I've been trying to stay busy with some new photography clients that I got through my running group. I've been spending my nights watching mindless TV after putting Enzo to bed and editing family pictures.

I'm lonely, there's no doubt about it. I was a chicken when I left a message for Cam telling him I just wanted to be friends. I was taking the easy way out to protect my heart, but the truth is, I miss him—his laugh, his teasing, the way he looks at me like there's no one else in the room. I miss the one night of incredible sex we shared. Mason showing up on my doorstep and crazy brunch lady definitely did not play in his favor, but I have to remind myself that he's not Mason.

I can't stop thinking about the *what could have been* between us. I feel like we were just getting started and I got spooked, shutting him out.

Mandy was right, I just needed to process everything logically. I don't believe the woman who showed up and poured the drink on him. I believe in Cam, in us. I want more...whatever that may be. I need to tell him all of this in person, but I can't seem to find him. Maybe he doesn't want to be found.

TJ WALKS INTO the office carrying a huge stack of magazines and dumps them on my desk.

"Hello, hello! Sare Bear! Kinky! Come out here! Lookie what Uncle TJ brought you! I bought the whole newsstand!"

"I see that," I grumble. I move my coffee out of the way as the magazines start sliding off one another across my desk. I pick up a copy as Sarah and Kiki come out of their offices. My eyes widen in disbelief as I smile up at the three of them.

"I thought we agreed you weren't to call yourself Uncle TJ without the kids around."

"Whatevs, piranha preggo, look!" Kiki gives him a dirty look as he holds up a glossy magazine and dances in place. "You are looking at the latest issue of *Nashville Go!* And lookie who's on the front!" he singsongs.

"Oh my god, give me that!" Kiki snatches the magazine out of his hand. "Andie, they used your photographs!" she squeals as Sarah starts to read from the article.

"*Move over Los Angeles, Nashville has some new star power in town. Kiki Reed, Sarah Ryan, and TJ Ryan are the movers and shakers behind the powerhouse branding team Nashville Stylists. Sarah specializes in hair and makeup, Kiki and TJ will style you from head to toe in all the latest trends, and they are even working on a wedding and home design. They have been listed in several top fashion magazines and have dressed several stars for the Oscars, Grammys, and country music award shows.'"* Sarah looks up, her cheeks flushed. "This is huge!"

She skims the article and chuckles. "Oh my god, TJ, did you read this? It says here, *'TJ Ryan may be as eccentric as his purple ostrich leather boots and his floral button-downs, but this guy brings his A game when it comes to men's fashion'."* Sarah squeals as TJ struts by us wearing pink skinny jeans and a pink flamingo-print button-down.

"Never underestimate the power of TJ's charm." He smiles confidently as he dons a white cowboy hat.

Kiki rolls her eyes. "Andie, look, they mention you too! *'Anderson Daniels is the latest team member to join forces with this dynamic trio with her superb photography skills and her eye for capturing those intimate moments that no one else sees. You can see her work on Kiki's blog, City Girl in the Heart of Country, or on her web page Anderson Daniels Photography.'* Andie, this is huge for you!"

A tear slips down my cheek as I read where Kiki just was in the article. "But I never interviewed with them...I never sent these photos in..."

Kiki, Sarah, and TJ all share a smile. "We know, Shorts, but we thought you deserved a shoutout too. And this is our way of officially asking you to join the team. You know, not just as office manager, but as our official photographer. Because after this article gets out, the phone will be ringing off the hook for you."

I swipe away at the happy tears that trickle down my cheeks. "You guys, I don't know what to say."

"Say yes, obvi." TJ rolls his eyes dramatically.

I let out a blubbery laugh as I cry. "Yes! Thank you, yes!"

I get up and we embrace in a group hug.

"This cover photo you took of us really is amazing. Dang, TJ, you look good all cleaned up in a suit and tie."

"Of course I do."

I flip to the front and look at the photograph I took of them for a shoot for their website last month. Kiki sitting in a velvet and gold-leafed chair wearing an emerald-green silk dress, while Sarah leans against her in a deep royal-blue dress looking angelic. TJ leans on the other side of Kiki looking dashing in a navy Armani suit. Three beautiful people. Three beautiful souls who took a chance on a little nobody from Inkdale, Alabama. *My* photograph on the front of *Nashville Go*. I can't believe it! I can't wait to show Mandy and Mama, they will pee in their pants they'll be so excited.

"Let's go out and celebrate tonight! Just the four of us. Can you get a sitter for Enzo?" Kiki claps excitedly.

"Oh, I don't know. I was kind of looking forward to putting on my sweats and watching a movie."

"Trés sad, Andie." TJ sits on the edge of my desk.

I look up to see all three of them staring at me. Sarah snaps her fingers. "Ooh! I've got the perfect plan. We can have a little party at my house! Maggie and Finn have the kids, so we won't have to worry about them. That way, Andie can wear her sweats and we can all have fun!"

"But I want to dance my booty off," TJ whines.

Kiki pinches TJ. "You can dance your booty off anywhere." She angles her head toward me. "Let's just stay in and have a party. We'll send Lex, Connor, and Tatum out to go do something."

"I don't know. I'll see if Becky's available. I hate to ask

Mrs. Miller again. She's been watching Enzo so much for me lately."

TJ claps his hands giddily. "Yes! We're going to celebrate the article and Andie becoming a part of Nashville Style!"

"Let's just see if Becky can do it first before you get all fired up." I smugly type out my text to her because I know she'll bail on me, she always does. I appreciate the three of them trying to celebrate with me, but I'm just not feeling it. I'm not feeling anything as of late.

My phone immediately dings and TJ snatches it from the desk.

"She's a go! Woop woop!"

Goddamn Becky. The one time I need her not be available, she is. I slump in my chair in defeat.

"Ooh! We can do facials!"

"No, let's dress up really fancy!" Kiki claps her hands. "Sarah can do our makeup! I can do hair!"

What happened to just kicking back in sweats and drinking wine?

"Uh, you're not touching my hair." TJ gives her a side-eye.

"One time, Tinker Jazz, and you're never going to let me live that down."

"What happened?" I muster up a smile.

Sarah smiles as she leans against my desk. "Kiki dyed TJ's hair a horrible greenish black. It looked like sewer sludge. It took me a while to undo the damage."

I cringe as I look at TJ's gorgeous head of strawberry-blond hair. TJ grimaces and snaps his fingers at me. "Exactly that expression right there. That sums it up perfectly. She swore she knew what she was doing. She watched a YouTube video and said Connor would go nutso for it. Girl, he laughed his ass off is what he did. Never again!"

"Hey, in all fairness, the YouTuber never said not to mix the two bottles together. He was just shaking one bottle. I got confused." Kiki giggles as Sarah audibly sighs next to me.

"Okay, so I guess I have a sitter. What should I bring?"

"Just yourself. We'll take care of everything else." Kiki winks at me and my stomach clenches. Maybe I could pretend to be sick? No, then they would just come to me. I sigh as I grab my pocketbook and shut my bottom drawer. "I guess I'll see y'all tonight then."

"Yes, bitches! Tonight, we go all night long, we're gonna party like Post Malone!" TJ dances in place. Kiki rolls her eyes as Sarah giggles.

"'Kay, I'm out before he pulls a muscle or decides to tattoo his face…see y'all in a bit."

I get on the elevator with a wave as TJ screams, "You're not going to kill my vibe, Andie! I will get you out of those tragic sweatpants!"

I ARRIVE AT Sarah's sprawling horse ranch a little after seven after I left every emergency number possible for Becky. I told her she could watch Netflix as long as Enzo was asleep, but absolutely no friends or boyfriends over and no gum. She rolled her eyes at that, but I told her Mr. Miller would be watching the house for me. A little harmless threatening never hurt anyone.

Kiki pops a bottle of champagne and makes us put on her latest wedding dress designs she's been playing around with for the business. Even TJ changes into a dress, which is pretty hilarious. Sarah sits me down on a kitchen barstool and slathers something cold and creamy on my face as Kiki sprays something in my hair.

"Aren't you worried we're going to ruin your dresses?"

"Nah, these all have something wrong with them, so they're just going to be used for scraps."

"Aw, really? They're so pretty."

"Close your eyes."

"Uh, should I be worried?"

"No girl, I got you." Sarah smiles as she gently smooths the cool mud mask under my eyes. "Kiki is just applying a holding spray. It's good for damaged hair—not that yours is damaged, you have beautiful hair. But it's like a protein builder."

"Uh, okay."

"Trust me." Kiki smiles over Sarah's shoulder.

"I want to…" I squeak out, making Sarah's smile widen.

"Kiki, you're next." Sarah applies the green gook on Kiki's face and then on TJ's.

He wraps a towel around his head and whispers to me, "Those bitches aren't getting near my hair."

I take a big gulp of champagne and peruse the cheeses on the charcuterie board Sarah has on her kitchen island.

"Let's play 'I never'!"

Kiki groans, "TJ, no, that's like we're back in high school."

"Oh come on, Kinky, it'll be fun! It will help us get to know Andie's most dirty, darkest secrets."

"What's 'I never'?" I munch on a cracker and brie as I turn around.

"What? You've never played? GAME. ON."

"Uh, only if someone explains it to me first." I stand my ground not wanting to strip off my clothes and run around the house naked if the game calls for it.

Sarah laughs. "Let's go into the living room." She grabs two bottles of champagne and leads us into a beautiful large white and gray living room.

"How on earth do you keep this so pristine with the babies and Jax?" I ask in awe as I step barefoot on her plush rug.

"Oh yeah, they're not allowed in here until they're older."

"Good luck with that." I laugh.

"Yeah, I know, it's a pipe dream. I had a meltdown when I caught Jax in here with a popsicle after school one day playing video games. It wasn't my finest moment." She smiles wryly at me as she sits down on the white linen sectional.

I stare at it and then at the cracker and champagne flute in my hand. "Um…"

Sarah waves a hand. "Oh it's okay, I've had it protected."

"Okay." I sit primly down on the couch as Kiki brings in the food and TJ plunks down on a comfy-looking chair. "So, what is this game?"

"I'll start." TJ straightens as his strapless gown slips down a notch. "Oh damn, this dress makes me show nip."

I cough as I laugh and take a drink of champagne at the same time.

"Well, no wonder, boy genius. That wasn't made for a six-foot muscular guy."

"Well, maybe you should make some for the taller ladies."

Kiki side-eyes him as she shoves cheese into her mouth. "Just explain the game to Andie before I go pregzilla on your ass."

"No need to get snippy, Kinks. I knew I would need these tonight." He chucks a mini Snickers at her head.

"Ow!"

"Just eat your chocolate and snap it. Okay, so I will say something like, I never brushed my teeth at night. And then if you don't brush your teeth at night you take a drink."

"That's gross. Seriously? How have I not known this disgusting factoid about you after all these years? You don't brush your teeth at night?" Kiki squints at TJ.

TJ rolls his eyes. "Of course I brush my teeth at night, it was just an example, Kinks. Cheez-Its."

Kiki eyes him suspiciously as she eats the Snickers. "'Kay, my turn. I never kiss on a first date."

The three of them take a drink of champagne and then they all stare at me.

"What?"

"You don't kiss on the first date?"

"Oh, oh! Sometimes I do, if there's potential there."

"Oh Andie, drink up, sweetie. We need to loosen up that sex kitten that's just dying to turn into a growling tiger. Grrr."

"Okay, okay, my turn," Sarah says. "I've never made out with two different people in the same night."

We all take a sip of champagne except for Sarah.

"Go Andie, maybe there is a little crazytown in you!"

I smile. "I'll up that one. I've never had sex in public."

The three of them take a drink.

"Y'all, no! Seriously? When? Where?"

TJ waves his hand. "On an airplane. This is BC—before Connor—it was dirty. I don't recommend it. Those bathrooms are revolting."

"And yet you did it anyway." Kiki smirks. "Tatum and I did it in a dressing room at Neiman Marcus. He was trying on clothes and you know me and clothes…shopping makes me so hot and then he was stripping and I lost my mind."

"Don't they have cameras in there?"

Kiki shrugs. "If they did, someone got a good show."

"What about you, Sare Bear?"

Sarah blushes. "Lex and I did it in an elevator. We didn't hit the emergency button, we just did it. I think the thrill of maybe being caught got us both wound up."

"I love it when Sare Bear gets all kinky on us!" TJ turns to me. "Andie, if you could do it anywhere, where would it be?"

"In public?" I squeak out.

"Yes, Laura Ingalls Wilder, in public."

"If I could do it in public and not get caught, because that would probably scar me for life, I'd do it…in a park, underneath the stars."

"Shorts is an exhibitionist, I love it."

"Wait, no I said if I was guaranteed *not* to get caught."

"Guarantees don't exist, sweets."

"Let's play would you rather. Ease Andie into this."

"Good idea, Sunshine." Kiki smiles.

"Okay Andie, would you rather eat a hot pepper or drink sour milk?"

"My Nana Rose has more fun at shuffleboard and shots night at her retirement community," TJ grumbles. "Make it sexy and spicy, Sare Bear!"

"Okay, hmm…Andie, would you rather suck on a guy's balls or give him a blow job after an hour of hot sweaty smelly yoga?"

"Cheese and rice, you just went right for it didn't you?" TJ snickers. "From hot peppers to sweaty balls."

Sarah smiles and shrugs as she takes a drink of champagne.

"Do I really have to answer that?"

"Yes!"

"Both are sweaty?"

Sarah nods. "Stinky clothes kind of sweaty. Like rivers of sweat while you're doing this."

"What the hell goes on behind closed doors with you and Sexy Lexy?" Kiki raises an eyebrow.

"Apparently he's like Richard Simmons in the bedroom. Oh my god, can you imagine Lexy in those little satin shorts? I'm going to have to change his name to Sweaty Lexy."

Sarah laughs. "Gross, he doesn't sweat. We're playing a game, remember?" She chucks a piece of cheese at TJ. "Andie, answer before these two jerks make up more delusional stories about my man."

I take a big gulp of champagne. "Ugh, I guess giving

head. Both are super disgusting, but I guess sweaty balls rate higher because they're under all the junk. The smell." I shiver in disgust.

"'Kay, my turn—"

"Wait, why am I the only one who has to answer the sweaty balls question?"

"You volunteered. I'm a no-go on either of those things." TJ wrinkles his nose. "Really nasty."

"I'm pregnant. I don't have to answer any questions that might hurt the development of the baby."

"Nice one, Kinks." TJ and Kiki high-five each other.

"But...that's not fair. Y'all are just mean." I scowl as I take another big swallow of my champagne. "Okay, my turn. Would you rather get caught naked in public or accidentally live video yourself in the act on social media?"

"Hmm...in public. Nana Rose would *not* want to see that on her Facebook page, even though she does love Connor more than me." TJ takes a sip of champagne as we giggle. "My turn—would you rather lick a gas station toilet seat or use your toothbrush to clean one and then brush your teeth with it?"

"Ugh! That's nasty shit, TJ. What is up with you and toothbrushes anyway?"

"And sweaty testicles isn't?"

"Lick a toilet." We all nod our heads in agreement.

"Would you rather have the most incredible sex of your life and never see the guy again, or just have mediocre sex but know that he'll never leave you?"

"Ooh good one, Kinks!"

I take another gulp of champagne and answer. "Most

incredible sex."

"Wait, do you know you're missing out on incredible sex if you're with Mr. Mediocre?" Sarah ponders.

"Yes."

"I don't know, because then you'll always be comparing him to Mr. One Night for the rest of your life. That's torture in itself." TJ crunches on a cracker. "But then again, Mr. Mediocre is dependable."

"True," Sarah agrees.

"I don't care. One night. I'd take the one night."

"Sounds like Andie's talking from experience." Sarah waggles her eyebrows.

I blush and give them a sad smile, but I don't say a word. Hands-down, I'd take the one night with Cam even if it meant everyone else was just a dud in comparison.

Kiki stares at me for a beat. "You know, Andie, that twat that came to brunch wasn't his girlfriend. She made it all up."

"I don't want to talk about it," I say glumly.

"I know, and we won't, but as his sister I just wanted to let you know everything she said was a lie."

"Okay."

"Ugh Sare Bear, when can we wash this crap off? It's making my face itch."

"Drink up, bitch, and stop complaining." Kiki winks as she fills his glass.

"Just because you're preggers and you're drinking sparkling cider doesn't mean you get to be pushy."

I start to pour myself another glass of champagne, but pause. "Sarah, do you have anything stronger?" I not only need to drown my sorrows but try and keep up with these three.

"Te kill ya!" TJ yells. "Wait, wait! I brought over cute little hats to take shots with." He brings the bottle over with four mini sombreros that he makes us put on. The three of us do a shot. "I knew I loved you, Andie!" TJ squeezes me into a suffocating hug.

"Sarah, do you still have your karaoke machine?"

"Yessss!" TJ claps and jumps up. "Now we're talking!"

"Wait!" Sarah stands up. "I have an even better idea! Help me move the couch back and the coffee table out of the way."

Chapter 32

Cameron

LEX OPENS HIS door going from the garage into the kitchen. Music is blasting as the four of us saunter into the kitchen. Shrieking laughter can be heard from the family room. Lex looks at Connor and they both shake their head.

"This doesn't sound good, bro."

"No, it doesn't." Lex grimaces as he leads the way to the family room. "I'm guessing it's TJ and Kiki's fault."

Tatum shakes his head and chuckles. "Jesus, even pregnant and sober she can still be a train wreck."

I almost run over Lex as he stops suddenly at the entrance into the family room. I look up and my eyes widen. What the hell?

"Uh, dude, I don't know what to say." Tatum laughs as he tries to cover his grin with his hand.

"There's nothing to say." Connor crosses his arms over his chest.

The four of them are all wearing big white poufy wedding gowns as they bounce up and down on a huge inflatable game of Twister. Kiki's hair looks like she stuck her finger in a socket, Sarah's straight blonde hair is now blue and spiraled, and Andie's hair looks like the bangs scene from *There's Something About Mary*. And they're all wearing mini sombreros.

"Are those wedding dresses? Why the fuck is TJ wearing a wedding dress?"

"What's on their faces? Why do they look like Shrek ogres?"

"Since when do they make an inflatable Twister? And why are they wearing little sombreros?"

"Mate, who the fuck knows. What's in Andie's hair to make it stand up like that?"

"I don't want to know," Tatum whispers. "Maybe we should back out of here slowly."

"On the count of three. Cameron, don't fuck this up."

"Why are you singling me out?"

"Because you're a rookie when it comes to dealing with these crazies when they're drunk," Tatum says.

"I've had plenty—"

"Hi, guys!" Kiki waves at us.

"Fuck, way to blow it, Cameron," Lex growls.

"Great." Connor looks at me, disappointed.

Tatum smacks me in the arm. "And you call yourself family."

"Like they wouldn't have spotted four large guys standing in the room," I mutter. We walk over to them like we're about to walk into a lion cage at the zoo.

Lex walks over to Sarah first as she sways to the music, a microphone in her hand. Her voice is megaphone loud as she speaks into the mic. "Andie, you are right foot red...Red right foot red...red red wine...you make me feel so good..." she drunkenly sings as she spots Lex and grins widely at him. "Aw, Sexy Lexy's home! Look, guys, it's my sexy-as-fuck Irishman. Hiya baby! You look scrumptious! Done worry, my hair isn't perm...no I didn't get a perm, that's just a curling iron. Perm-ann-nan-ant. Goddamn, this word is so hard to say. Why is it so hard to say you guys?" She starts laughing hysterically and then hiccups. Lex glowers at me as he takes the microphone from her and turns it off.

"Dude, I didn't provide the alcohol." I throw my hands in the air.

"Hey, you can't take our microphone! I need Sarah to spin and shout out where I'm supposed to move next," Kiki says grumpily as her limbs are twisted with Andie's on the inflatable gameboard.

"TJ, what's on your guys' faces?" Connor tries to rub off the lime green on his cheek.

"Some crap Sarah made us put on, but it's so hard now I can't make any facial expressions. Right now, I'm really smiling at you." TJ tries to move his lips but his eyes just crazily race around the room. Andie starts to giggle and ends up losing her balance and falling on Kiki. They both crack up hysterically.

"Do you need help?" I ask them as I reach down. "Don't hurt the baby. Jesus, you guys."

"I got it, I got it." Andie snickers as she rolls to her knees and unsteadily gets up. She falls off the inflatable, trudges over to the sectional, and falls face down in a big cloud of wedding dress.

Tatum helps Kiki get up. "Babe, Cam's right, you shouldn't be rolling around on this thing."

Kiki rubs her belly. "I've been careful."

"What happened to your hair?"

"Oh, do you like it? TJ did it."

"It's um…it's…yeah."

"Did you guys have fun at the game?"

"Not as much fun as you, apparently." Connor smirks as TJ twirls around in his wedding dress.

"Hey Cam, can you do me a favor?" Kiki gives me her puppy-dog expression which means whatever she wants is not going to end well for me.

"Depends."

"Can you take Andie home? I don't think she's suitable to drive."

We look over at Andie face-planted on the sofa as she softly snores. "Yeah, sure."

"Thanks, you're the best big brother."

I'M PARKED OUTSIDE of Andie's house and I'm not sure if I should wake her or try to carry her in since she's still passed out. Even passed out, snoring, with her hair mysteriously gelled to stick straight up in front, she's fucking beautiful. I've missed her more than I care to admit. My feelings are all over the road. I want to be with her, but she just wants to be friends. I question if I can be the guy she wants me to be. Her having a son complicates matters—I'd be naïve to think it didn't. My business has me flying back and forth to the West Coast weekly and if I'm not there I'm at the bar here or in Chicago.

I scrub my hands over my face in resignation. She's right, friends is all we'll ever be. We just can't make it work.

I get out of the car, come around to her side, and gently scoop her into my arms. She doesn't even stir as I shift her weight. What the heck did those three make her drink? I get to the front door and softly knock, not wanting to wake up Enzo. Panic has me tightening my gut. I swear to god if that douche opens the door I'm going to dropkick him.

I knock again as I gently put Andie down on her feet and try to wake her up. She slumps against me and I wrap my arm around her waist to hold her up. The door opens a crack and then wider as an older woman spies me holding Andie.

"Oh goodness, is she okay? Is she ill? Come on in."

"She just had a little too much fun tonight. I'll take her back to her bedroom?"

Andie mumbles something. I quickly pick her up again.

"Oh, sorry, honey, sure, it's this way." The woman leads me down a short hallway to Andie's bedroom. I don't want to tell her that I already know where it is. I lay Andie gently down on her bed. The white wedding dress she's still wearing poofs up all around her. "Oh my, will she be okay? Should I get her something?" The woman worriedly wrings her hands as she looks over my shoulder at Andie passed out cold. "Why on earth is she wearing a wedding dress? And why is her face green?"

"Oh, she was just having fun with my sister. She's been designing wedding dresses and I guess they decided to try them on. I'll get a washcloth and get the face mask off." I shrug and try to give her a charming smile because I'm sure this is a first for her. "I'm Cameron Forbes, a friend of Andie's."

"Oh, where are my manners, I'm so sorry, Nancy Miller. I live next door. Andie had Becky babysitting, but she had to leave, so Becky asked if I could watch Enzo. Would you like me to help you with Andie? Should I get her out of her dress? I could get a warm washcloth ready for you."

I walk Nancy back to the living room. "Don't worry, I'll take care of her. Thank you for the offer. I'll sleep on the couch to make sure nothing happens to Andie or Enzo."

Nancy exhales and smiles gratefully. "Oh, thank you, that would make me feel so much better."

"How much do I owe you for this evening?"

"Oh honey, nothing. I wasn't over here that long." Nancy gathers her coat and gloves as she heads to the front door. "I'm just glad she had a good time. Andie deserves that. She hasn't had much fun in her life since she's moved here." She smiles at me sadly and it makes my heart pause. "Anyway, I'm right next door if you need anything."

"Thank you for your help, Mrs. Miller."

"Dear, please, call me Nancy." Smiling, she heads out the front door.

I make my way back to Andie's bedroom. She's curled up on her side, breathing deeply. I get a warm washcloth and try to wipe some of the green crap on her face, but it's not coming off. Oh well, she can shower it off in the morning. I place a warm blanket over her and push a soft caramel curl away from her cheek, and she sighs in her sleep.

"I wish I could give you more, Andie." I bend over her and quietly kiss her temple. "But I can't."

Chapter 33

Andie

I WAKE UP to the amazing smell of bacon. I'm betting there are eggs and toast accompanying that incredible aroma…and coffee. Oh god, I'd kill for a hot mug of coffee with a little bit of cream. I groan just thinking about it. I roll out of bed and immediately drop to the floor. What the hell? I'm engulfed in a cloud of white chiffon. I forgot I passed out in this poufy wedding dress I just tripped on. I try to reach for the back zipper but I can't reach it or the hooks that close it. I glance at the clock on my nightstand and freeze. It's ten a.m. Shit, shit, shit! This means Enzo has been up for hours. Why didn't anyone wake me? And who the hell is in my kitchen making breakfast?

I slowly stand up on my sea legs and reach for the glass of water and two aspirin on my nightstand, grateful for whoever put them there. I don't remember getting home from Sarah's last night which is discomforting. The last thing I remember is playing Twister. I push my hair out of my face and shuffle to the kitchen to face the music. I can hear Enzo babbling and banging something on his highchair table.

I stop short in the doorway. Connor is at my stove looking incredibly sexy cooking breakfast in my pink floral apron and TJ is at the table with a big mug of coffee handing Enzo a wooden spoon he just threw on the table. TJ looks up as he notices me in the doorway.

"Aagh! I mean…good morning, Shorts! Are you trying out for a part in *Wicked*? I'm not sure which witch you're trying to channel, Glinda or Elphaba…or maybe there's a third witch named Stacy." TJ snaps his fingers. "Yes, that's it! Stacy who wants to be green, but sadly looks more like a jilted eighties bride that went on a bender."

"What are you talking about?"

Connor grins. "Go look in the mirror."

I duck out of the kitchen and go look in the mirror hanging in the guest bathroom. "Oh dear God…" My face is smeared green. My hair is sprayed up in the front and stiff. Did someone give me bangs? Sequin sparkles from my gown are stuck to my face and in my hair. Is that a crumpled sombrero in my rat's nest? What the hell?

I come back into the kitchen. "That's pretty bad. How did you get your face mask off? It feels like concrete."

"Sledgehammer."

"Great. What are you guys doing here this morning? How come you didn't wake me when Enzo got up?"

"Because you needed your beauty sleep, Princess." Connor winks at me. "We're happy to help."

"Where did you guys sleep? I hope you didn't squeeze on the couch. I'm so embarrassed I was such a train wreck last night."

TJ and Connor look at each other. "Uh, we didn't take you home last night or spend the night."

"If you didn't, who did?"

TJ clears his throat. "Cam brought you home and slept on your couch. He uh, had a meeting this morning, so he called for us to come over and take care of you and Enzo. He's such a little stud, Andie."

I hold a hand to my throbbing head as I move toward the kitchen table. "Cam's a little stud?"

"Well he is a stud, definitely not little, but no, I was referring to your mini me, Enzo."

I smile down at my precious baby and kiss his head. "He's pretty special. So, Cam slept here? And got up with Enzo?"

"Yeah, he left about an hour ago." Connor places a plate of eggs, toast, and bacon in front of TJ and me.

"Oh my god, this looks amazing, but I need to change out of this dress and wash this crap off my face first. Can you help me, TJ?"

"Sure thing, Shorts." He unsnaps the hooks and pulls the zipper down as I hold the dress in place. I quickly walk back to my bedroom. I can hear TJ talking animatedly to Enzo. I smile as I shed the dress and throw on a sports bra, my soft comfy t-shirt, and sweatpants. I tie my hair up into a top knot, scrub my face, and reenter the kitchen already feeling more human. Connor sets a coffee cup in front of me and I want to kiss his handsome face in gratitude.

"I can't thank you guys enough...for helping me out. I'm ashamed I didn't act more responsible."

"Pssh, Andie, the whole point of last night was to make

you have a little fun. You deserve it, girl." TJ slips a piece of bacon to Vader under the table.

I scoop a little of my scrambled egg onto Enzo's tray and then chomp on a piece of bacon. "I did have fun"—I smile wryly—"but I feel bad that Cam had to take care of me last night. We haven't exactly been on speaking terms."

"I wouldn't worry about him. He seemed like he was doing pretty good when we got here." Connor smiles at me.

"Really? What was he doing?"

"Let's just say that man looks pretty fine with bedhead while holding a baby." Connor gives TJ a look. "God, I love it when you're jealous, Boo Boo Bear."

Boo Boo Bear? I smirk at TJ's nickname for Connor and quietly drink my coffee, lost in thought as they squabble about who is jealous of who. I can't believe Cam brought me home and I have no recollection of it. And then he slept on my couch and got up with Enzo this morning? I'm kind of hurt and confused as to why he didn't sleep in my bed last night, but then again I do look pretty damn scary. And why didn't he stick around this morning? I mean, who has a meeting at nine a.m. on a Saturday? And oh my god, he had to deal with Becky. I'll be mortified if he paid her. I better call her and make sure.

"Earth to Andie…"

I look up and see TJ and Connor smiling at me. "Oh sorry, lots of thoughts running around in my coffee-deprived brain. TJ, how are you not hungover?"

"I only did one tequila shot to your four."

I groan. "Ugh, please don't mention that word."

Connor gets up and brings our plates to the sink. TJ

takes Enzo out of his highchair. "We were going to go run some errands. Do you want us to take Enzo with us? Give you a little time to recoup?"

I can feel my eyes mist over with gratitude. "You guys would do that for me?"

"Of course, we would. *Mi bebé es su bebé.*"

I laugh as I wipe a tear away. "I don't speak Spanish, but I'm pretty sure that's not right."

Connor shakes his head and laughs, grabbing Enzo's diaper bag off the counter. "It's definitely not right. Come on, my love, let's give Andie some space. Andie, we'll be back in a few. Rest up, Love."

"Thanks, you guys. A hot shower and another gallon of coffee will have me right as rain."

"You're not alone anymore, Andie. You're part of our family now." TJ kisses my cheek as he walks out the door with my world.

Chapter 34

Andie

I TEXTED CAM a heartfelt thank-you for taking care of me and waking up with Enzo last weekend. He responded with a friendly but short "you're welcome." I know just being friends with him is the right thing to do, but I miss him.

TJ, Kiki, and Sarah's night in was just what I needed to pull me out of my slump. I'm feeling better and excited about the mention in the magazine. My mom and Mandy went nuts over it and have been parading it all over Inkdale. Mandy even left one on Mary Kates's doorstep with a smiley face Post-it Note stuck to it.

TJ was right, the phones have been going crazy since the publication. We've even had to turn people away. I've got three families booked for photo sessions next week and a private event. The best phone call I got was from Stephie, the woman with the horrible twins from the mommy group I joined when I first moved here. She clearly didn't remember who I was as she blabbed on and on about her adorable twins and how she'd heard what a fantastic photographer I am. She was dying to have me take her family portraits. I happily told her that I was booked out until next year and I'd give her a call when availability came up. Mandy said I was way too nice, but just knowing Stephie is waiting for a phone call that will never come is enough satisfaction for me. Karma's a bitch, Stephie. Things are going well and I'm learning that good friends and family are what I really need in my life right now.

I hang up the phone after jotting down an appointment in Kiki's book just as the elevator dings. Two tall brunettes step off and look around the room. "Where's the hairless cat?" one of them asks.

"It's not hairless, Amanda," the other says, "it's hypoallergenic."

"Same diff."

"Hi, welcome to Nashville Stylists! How can I help you?"

The taller brunette with an Ariana Grande-style ponytail looks at me with disdain as she folds her arms over her chest. "You're new."

"Hi, yes, I'm Anderson." I smile brightly at her. "What can I do for you?"

She stares at me with a reptilian-like smile, making me squirm in my seat. "I have an appointment," she says coolly through her teeth.

I quickly reach for the appointment book and flip to today. At the five p.m. slot written in big block letters and underlined three times is the name "Sonja Big Ole B." I quickly snap the book closed and look up. "You must be Sonja." I smile.

"She's a genius." Sonja turns to her friend who giggles.

I keep my smile frozen on my face and ignore her dig. "Are you here to see Kiki or Sarah?"

She stomps her high heel in irritation. "Why can't anyone in this fucking place ever know what the hell is going on? I'm sure the next thing you're going to tell me is that you don't have my champagne and charcuterie board ready!"

Uh... "Why don't you and your friend just have a seat over there and I'll get Kiki. Do you both have appointments?" I smile graciously.

"My name is Amanda." The friend pops a bubble with her gum that gets stuck all over her upper lip. I stare at her curiously as she tries to peel it off unsuccessfully with her tongue. "I'm Sonja's BFF." She gives up on the gum and starts typing on her phone.

Oohkay... "Let me grab Kiki."

"Yeah, why don't you do that." Sonja continues to stand as she looks at me like I'm a cockroach she'd like to grind to a pulp with her Jimmy Choos.

I take my sweet time as I push back from my desk and walk to Kiki's door. I knock and then quickly open it and stick my head in. I whisper, "Kiki! Some mega bitch is here and I'm not sure if it's for you, Sarah, or TJ and she's super pissed that I don't know. I'm so sorry! All that was written in the appointment book was her name, Sonja."

Kiki's eyes widen. "Shit, shit, shit. I totally forgot she was coming in tonight! Damn pregnancy brain. She's going to see Sarah first and then I'll have to deal with her. Crap, I forgot to get her champagne. Run down to my brother's bar and grab a few bottles of Veuve Clicquot, I'll get her food. Dammit, we cleaned out the fridge this week, didn't we? See if my brother has anything to eat too. Go down the back stairs so you don't have to deal with her. She's awful."

"Okay! I'm on it." I quickly walk down the back stairs and try the handle on the patio door leading into the bar. It's loud and crowded with happy-hour patrons. Chatter and laughter wash over me as I walk past the bar. Connor is elbows-deep helping customers. I catch his eye and he smiles and nods. "Just going to grab some champagne!" I shout over the noise.

He waves and points to the storage room down the hall. I've rummaged around their stock room enough for Kiki that I feel confident I know where to find the champagne. I pass Cam's office, but the room is dark. The storage room is on the left at the end of the hallway. I peruse the glass doors of the refrigerator shelves but I can't find the champagne. Maybe it's not back here. I step up on a low wood box and reach up looking at one bottle on the top shelf. A throat clears behind me making me almost drop the bottle.

I twist my body around as I hold my hand to my chest. I drink in the sight of Cam leaning against the doorframe. He looks different tonight in the dim light. Rugged, incredibly handsome in jeans and a crewneck gray sweater that match his eyes. The sweater hugs his broad shoulders, tapering down to his trim waist.

"What are you doing?" His voice is silky smooth like rich caramel poured over chocolate.

"I, uh, I'm..." My voice trails off as he arches an eyebrow. Oh sugar, he is so sinfully sexy I can't breathe. Damn, I've missed him. It's been weeks since he last touched me and my body is so attuned to him that every cell cries out for him.

He steps up to me, invading my personal space. I can't think rationally with his close proximity. I turn back around and face the shelves because this man is making me die inside with need. I inhale his luxurious scent of leather and something expensive and woodsy. I was fooling myself when I said I was happy with just my friends and family. Fucking lies. I need this man like I need air.

He reaches above me and straightens a wine bottle on the shelf. His other hand grabs my waist. "Are you trying to sneak a bottle out of here, Alabama?" he asks huskily next to my ear.

Mercy me.

"I, um, no, I mean kind of, but it was for Kiki's client, not for me." I stumble over my words as my knees weaken. "She asked me to." *Goddammit, I'm panting again. Why does this man make me pant?*

"What do you need?" His breath feathers against my neck making my skin break out in goosebumps.

I need you! Strip me down and have your way with me, that's what I need. Jesus, I need to get a grip if just his breath on my neck is making my panties wet. *Just breathe and be normal.* Act like he doesn't ignite every nerve ending in your body causing a volcano eruption of lust.

"Champagne…" I moan as I bite my lip, the nearness of him making my brain fuzzy. There goes that goddamn panting again. I sound like Vader after a run. "Something with an orange label? I don't really know or care right now."

"Andie." He cages me in, his hands gripping the shelf above my head. His lips graze my neck.

"Yeah?" I squeak out as I stare at the shelves of alcohol, trying to concentrate on the alcohol percentages typed out on the label. Trying to do anything but turn around and glue myself to his front. This is fucking torture.

"Do you think about me? Because you're all I think about. I can't get you out of my head." He softly kisses my neck and my legs turn to jelly. "Turn around," he says gruffly.

No, no, no, no.

I slowly turn around and his hands are on my hips as he gently tugs me off the step into him. My hands automatically fall to his shoulders as he catches me. I slide down the hard plain of his body, and bless his personal trainer, because he maintains a rock-hard body with the discipline of a monk.

"You keep me up tossing and turning at all hours of the night thinking about kissing these soft lips again." His eyes search mine asking for permission. My fingers curl into his hair as I press my body against his. "I don't want to be just your friend."

"Cam," I whisper, half pleading, half surrendering, my body trembling with need. Maybe I'm not the right girl for him, and maybe I don't need happily-ever-after. Maybe I just need to live in the moment and take the bull by the horns and go for it. Maybe I just need the one night of unbelievable hot sex to hold onto.

He bends just as I tug him closer. I kiss his lips, cautiously at first, relishing the shape and smooth texture of them. I sigh into him as he tugs me closer, parting my lips with his expert tongue. He groans, deepening the kiss, tasting me over and over. The kiss becomes frenzied as he pushes me up against the shelf. I gasp when I feel his hard-on rub up against my core.

"Jesus, Andie," he growls before he reclaims my lips, our tongues tangling in a war of who can kiss who better. He lifts me up against the shelf and both my legs wrap around his waist as I grind shamelessly into him. He pulls up my shirt, his fingers trailing over the soft satin of my bra. I arch into him and he slams back into me, pushing me up against the shelf. A couple wine bottles come crashing to the ground.

"Cam, is that you? Where are you?"

We both freeze, the voice dousing the flames that had licked up between us.

"Shit, this can't be happening." He places me gently away from him as I gather my wits.

"What's happening? Who is that?" I hiss as I straighten my shirt and smooth down my hair. "I swear to god, Cam, if that's crazy brunch lady…"

"I'll explain later. Whatever happens, just say yes, okay? Please, Andie, I need your help to survive the next two hours. I'll owe you big time for this. *Just say yes.*"

I eye him warily as I try to pick up the broken glass on the floor. "Cam, I can't—"

"Cam? Are you back here?" a female voice calls.

"Don't clean that up, you'll cut yourself," he says tersely as he turns his back to me. There's the old bossy jerk I first met.

"Finally, geez I've been looking everywhere for you! What the hell happened in here?"

I look up and see a skinny blonde with perfectly curled hair and flawless makeup standing in the doorway with her hands on her hips. She looks expensive in her black cashmere sweater dress and knee-high boots. She looks like the type of girl Cam would date. I suddenly feel sick to my stomach. Was he here on a date and just made out with me in the storage room? No way, this can't be happening again. I protectively fold my arms over my chest as my claws come out.

"Who are you?" I ask icily.

She rears her head back and raises her eyebrow. "*Excuse me*, who are you?"

Cam sighs as he looks at the floor unable to meet either of our eyes. He says an expletive under his breath. "I thought you were meeting us at the restaurant with Kiki."

"Well, Kiki forgot she has a client, claimed she has 'pregnancy brain' which I call bull on because *I* never had that, she's just trying to get out of dinner. Anyway, I wasn't about to sit around upstairs with that mangy cat of hers. I'm highly allergic."

I look between the two, confusion clearly written across my face.

"Andie, this is my sister Brooke. Brooke, this is Andie. Andie is Kiki's office manager."

She rolls her eyes. "Oh great, another Susan and TJ, just what this world needs."

"Susan?"

"Brooke, behave," Cam grits out. "She means Sarah."

"Well, are we going or what? What a mess in here, what were you guys doing anyway?"

I look between the two, stunned that this is their sister. She doesn't look like either of them. I've never heard her mentioned before by anyone, and on top of that, she's not very friendly. I guess it doesn't help that I wasn't Miss Congeniality a minute ago.

"Yes, we just need to drop this champagne upstairs and let Andie grab her coat and purse."

"Oh, no I'm not—"

"Yes? Remember dinner? *Yes?*" Cam turns around and gives me a desperate look.

"Uh…"

Brooke taps her foot and rolls her eyes. "She must be suffering from pregnancy brain too. Can we go? Now? Mom, Dad, and Graham are meeting us with the boys."

Cam turns to me and grabs my hands. He bends his head and looks beseechingly into my eyes. "Please, Andie," he whispers. "I know I don't deserve to ask anything of you but can you please do this for me?"

I'm curious to know why he needs me to be his date at this dinner so badly, and his pleading look softens my stubborn heart. Besides, I do owe him for getting me back to my house and taking care of Enzo. "Let me just drop off the champagne. I'll meet you back by the elevator."

He squeezes my hands. "Thank you."

"Hello? If Pollyanna can get a move on. We're going to be late," Brooke bitches from behind us.

"I'll be quick." I flash her a smile as I grab the bottle of champagne Cam miraculously procured out of thin air and I scoot out the door. I grab a couple bags of chips, a jar of pickles, and a tin of mixed nuts from the kitchen before I head upstairs.

Did I just agree to dinner with Cam and his family?

Don't start hyperventilating now, Andie, it's just dinner. I better call Mrs. Miller and see if she can keep Enzo a little longer.

I HUSTLE INTO the breakroom and throw all the nuts, pickles, and cheese puffs on a platter. It's kind of a weird cheese board since there's no cheese, so I open the fridge and find a few baby bell cheeses and throw them on the tray. I rush the tray into Sarah's office.

"Ugh, it's about time. I think I've had faster service at the Golden Corral."

"So slow." Her friend Amanda stuffs a cheeseball in her mouth and then removes the cheesy wad of gum from her mouth a few seconds later and puts it on the plate. I grimace as I watch her.

"Hello?" Sonja snaps her fingers as Sarah sprays her face with something. "What's your name again? Can you pour me some champagne?"

"Oh sure. It's Anderson."

"We don't need to know your last name," Amanda snickers from the couch. I roll my eyes as I pop the cork, wishing for it to go flying into one of their eyes, but no such luck. I pour two glasses and hand them each one while Kiki rolls a rack of clothes into the room.

"Oh, thanks Andie!"

"Do you need anything el—"

"Ugh, what *is* this? It's not sweet. Is this Prosecco?" Sonja spits the champagne back in her glass like the classy lady she is.

I look at the bottle of Veuve Clicquot Cam had given me downstairs. "Didn't you want this?" I show Sonja the bottle.

"It must be a bad bottle." Amanda hiccups.

"Must be." Kiki rolls her eyes. "I'll get you another bottle in a minute."

Sonja sniffs as she turns from me. "Help is so hard to find these days. I feel your pain."

Kiki looks like she wants to have a throwdown with Sonja as she turns to me with a brittle smile on her face. "Andie, thank you so much. You are such a big help. We should be good now."

"Yeah, thanks Andie! You're amazing!" Sarah straightens up and smiles at me.

They don't have to tell me twice. I gather up my things. "Have a good time tonight, y'all." I'm talking to Sarah and Kiki, but of course Amanda thinks I'm talking to her.

"Oh we will. Blondes have more fun, right, Sonja?"

"I guess. I'm not blonde, and neither are you." She rolls her eyes at her idiot BFF.

"Oh right. That was last month," Amanda says sadly as she inspects a mini pickle. "Wait, is her name really Andie Anderson?" Amanda shoves the whole pickle in her mouth and crunches down on it. "That's so weird."

I seriously wonder how this girl survives out in the real world. I'm not sure which is the shoddier choice, staying here with these two high-maintenance mean girls or going to dinner with Cam's sister. Here's to hoping I'm making the right choice.

Chapter 35

Cameron

I WATCH ANDIE hurriedly walk out of the store room.

"Really, Cameron?" Brooke says drolly. "Having sex with the receptionist in the storage room?"

"Fuck off, Brooke, we weren't having sex. Besides it's none of your business."

She shrugs as she tucks her clutch under her arm. "Whatever, it's not like you're going to keep her around for long. Does Kiki know?" She chuckles. "If she's any good and you cost Kiki her receptionist, she's going to be super pissed at you."

"No, she doesn't know anything, because nothing is going on. We're just friends."

She leans in and rubs my cheek. "Might want to get the lipstick off that your *friend* left." She cackles as she walks out of the storage room. I take the bottom of my sweater and rub my face.

I quickly sweep up the broken wine bottles, thinking about Andie and that incredibly hot kiss. Seeing her butt in those jeans made me lose my grip on whatever control I thought I had. She makes me lose my mind. First Lisa, who thankfully has taken the hint and stopped leaving me messages, and then crazy Kendra. Andie's different though. Whenever I see her it's like I can breathe again. She makes me want to try.

I NERVOUSLY GLANCE at Andie in my rearview mirror. She hasn't said much on the way over to the restaurant, but then again, Brooke hasn't let anyone get a word in since she's been incessantly complaining about Kiki's decision to have her baby shower at her lake house.

"I mean, I don't understand why we have to drive an hour to get to this place. And it's going to be buggy and swampy."

"Well, it is on a lake."

"But why? Why not have it at a local restaurant or the country club? A lake sounds so…"

"Pretty?" Andie pipes up from the back seat and it makes me smile.

"That would have been the last adjective I would have used, *Polly*."

I growl in irritation. "Brooke, her name is Andie."

"Isn't that a boy's name? No offense or anything, but it's not very feminine sounding."

"No offense taken." Andie blows out a breath sounding incredibly bored. I can't believe I pulled Andie into this mess, but I'm not going to lie, I didn't want to go to this dinner by myself especially with Kiki having to miss it. I open Andie's door after finding a parking spot and help her out of the Range Rover.

"I'm so sorry," I whisper in her ear causing her to shiver.

"It's okay, it's just dinner, right?"

"Right." God, I hate it that my sister can be such a bitch. Her love for Jesus has not softened her at all, and she's learned nothing from her husband having an affair. If anything, she's even more spoiled now because Graham gives in to whatever she demands.

I open the door and follow them into the restaurant. I see my mom and dad sitting at a large round table with Graham and my two nephews.

"Mom, Dad, this is my friend Anderson Daniels."

"Oh, you can call me Andie. It's nice to meet both of you." She smiles graciously as she shakes their hands before sitting.

"Oh Andie, it's lovely to meet you. Kiki has told us so much about you. I didn't realize you were friends with Cameron as well." My mom smiles at me before returning her attention to Andie. "Where are you from, dear? I detect a Southern drawl."

Andie blushes. "I'm from a small town in Alabama."

Brooke snorts, "Of course she is. Where is that anyway? Has to be somewhere in the middle."

"Where is Alabama?" Andie looks at me as if this is a trick question. Knowing my sister, I wouldn't put it past her.

"Jesus Brooke, how did you graduate high school?"

"Oh, I'm from California. I don't have time to pay attention to those middle states." She waves a hand dismissing the topic. "Andie, this is my husband Graham and my boys, Heath who just turned twelve, and William who is nine."

"Nine and a half!"

"Nice to meet you. Thank you for having me at your family dinner."

"Oh of course. Any friend of Cam and Kiki's is welcome." My dad smiles at her over the menu.

I look up to see Graham staring intently at Andie as she looks down at her menu and it makes me bristle. He's such an uptight loser. I can't stand him, but I tolerate him because of my sister. I'd be happy to make it crystal clear to him that he can keep his eyes solely on his wife.

"So Cameron, what's the latest on Charles?" my mom asks after she places her order with the waitress.

"Well, obviously he's been fired. We're settling with the women out of court for punitive damages. Josh has stepped down from his position, signing the locations over to me."

"Oh no dear, I know how much you wanted to step away from them yourself."

"Yeah, I'm not sure what I'm going to do. I've put finding a second location here on hold unless something spectacular comes up. But I'm busy enough right now."

I feel Andie's hand land on my thigh and I look over at her in surprise.

"I'm so sorry, Cam. I know how much you wanted the second location here."

I shrug. "Sometimes things out of our control make us have to change course."

"Charles was disgusting. A womanizing cheat." Brooke

sniffs. "It's too bad he won't get jail time." I look over at Brooke and then at Graham. The vinegar in her voice makes me wonder if there was ever something between Brooke and Charles.

Graham clears his throat. "If you need a lawyer, I can always help—"

"Stop!"

"You stop! I hate you!" Heath grabs a piece of bread from the basket and mashes it over William's head. William gets up from the table crying and starts to run through the restaurant.

"Graham! *Do something*," Brooke hisses at her clueless husband.

"William, please return to your seat!" Graham yells as he finishes off his gin and tonic. "Heath, go retrieve your brother. He's over there by the bar."

"No, I don't want to." Heath pouts as he folds his arms over his chest. I look over to where William is jumping around between patrons' tables.

"Well, someone needs to go get him, that's rude to other diners." I growl. My mom gets up and I want to pull her back in her seat, but I don't want to cause a scene. "I can't believe you're making Mom deal with your kids, Brooke."

Brooke pretends like she doesn't hear me as she takes a sip of her chardonnay and looks around the restaurant. Mom brings a whining William back to his seat. Graham pulls two iPads out of Brooke's purse. "How do you turn these things on?"

"It's the button on the side," Heath directs while Brooke types something out on her phone.

"Are you sure it's not the button on top?"

Heath snatches them from his dad and gives one to William who starts howling like a monkey in excitement at the table.

Brooke huffs. "Graham, they're not supposed to have their electronics during dinner. We've talked about this, Sweetcakes."

"Well, they already have them, it's not like I can take them away now." Graham shrugs as he takes a big gulp of his refreshed gin and tonic, eyeballing Andie over the glass.

Heath takes William's iPad and throws it on the floor.

"I hate you!" William screams as he kicks Heath in his chair.

"William, remember what we talked about. Jesus would *not* like you speaking to your brother like that."

"Fuck that!" William shouts causing several diners to look over at our table. My mom gasps next to Andie.

Oh shit.

"William Devon Parker! Do not swear! Where did you learn to speak like that?" Brooke takes a big drink of her chardonnay. "Graham, say something!"

"Now I've had enough from the both of you. Find an educational game on your iPad and shut your mouths or else I won't get the new hockey game you're dying to have." Graham orders his third gin and tonic as the waiter passes by.

"Remember, Heath and William, what would Jesus do…"

"Jesus would drink more wine is what he would do," Andie mumbles next to me making me laugh.

"Oh my gosh, they are so funny. *Boys*, what are you going to do?" Brooke laughs nervously. "Blessed is the best! Do you have kids, Andie?"

I look over at Andie and she looks like she's being held up at gunpoint, a hostage at this dinner table from hell. She clears her throat. "I um, uh yes, I have a twenty-month-old."

"Oh no, you're one of those."

"I'm sorry, one of what?"

"Oh you know, the mom who says her child's age in months. Like my kid is thirty-six months when we all know he's three years old." She snorts at her own joke. Graham blatantly eyeballs Andie as he drinks and it makes me want to reach across the table and punch his lights out.

"So you'd like me to say he's a year and eight months old? Or if we want to get really technical, I could say he's one point six nine years old."

Brooke gives Andie a vapid stare as she takes a sip of wine.

"Uh, if I remember correctly, you did exactly that." I give her a level look.

"Oh, I don't remember." Brooke waves me away as our food arrives. "So Andie, are you married? I don't see a ring on your finger."

"Brooke," I warn.

"Cam, relax, I'm just making pleasant conversation."

"It's okay," Andie says quietly next to me. "No, I'm not married. In fact, Enzo's dad isn't in his life."

"Oh Andie, dear, I'm so sorry to hear that," my mom says kindly.

"Thank you, Mrs. Forbes. Unfortunately that's sometimes how life goes."

"Yes, but it can't be easy, and please call me Linda."

"We manage." She smiles but it doesn't reach her eyes. I want to wrap her in my arms and take all her hurt and struggles and make them disappear.

"So…what happened? Did he die?"

"Brooke, honey…" my mom admonishes as Andie tenses next to me.

"What? I'm just curious."

"No, he's alive, it just didn't work out between us." Andie sets her fork down. Apparently, both of us have lost our appetites.

"So, now you're…dating my brother? Are you hoping he'll support you and your baby? Because I've got news for you—"

"Brooke!"

"What? You're so tetchy tonight, Cam. I'm just trying to get to know your new flavor of the month."

"That's it. I've had enough." I throw my napkin down and pull up a surprised Andie by her arm. "We're leaving. Mom, Dad, I just can't. Not tonight."

"Do you need me to take Andie home?" Graham pipes up from guzzling his drink. I ignore him as I turn to my sister. She looks up at me innocently.

"I don't see why you're so upset."

"Because you're rude and disrespectful to my…to Andie."

"Geez Cam, can't you take a joke? You're overreacting. I was just teasing."

"Teasing is playful. You're just mean. Your kids are rude,

your husband is drinking too much, you use Mom like she's your servant—"

"You're the one being rude, Cam! You're upsetting everyone." Brooke looks around the restaurant.

"Cam, honey, settle down."

"No, Mom, I won't. I'm tired of Brooke getting away with her shit."

I turn to my parents. "I'll see you all tomorrow at Kiki's house."

Mom stands up and gives Andie a hug. "Andie, it was so nice to meet you, honey. Will we see you tomorrow?"

"Yes ma'am, I'll be there."

"Great. Have a good night, you two." Mom smiles ignoring the fact that my sister just acted like a royal bitch at the table. My dad looks up from his game of *Words with Friends* on his phone. "Night, Cam! See you tomorrow. Andie, it was nice to meet you." I don't bother saying goodbye to Brooke or Graham.

I pull Andie out of the restaurant and wish tonight had never happened. What a shitshow my family is and we get to do it all again tomorrow.

Chapter 36

Andie

I FINISH PUTTING gloss on my lips when there's a knock at my front door. I look at myself in the mirror and take a deep breath. I'm going with Cam to Kiki's baby shower, but after last night I'm kind of dreading it. His sister is an absolute bitch and her husband was giving me major creep vibes as he stared at me all through dinner. The kids were total assholes and everyone pretended like it wasn't happening. Poor Cam apologized all the way home after we went through a drive-thru and grabbed some burgers since we didn't get to eat our food. I agreed to go with him today because I figured this would be the perfect time to talk.

I pick Enzo up out of his playpen and give Vader a treat before opening the front door. Cameron greets me with a gut-punching smile. I could answer the door a million times and he would take my breath away every time. He looks gorgeous in a button-down with the sleeves rolled up and dark jeans.

"You look beautiful." He smiles and then turns his attention to Enzo. "Hey buddy, don't you look stylish."

"Mama."

"Yes, your mama is breathtaking." Enzo reaches for Cam which surprises me. Without hesitation Cam takes him into his arms. "You're showing me up with this bow tie, little man." Enzo slaps his hands on either side of Cam's cheeks and presses a kiss to his cheek. Oh my god, melt my heart these two.

"Okay, we can either take my car or move my car seat over to yours if you brought the Range Rover."

"We'll move the car seat to mine."

We get the car seat transferred and on the road to Kiki's lake house.

"Are you nervous?"

I laugh. "A little. Your older sister is kind of scary and your brother-in-law creeps me out."

"I know." His jaw clenches. "I'm sorry about that, but I promise I won't let her be a bi…" He looks back at Enzo in the rearview mirror. "I promise I won't let her be a bird today, and I'll make sure he stays away from you."

"Okay." I laugh. "Thank you for protecting me against the bird and the lecher."

He looks over at me and smiles, slipping his hand into mine. He looks so damn good with his aviators on and his sun-kissed arm resting on the console. Something niggles my brain from dinner last night. I don't want to ruin this blissful peaceful moment, but I need to get it out on the table.

"Cameron, about what your sister said last night."

He sighs. "Don't listen to a word that comes out of her mouth."

"I know, but I just want to be transparent with you. I'd never date you just so you can take care of Enzo and me. I'm not looking for a sugar daddy, or a baby daddy...I just...I just wanted you to hear that from my lips."

He glances at me before his eyes turn to the road. He squeezes my hand. "I know."

"Okay, good."

Silence descends upon us. I look back at Enzo and he's zonked out in his car seat.

"I never got a chance to tell you, I met your ex."

Thank god I'm not driving because I would have swerved off the road. "You what? When? How?"

"Breathe, Andie." He chuckles. "I came by your house one morning and he was there sitting on your porch. It was the morning after brunch, I think you had left town. What's up with the two of you anyway? Does he come by a lot?"

I take a deep breath. I didn't stick around to find out if Mason would return, but apparently, he did. "What did he say?"

"Not much. He tried to punch me, but he missed."

I look at him in horror. "Oh god, he tried to punch you? He, I...I don't even know what to say. I'm so sorry. This is so messed up."

"What is he to you?"

"Nothing. He is *nothing* to me. He got my address from his girlfriend who got it from my mama. He showed up the afternoon I got back from the brunch and insisted on seeing Enzo. I told him it wasn't a good time, but he just steamrolled over me. He stayed for about two hours and then I asked him to leave. When he told me he'd be back in the morning, I hightailed it out of town. I knew he would try to somehow worm his way back into my life."

I peek a look over at Cam. His jaw is clenched tight as a small muscle ticks in annoyance. "Does he pay you child support?"

"Ha, that's a joke. He left me a hundred bucks when he walked out on us. That's all I've ever gotten from him."

"What a piece of shit. You need to talk to a lawyer, Andie. Promise me you'll do that. You need to know your rights."

I nod. "You're right. I can't keep hoping he won't return."

"Guys like that will always come back. If he wants something, he'll use Enzo against you to get it."

I chew my thumbnail nervously as I look out my window. "That sounds like something he'd do."

"Just…promise me you'll talk to a lawyer, okay?"

"Okay. Can I ask you a question since we never really talked about it? Can you explain crazy brunch lady?"

Cam blows a breath out. "That was Kendra, a woman I went out on one date with in California. I ran into her at a restaurant in Nashville back in October and she tracked down my number. We went out for drinks. I was hoping she could help me out with real estate; she was hoping for a boyfriend. I never called her again and what you saw that Sunday was the result."

"Yikes."

"Yeah. I'm so sorry you had to witness that."

This time I squeeze his hand. "It's okay. TJ mentioned someone named Lisa. Is she someone special?"

He sighs. "Lisa is an ex-girlfriend of mine. We dated for a little over a year before I ended it."

We sit in silence but the curiosity is burning off of me in waves. "Why did you end it?"

"She wasn't the right one for me. She didn't like that I was married to my work. She wanted me to be married to her. I didn't. She made an ultimatum and I didn't choose her."

"Oh."

He sighs heavily. "Look, Andie, I know we're kind of at an impasse. I want to be more, but with everything that's happening in California, I can't guarantee you anything."

I look at him curiously. "Tell me what's going on in California."

"With Josh turning the California locations over to me, I'm going to be out there weeks at a time now. I've lost a manager and a co-owner. I have this lawsuit I'm trying to get settled, it's a mess. Connor will basically be running this location for me. I'm sorry, but I won't be around much." He flexes his hands against the steering wheel. "To be honest, we both have a lot to think about. You need to figure out what you're doing with your ex and I need to figure out the business. It's not fair to either one of us to be half in."

I swallow as tears prick behind my eyes. I look out the window so he can't see my face flush. Just when I think the pieces have finally fallen into place, the rug gets ripped out from underneath me again. I swallow past the heartbreak in my throat. "When are you leaving?"

"Tomorrow."

"How long will you be gone for?"

"I don't know." He looks over at me briefly. "Awhile. I'm sorry, I didn't want to bring this up and put a damper on the party. I'm hoping you'll want to spend the day with me, but I'll understand if you need to put space between us."

A tear leaks down my cheek and I swipe it quickly away before he can see it. He's asking for one day to be with me, but beyond that he can't promise me anything. This is not how I thought our relationship would go. I never dreamed he'd be going back to the West Coast for a long stay, maybe even permanently. It may not be what I want in the long term, but I'm not ready to say it's over either.

I put on a brave face, but I feel like I'm crumbling inside. "I guess we've got today then, huh?"

He squeezes my hand. "I was hoping you would say that."

THE PARTY IS simple and elegant as we gather on the back stone-flagged patio that overlooks the placid blue lake. Partygoers are mingling by the buffet table and sitting at the white tables decorated with pastel floral arrangements. Waitstaff are passing around flutes of champagne and there's a full bar offering whatever drink you could want. I spot Sarah first as we walk in.

"Hi guys! Enzo, you look so darling! Oh my god, Andie, I will need to borrow this cute little outfit for Wyatt."

I smile. "It's yours."

She claps her hands happily. "So, we have two nannies in

there that are watching the babies if you want Enzo to join them."

"Oh, that would be amazing."

"Come on, I'll show you." We start to head in as Cam announces he's going to find his parents. "Are you okay? Your cheeks are rosy."

"I'm okay, just had kind of an intense conversation with Cam on the way here."

"Is everything okay?"

"Yes, no. I don't know," I say miserably as I put Enzo down on the floor with Chase. I leave my diaper bag with the nannies and head back outside with Sarah.

She links her arm in mine. "Hey, trust in each other. It will happen."

"I don't know, Sare. He has to go run the California locations. He doesn't know when he'll be back. There's just no future in that." Sarah squeezes my arm in comfort. "I'm feeling…" I gasp. "Oh no, hide!"

"What?"

"There's Brooke, Cam and Kiki's sister. I met her last night. She's a real piece of work."

"Oh god, I can't stand her. Let's go this way." We dodge Brooke and spot TJ hiding crouched down by the gift table.

"What are you doing over here?"

"Hiding from the wicked witch of the west." TJ looks over his shoulder as he stands up and pretends to straighten the gifts on the table. "She already made Kiki cry this morning."

Sarah grinds her teeth. "I hate that woman."

"You know, you can't hide out over here all afternoon."

We all yelp and turn around in surprise. "Oh thank god, it's only Lex."

"Only Lex?" He arches an eyebrow up at Sarah.

She kisses him. "*The* Lex. The hottest guitarist this side of the Mississippi."

"Hmm." He nuzzles her neck as he wraps her in a hug as she giggles.

I love the two of them. They are the epitome of what happiness should be. I'm suddenly in the dumps knowing what I have can't commit.

"TJ, I've been sent by my brother to tell you the baby gender reveal is happening soon. Andie, Cam's looking for you, Love."

"Yes!" TJ grabs my hand. "Come on guys, help me gather everyone up. We've got a baby to reveal!"

We gather everyone under a big old oak tree. "I have to say, TJ, I'm kind of surprised Kiki left you in charge of this."

Lex snorts and shakes his head.

"Hey, I can gender reveal with the best of them! I had so many brilliant ideas, but that little preggy ogre can be such a killjoy. I wanted to do a Game of Thrones dragon egg, but she vetoed that fab idea. Then I wanted to do a paintball reveal where we all shoot her with paint balls, but she said that could hurt the baby and who wants to be covered in paint for the rest of the party? She's such a grump. Then I thought fireworks would be amazeballs, but doing this during the day kind of put a damper on that."

I bite my cheek and smile. "She's lucky to have you as one of her besties."

"I know, right? Okay, I'll be right back!"

TJ hurries over to Kiki and Tatum and starts calling people to gather around them. Cam finds me and joins Sarah, Lex, and I as we watch on in amusement. TJ circles the group, lighting little round things. Tatum and Kiki hesitantly take a step back.

"Oh god, what is he doing? Are those firecrackers?" Sarah asks worriedly.

"I don't know, but if TJ is involved it's going to be a shit-fest." Cam grimaces, making me giggle. He smiles down at me, and pulls me against his chest, his arm wrapping protectively around me.

We watch as smoke starts swirling out of the little bombs around us.

"It's purple...what does that mean?" Cam whispers to me.

"I have no idea." I grin.

The purple smoke turns to green. The acidic and pungent smell disperses through the crowd. Several people try to wave the smoke away. "Purple and then green...I'm so confused."

The four of us start to laugh as Kiki throws her hands up in the air in frustration. Guests start fanning the air around them as the stinky smoke lingers.

"Should have gone with the dragon egg," Lex murmurs.

"I have a pinata! Let me just get it! Just wait everyone!" TJ shouts desperately as he fans smoke out of an elderly woman's face.

"Babe," Sarah tells Lex, "you better go get the backup plan I brought. It's in the car. The last thing we need is Kiki hitting TJ with the pinata stick." Lex nods and hustles into the house with Cam following.

"Good thing you brought a backup." I giggle to Sarah.

"Oh girl, I've learned you always need a backup when it comes to TJ."

We both laugh as Lex and Cam return with two large confetti poppers. Kiki's face relaxes in relief as she mouths *thank you* to Sarah. TJ comes over to join us.

"I mean, I don't know what happened! I'm going to cry. I knew I should have done the dragon egg or the paint guns."

I rub his back. "It's okay, the purple was really pretty."

"It was like a bad fog machine at a Disney Descendants party."

"Okay…I'm not sure what Descendants is…but, it was a lovely effect."

Tatum turns to all of us. "Thank you everyone for coming this afternoon and celebrating our second baby. It means a lot to us that you are here and sharing in the excitement of what we're having." He looks down at Kiki. "Whatever it is, Coffee Girl, I'm just so excited it's ours, and that our little family is growing. There's no one else I'd rather have by my side doing this with." He reaches down and wipes a tear from her cheek. "Even if it's green…or purple."

"Even if it's green or purple." Kiki laughs as she kisses him back. Several people, myself included, wipe a tear away.

"On three!" Tatum shouts. They stand together and point the confetti cans in the air. "One, two, three!"

They shoot the poppers and blue confetti rains down on the two of them. Kiki and Tatum kiss in pure joy.

"No!" TJ shouts, causing several people to turn and look at him. "Oh sorry, if you knew their son Chase you'd understand." He shrugs and then runs over and hugs Kiki.

We all wait our turn to hug them. Brooke and Graham walk up to Cam and me, both of them eyeing me up and down. She zeros in on our clasped hands and rolls her eyes. "Polly." She eyes me briefly before turning toward Cam. "So Cam, looks like we'll have another nephew."

Cam smiles and lets go of my hand. Just when I'm about to step away, I feel his hand wrap around my waist and tug me possessively to his side. "Looks like it."

"Graham, be a dear and go fetch me a glass of chardonnay." Graham dutifully rushes over to the bar set up outside. Brooke's eyes narrow on Cam.

"I think you owe me an apology, don't you?"

"For what?"

"For what you said last night."

"I stand by what I said. If anyone deserves an apology, it should be Andie."

Brooke scoffs, "I'm not apologizing because I didn't do anything wrong."

I don't understand this beautiful woman standing in front of me. She could have it all, but instead she chooses to be a hateful little witch.

TJ comes walking toward us and then tries to do an about-face when he sees who we're talking to, but Brooke sees him before he can slink away.

"Well, if it's not the gay David Copperfield. Nice smoke illusion," Brooke sneers. "Are you going to make yourself disappear next?"

TJ sighs heavily as he turns around. "Don't be so *despacito*, Brooke. That's a nice weave you have by the way. Is that real horsehair?"

"It's not a weave!"

"Oh sorry, a wig then." He studies her forehead. "Aah yes, I can see the line now. Classy. What's that smell?" TJ looks down at Brook's heels. "Oh honey, should have worn the scrubs. That will never come out of suede."

Brooke lifts her suede heel, covered in dog poop.

"Ugh, I hate you!" she shouts and storms off.

Cam sighs. "TJ."

"What?" TJ shrugs. "It's not like I pushed her in dog poop, although I wish I had."

I cough in my hand to cover my laugh and excuse myself to go get a drink and check on Enzo. I give TJ a high-five behind Cam's back as I pass him. That bitch deserved it.

DESPITE BROOKE AND the sulfuric smell, the afternoon was relaxing and fun, and went by way too fast laughing with my friends. The guys played a few songs entertaining the crowd, and even Matt was fun to hang with since he no longer hits on me.

"You ready to head back?" Cam comes up from behind me, slipping a hand around my waist. I nod, unable to speak with his close proximity. I lean my head against his chest and close my eyes wishing it could always be like this. "Let's grab Enzo and say our goodbyes." He kisses the shell of my ear and it makes me shiver.

"Okay." I don't want this afternoon to end because that

means it's closer to having Cam leave. We say our goodbyes and drive the hour back home. We don't say much in the car, because really, what's there to say? He's leaving tomorrow and I don't know when I'll see him again. Maybe back in a month for a day or two? Maybe six months? I don't know and neither does he. I could beg him to do long distance and try to make this work, but let's be realistic. He's not in a position to make Enzo and me his top priority and that's what I need. We both know that. The most I can hope for is his friendship.

We get back to my house and he helps me warm up a bottle of milk while I give Enzo a bath. After getting him down to bed I find Cam standing in my living room waiting for me.

"Are you leaving?"

"Do you want me to?"

"No."

"Then I'll stay."

Damn, why can't it be that simple? Why can't I ask him to stay permanently? "Stay," I murmur as I look at his chest and run my fingers up to his broad shoulders.

"I'm here." He lifts my chin and kisses me breathless. "I love you, Andie." He trails a finger down my jaw and I melt under his touch. "I want you to know that, no matter what happens between us, you've got me so tightly wrapped around your finger."

His eyes search mine, but my throat is constricted with sadness and fear. My fingers thread through his hair and I tug his lips down to mine. "I love you." It hurts to admit that to him. It leaves my heart feeling vulnerable and open for him to crush it. But I need for him to hear it as much as I craved for him to say it.

He smiles devilishly down at me, breaking the intensity of the moment. "This sundress has been driving me crazy all afternoon. You're gorgeous in it, but I need it off of you."

I smile against his lips. "Then take it off."

He growls as he finds the zipper at the back and slides it down. The dress pools at my feet and he stares at me in my lace panties. I've never had a guy look at me with such reverence, with such want. "Andie, you're so beautiful...god, I need you."

"Yes," I whisper against his mouth as he lifts me, wrapping my legs around his waist. He carries me back to my bedroom. He turns the bedside lamp on and I let him because I need to see him tonight, and I want him to see me. I want to memorize every touch, every detail.

Tonight it's different as his body covers mine. We make love slowly...languidly, as if we can't get close enough to each other. And I let him own me completely, touching places of my heart I've never let anyone else get to, because tonight this is for me. It's my one night with him that I will never have again. My one night that will get me through the lonely. No one will ever live up to the way he makes my body hum with pleasure.

My one night I will keep for myself.

In the morning I wake up to find him gone. He didn't even say goodbye, but it's probably for the best. My heart wouldn't have survived it.

Chapter 37

Andie

Two Months Later

I OPEN THE door and sigh. "Mason, what the fuck do you want?"

"Geez Andie, is that any way to answer your door to the father of your child?"

"Oh, you've seen Enzo's dad? I haven't seen him since the day he was born." I fold my arms over my chest not letting him through the door. "Tell him he owes me child support."

"Come the fuck on, Andie. Let me in."

"No."

"Don't make me move you."

"Lay one finger on me and I will call the cops faster than you can blink. You should also know I'm recording this."

Mason takes a step back looking affronted. "Are you *threatening* me, bitch?"

"Uh, yeah I am."

"Is your stupid rich boyfriend around?"

"I don't have a rich boyfriend."

"I popped him one good. If he ever comes sniffing around here again, I'll do more than give him a black eye." He sways on his feet and I eye him with contempt.

"Well, if I see him, I'll pass along that little love note."

"I came here to see my son." He stumbles toward me and I wrinkle my nose.

"Are you drunk?"

"No."

"You smell like stale beer. You're not seeing my son."

"Our son."

"Oh, that's laughable. The way I see it, you're just an unfortunate sperm donor. I've met with a family lawyer and filled out an application for child support."

"I can't afford to give you child support!"

"Oh, hmm, that's a shame. Wages can be garnished."

"I get paid in cash!"

"Even better, then you can just send me cash every month. It's required by law, Mason."

"Dumb bitch, I'm not giving you a cent."

"That's unfortunate." I reach in my back pocket. "Here's my lawyer's card if you have questions about visiting Enzo. He'll need you to fill out paperwork as well."

"Come on, Andie! What happened to when you loved me? You were so sweet back then. Where did that girl go? Don't you love me?"

I prop my chin on my hand. "The question is, did you ever love *me*, Mason?"

"Aw, come on! We made a child together."

I roll my eyes. "Not intentionally, the condom broke.

You know what I think? I think you're in love with Mason Mahoney. You didn't give a twig about anyone else."

He scoffs as he stretches his arms out to his side. "I had dreams!"

"Don't we all."

"Fuck this shit." Mason agitatedly takes off his cowboy hat and runs a hand nervously through his hair. He grabs the card I'm holding out toward him and stuffs it in his back pocket. "Fuck this. I never wanted a kid!" He turns and stumbles down my front steps.

"Call Larry, Mason! He'd love to chat with you about Tennessee child support laws and visitation rights! Byeee!" *Good riddance, asswipe.* I walk back into my house and slam the door shut.

Chapter 38

Cameron

"Hɪ Cᴀᴍ, ᴄᴀɴ I come in?"

I slowly lower my arm and let her into my condo. I close the door and follow her over to the couch. "What are you doing here Lisa? It's late."

"Look, I know I'm the last person you want to see, but I was hoping…"

I shake my head. "Please tell me you didn't fly all the way to San Francisco on the hopes of you and I getting back together."

Lisa looks crestfallen. "Cam, just hear me out, okay?"

I lean over and run my hands through my hair. "Yeah, sure." If she flew all the way to San Francisco, the least I can do is listen to her.

"I've missed you. God, I've missed you so much. You broke something in me and I don't know how to move forward."

"Lisa…"

"No wait, let me finish." She fidgets with a gold bracelet

I had given her on her wrist. "I messed up. I get that. I pressured you when you weren't ready and I am so sorry. I won't do that again. I understand The Social Hour is the most important thing to you. I'm so sorry I made you choose between your baby and me. I will never make that mistake again. I am willing to wait for however long it takes." She inhales deeply. "Even if we never get married or have children, I will be by your side."

I look at her incredulously. "You are willing to give up everything you've dreamed because I'm a selfish asshole who's not willing to sacrifice for you?"

Her eyes dart around the room nervously before returning to mine. "Yes."

I sigh as I lean back in my chair. "No."

"What do you mean *no*? Cam, I'm throwing myself down across your doorstep begging you to take me back. We were so good together! You are my world! I am willing to give up fucking everything to be with you!"

"That's just it, Lisa, I don't want you to. I am exactly what I said, a selfish asshole. I would never ask someone to gie up their life to fit into mine. Go find someone who will make your dreams come true. I'm not him." I get up from my chair as she flings herself at me hysterically crying.

"No, Cam, I don't want anyone else!" she wails. "I want you! I want the life we had."

"The life we *had*." I detach her vise-like grip on my arm. "I'm sorry, but I'm in love with someone else."

She pushes back from me angrily. "Who? I haven't heard you were dating anyone else."

"It doesn't matter who. Move on, Lisa, it's time."

She crumples to the floor and bawls. Shit, this is all I need right now. I crouch down beside her and try to soothe her. "Lisa, honey, it's time to go back to your hotel. I'm sorry, okay? I'm sorry it didn't work out. You're an amazing woman who will make some guy incredibly lucky, but it's not me."

"Why can't it be you!" she cries, but I don't answer her. There's nothing more for me to say. She hiccups as she sits up. "I don't have a hotel. I came straight here from the airport."

Shit. I look at my watch, it's almost midnight. "Okay, you can sleep in my guestroom."

"Okay."

She gets up and shuffles to the bedroom. How did my life get so fucking messy?

Chapter 39

Andie

I'VE BEEN TRYING to call Cam at least once a week to see how he's doing. I miss him like crazy. He's been gone for three months now and I'm understanding why he couldn't commit to me the night of Kiki's shower. It's just too hard. I'm busy with Enzo and work and he's struggling with The Social Hour.

I pick up my phone after putting Enzo down for his nap and check the time. It's nine a.m. West Coast time, so he should be up. I love hearing his gravelly voice when I call him in the mornings. It makes me think of our last night together.

I need to hear his voice, and I want to tell him about Mason showing up yesterday.

"Hello?"

I look down at my phone, and sure enough it's Cam's number, but a woman answered. I take an unsteady breath as dread fills my belly. "Uh, hi. Is Cam there?"

"He's in the shower," she purrs. "Can I take a message?"

"Um, who is this?"

"Lisa. Who is this?"

"Lisa, his ex-girlfriend?" My voice sounds tinny like I'm in a tunnel.

"Lisa, his current girlfriend," she huffs. "Who is this?"

"This is...no one." I hang up the phone. I want to throw up. I want to throw my phone against the wall and watch it shatter into a thousand pieces. I want to scream and kick and call Cameron Forbes a million names and wish that he dies a horrid death, but I don't.

I wait for my heart to break apart, but instead a wintry blast of ice freezes over it.

Chapter 40

Cameron

I RUN TOWARD the hospital doors into the sterile waiting room. I check my phone again for the directions Tatum had sent me. I take the elevator up, impatiently tapping my foot as I shift the flowers I'm carrying in my arms. Rushing over to the nurse's station I ask which way to room 408. I jog down the corridor, the neon lights making me feel sick. I hear yelling and I know I'm in the right place.

TJ meets me as he quickly walks out of the room. "Oh Cambam thank god you made it in time. She's been asking if your flight landed. Careful, she's a beast. Tatum went in search of ice. Here, I'll put these in water."

"What's that smell?"

"Oh, apparently it's a no-no to burn sage in hospital rooms. Who knew?"

"Everyone who's anyone."

"The nurse practically tackled me and threatened to expel me from the hospital. Can you believe the nerve of her? Luckily, I was able to wave a little in Kiki's face before she put me in a choke hold."

"Why were you attempting to burn sage again?"

"Listen, that sister from another mister in there is acting like a demon beast right now. She needs all the help she can get."

"Uh, TJ, why are you wearing a shirt like the guy in *Tiger King*?" I'm blinded by the black-and-gold sequin tiger print silk shirt. "You look like an Ice Capades dancer. Is that a *Karate Kid* bandana?"

"I'm dealing with a tiger in there Cam. I have to dress the part for total zen concentration."

I shake my head as I hand the flowers over to TJ. "I don't even know what to say to that." I smile as I enter the room. Kiki is hooked up to beeping machines reading a magazine. Well, I wouldn't quite call tearing through pages at lightning speed reading, but she seems occupied. She looks up when I enter.

"Well it's about time. Thought you were going to miss your nephew being born. Mom and dad still in the waiting room? Where the heck is Tatum? He left like twenty minutes ago! God, it's hot in here, are you hot? Oh shit, get over here Cam, I need a hand to squeeze. Hurry, I feel a contraction coming on!"

I nervously look over at TJ who's arranging the flowers in a vase he procured from somewhere. "Don't look at me, I just do the breathing with her."

"Well, shouldn't you be doing that?"

TJ shrugs. "I'm kind of scared of her."

"Will one of you pansy asses get the fuck over here!" she growls.

I swallow and approach her bedside and gingerly reach out my hand for her to hold. She grabs it and starts to squeeze. *Hard.* I wince as I try to pull away a fraction. "Where's your husband?"

"Agh! God, this is a bitch! Where's the goddamn doctor?"

"Hee hee hoo. Hee hee hoo. Breathe through it, Kinks. Do it with me now." I look over at TJ as he bounces on a large pink rubber ball next to her bed.

"Shut the fuck up, Tammy Jean!" she cries. "Hee hee howamotherfucker!"

She squeezes my hand tighter and I'm pretty sure she's broken some of the smaller bones. I grind my teeth together and let her crush my hand as she slowly releases it and gets her breathing back under control with TJ. I take my hand back and shake it out.

"Maybe I should send mom in here."

"No, I made her leave because she kept asking me if I was following Brooke's list for having a baby and dad was driving me nuts asking for synonyms for his crossword puzzle during a contraction."

"Oh geez, I don't even want to know."

"Let's just say it started with getting a professional blow out and your makeup done so you look your best while having the baby. Mom asked me why I wasn't wearing makeup and I almost chucked her phone across the room."

"Here, Kiki, we need to get you out of bed. Come bounce on the ball with me." TJ rolls a purple one out from behind a chair. I help her out of bed and she slowly lowers herself to the ball. TJ holds her hands and then quickly drops them.

"Hey, why won't you hold my hands?"

"Because you're like King Kong with those things. No thank you."

"Come on, TJ, I need help balancing. I promise I won't hurt you." TJ reluctantly puts his hands in hers.

"Where's Sarah?" I ask as I check my text messages. I send one quickly to Andie to let her know I've landed and I'm at the hospital. I missed our weekly call last week, but I thought she would have responded when I texted her that I was flying in to Nashville today.

"She and Andie are on their way...yayyay oh god!" she pants. "Lex and Connor are watching the kidssss...Godzilla!"

"Breathe, Kiki! Jesus, just breathe! Ow, you're hurting me!" TJ tries to pull his hands away from her. "Hee! Hee! Hoo! Do your fucking breathing, Kong! Hee to the Ho to the Bee Bop Bo—"

"I swear to fucking god I'm going to strangle you with Mr. Miyagi's bandana if you don't stop rapping!" she screams just as Tatum, the doctor, and nurse enter the room, eyes wide as they take in the scene.

The doctor checks her print outs. "And five, four, three, two, one. Well, that was an intense one, wasn't it?" She smiles at all of us like we just finished an invigorating session of yoga.

"I think I'm paralyzed...and traumatized. She's like a scary ass honey badger who looks sweet and innocent and then claws your eyes out when you least expect it." TJ hides behind me as Tatum helps Kiki off the ball and back into bed.

"Tater Tot, I need the drugs. Get me the drugs. I'm can't do natural like I planned. I thought I could, but I can't. Chase turned out okay, and I had an epidural with him. Give me all the drugs."

"Can I just point out that Chase did not turn out okay? He is wild," TJ chimes in behind me causing me to laugh.

"Tater Tot, don't listen to them, pleeeaase!" She grabs his shirt and pulls him to her face. "I'm not strong enough like Brooke."

I snort. "What are you talking about? Brooke had planned c-sections with both so she could have a tummy tuck right after."

"What?! That lying B. She told me she had both boys *au natural!*"

"The only thing natural on her—"

"Okay, TJ, we don't need to finish that statement in front of the hospital staff. Dr. Rosen, do you think Kiki could have an epidural?" Tatum softly kisses her forehead as he smooths her hair back.

"We'll have to check her progress which is why I came in. If you all could give us a moment?"

"Oh thank god!" TJ and I don't have to be asked twice as we hightail it out of the room.

"Bejeeze wax she's a scary little preggo monster. Oh, there are the girls!" TJ skips ahead down the hall to the waiting room where Sarah and Andie are talking to my parents.

"Oh Cameron, honey, I'm so glad you made it!" My mom stands up and hugs me. My dad thumps my back.

"How's our girl?"

"Uh, she's a bit…" I look over at TJ for help.

"You know when a mama bear has cubs in the area and she gets super aggressive and her claws come out and she wants to rip out your throat? Guts and blood and bodies torn apart. Ugh, I can't even!" TJ shivers. "That's Kiki right now."

"Oh, well, that paints quite a picture, TJ." My mom laughs nervously. "I think we'll just stay out here until she calls for us."

"Good idea, Mom. Hey, Andie, can we have a minute? Alone?"

Andie gets up and wipes her hands on her jeans as she stands up. She looks at a spot over my shoulder. What the hell is going on with her? I know these past few months have been hard, but I at least expected a smile or a hug. "Welcome back," she says flatly.

"Thanks." I grab her hand as I lead her down an opposite hallway, but she quickly wrenches it out of my grip. "How have you been? I missed your call last week. I tried calling you but you didn't answer."

She looks down at the floor. "Hmm."

"What's wrong?" I turn her to me and place my hands on her hips. "I've missed you."

"Cam, please don't."

I lean my forehead against hers and breathe in her heady scent. "I've missed you so much. Can we grab dinner tomorrow night?"

She exhales deeply as she steps back from me. "Cam, drop the act. I know—"

"Cameron, Andie! You're being summoned!" TJ shouts

down the hall at us. A nurse shushes him. "Come on!" he whispers loudly.

"We'll talk later." I gently squeeze her hips before I drop my hands and walk with her to Kiki's room.

"There you guys are!" Kiki beams at us from the bed. The room is crowded since we are all in here now.

Andie rushes over and gives her a hug. "I'm so excited for you guys! You're going to do great. Can I get you anything?"

"I'm great, thanks! I'm so ready to meet this baby boy."

I look over at Tatum who's lounging in a chair rubbing his hand. TJ looks at her print out.

"Uh, Kinksadoodle, are you okay? You're having a big contraction right now."

"I am? Huh, just feel a little tug. Crazy." She beams at all of us.

"She just got her epidural." We all breathe a sigh of relief.

"Hats off to the mamas who do it *au natural*. I tried." She smiles at all of us.

"It's okay, CG. No one needs you to be a martyr. You're doing awesome." Tatum gets up and kisses her and she smiles up at him gratefully. "I'm sorry I hurt your hand, Tater Tot. So guys, we brought you all in because the doctor says it's going to be soon."

"Aw! I can't wait to meet Baby Reed!" Sarah gushes as she hugs Kiki. "We'll be right out here if you need any of us."

"Tatum and I talked it over and we'd love to have all his aunties and uncles in the room with us when he's born. Do you guys want to stay?"

"I for one, do not need to witness this." I kiss Kiki's head. "But I can't wait to meet him. Dad and I will be out in the waiting room."

"Kiki, sweetheart, Brooke's list says you should only—"

"Mom, you're out. Go wait with Cam and Dad."

I wrap an arm around my mom, her crestfallen face resigned as I guide her out of the room. "It's better this way, Mom." Andie, Sarah, TJ, and Tatum stay back as we wait for baby Reed to arrive.

IT'S EARLY EVENING when I park my car on the curb outside of Andie's house and jog up the stairs. I knock on the door in case Enzo is sleeping. I wait a minute and then impatiently start knocking again. The door swings open and I'm surprised because I'm expecting Andie, but instead I'm looking down at her teenage babysitter. She glances up at me from her iPhone as she blows a bubble with her gum.

"Yeah?" she asks impatiently after she snaps the bubble.

"Uh, hi. Is Andie home?"

She blows another bubble and it snaps as she looks me over. "No." She starts to shut the door in my face but I quickly reach out and stop the door with my hand. The girl sighs and looks back at her phone.

"Look um…" I look at her questioningly. "What's your name again?"

She glances up at me and rolls her eyes as she chews her gum. "Becky. So what are you, like the pizza guy or something?"

"Do I look like I'm delivering pizzas?" I look down at my Tom Ford suit and Italian wingtips.

"I dunno, but I didn't order pizza."

"Very perceptive. Becky, can you stop looking at your phone for two seconds?"

She stares at me with a blank expression on her face as she pops her bubblegum.

"Becky, where is Ms. Daniels?"

"What do I look like, a thesaurus?"

I stare at her a beat. "That doesn't even make sense."

She shrugs as she looks back down at her phone. I want to throw it across the room. "Earth to Becky? Where's Andie? This is important."

"What are you like the FBI or something?"

I smirk. "First a pizza guy and now I'm the FBI?"

Becky raises one eyebrow and looks at me like I'm a total creeper. "Maybe you're an FBI agent disguised as a pizza delivery guy."

I lean in closer. "Don't you think I'd be carrying pizza boxes if I were delivering them?"

She looks around me as if pizza boxes will magically appear. "Whatevs, I don't care." She texts something on her phone and pops her gum. God forbid this girl ever have to identify someone in a lineup.

"Are you babysitting Enzo?"

"Who?" She blows a bubble as she continues to text.

"Enzo? Andie's little boy?"

"Oh yeah, why do you want to know?"

"Because I'm concerned for his safety."

Becky rolls her eyes as she types away. I snap my fingers in front of her face and she doesn't even flinch. Jesus, where did Andie find this girl?

"Becky? *Becky*! When is Andie coming back?" I feel like I'm shouting, probably because I am.

Becky sighs as she looks over her shoulder and shrugs. I'm sure she's watching some mind-numbing show on Netflix she can't miss. "Dunno." I'm seriously afraid for our future if Becky is any kind of representation.

"Becky."

She looks back at me and her eyes narrow. "Hey wait, don't I know you?"

Now we're getting somewhere. "Yes, I've me—"

She snaps her gum. "You're the guy that bought us beer the other night at the Eleven."

Jesus Christ. I want to bang my head against the door. I get my wallet out of my pocket and pull out a fifty. I'm not sure how long she's been here, but I can't imagine Andie would leave Enzo with this girl for very long.

"Becky, listen to me," I say slowly, "I'm going to pay you and you're going to leave and go back to whatever spaceship dropped you off."

"Yeah, whatevs."

I hold the fifty in front of her face and she snatches it quicker than I can blink. She grabs her backpack and slides by me.

"Laters, hot pizza guy."

I walk into Andie's house. Her dog Darth Vader comes bounding up to me. We bonded the night I had to sleep on her sofa. He took up half of it and then proceeded to light off gas bombs all night long. For being such a short squat thing, he sure can clear a room.

"Hey Vader, where's your brother?" I look around and spy Enzo on the couch watching the television, eyes the size of saucers as he sucks on a block. I look at the TV and watch for a second before I find the clicker and turn it to a hockey game. Sure enough, Becky was watching some TikTok crap.

"Mama da!" Enzo shouts as he gives me a gummy drooly smile.

"Hey buddy, I don't know where your mama is, but we'll hang out like some regular dudes. That be okay?"

He claps his hands and reaches for me. He really is a sweet adorable kid. I take my coat off and lay it over a chair. I pick him up as I loosen my tie and head into her kitchen to grab a beer. I look at the clock and notice that it's five p.m. Probably dinnertime for Darth Vader and Enzo.

I open some cupboards and snoop in her pantry gathering some noodles. I know my nephew Chase loves noodles. I find where she keeps the dog food and Enzo helps me scoop some food into his bowl. The dog finishes before I even get water boiling for Enzo's pasta. I set Enzo in his highchair and give him some milk in a sippy cup with a wooden spoon to bang around while I make his dinner.

"Do you like plain noodles, little man? I don't know if you have any allergies, so I'm afraid dinner will be pretty basic." Maybe I should text Andie and let her know I told Becky to go home, but it might really piss her off that I'm here. I text Kiki instead.

Me: *Do you think it's okay to give Andie's kid plain noodles for dinner?*

Kiki: *Why are you asking me? Ask her.*

Me: *She's not here*

Kiki: *She left you alone with Enzo?*

Me: *You make me sound like I'm some child creeper.*

Kiki: *Sorry, not what I meant. I'm just surprised you're over there watching Enzo.*

Me: *Me too. Long story. Can I feed him noodles or not?*

Kiki: *Don't get impatient and bossy with me. You need me right now.*

Me: *I'm sorry. Noodles? Check yes or no.*

Kiki: *That George Strait song just popped into my head. Thanks a lot. Now it's going to drive me crazy.*

Me: *I thought about texting TJ over you but I thought no, that would lead me down a rabbit hole I'll never get out of. I was wrong.*

Kiki: *I don't know why but now that Drop Dead Fred song I'm too sexy for my shirt just popped into my head. Why is that? Crazy.*

Me: *It's Right Said Fred. Drop Dead Fred was a movie. I hate you right now.*

Kiki: *You're singing it too aren't you…*

Me: *I don't know why I ever ask you for help.*

Kiki: *Tatum just walked into the room. Damn, he looks sexy in his shirt.*

Me: *I'm not Sarah or TJ. Please don't ever think I want to know if and when Tatum looks sexy.*

Kiki: *You really need to loosen up. Gotta feed the baby. Noodles are fine. Bye!*

"Enzo dude, don't ever have a sister, 'kay buddy? Both of

mine are crazy in their own ways." I chuckle as I pour macaroni noodles into the boiling water. I take off my tie and undo a couple buttons, then roll up my sleeves to stir the noodles. "So buddy, on a scale of one to ten, how pissed do you think your mom will be when she sees me here in her kitchen?"

"Dah! Mmmbee ma!"

"A three? That's not too bad."

"More like twelve. What are you doing here?"

I whirl around and see Andie leaning against the kitchen entrance. Her arms are folded across her chest and her eyes are shuttered so that I can't tell what she's feeling. "Hi, I stopped by, but you weren't here."

"I just left the hospital." She walks into the kitchen and drops a kiss on top of Enzo's head and then sighs, facing me. "What are you doing here, Cam?"

"I'm only in town for another day. I wanted to see you. Your sitter Becky was here, but she couldn't look away from her phone long enough to tell me when you'd be back and I was worried about Enzo." She starts to open her mouth, but I push on. "Rightfully so, she had him alone on the couch watching some teen crap."

Andie snorts as she buries her nose against Enzo's neck.

"Seriously, Andie, that girl isn't qualified to watch a fly."

She rubs her hands down her face. "So?"

"So…"

She laughs, but it doesn't sound happy. "What do you want, Cam?"

I ignore her question as I scoop out pasta onto a plastic kid's plate. "I hope pasta is okay? Should I put sauce on it or butter?"

She shakes her head. "He likes it plain." She gets a container of blueberries from the fridge and puts some on his tray. "He loves blueberries."

"Good to know."

"Is it?"

"Is it what?"

"Good to know." I feel like I'm being set up, so I keep my mouth closed, but she continues. "Because what would be the point of knowing his likes or dislikes if you don't plan on sticking around? And why are you here tonight helping me out? Don't you have to go check on The Social Hour?"

"I deserve that. I came to talk to you to try and figure this out." I wave my hand between us then lean against her kitchen counter. "To be honest, I can't stop thinking about you. I've missed you so much these past few months and...I'm in love with you. That's never happened to me before. I keep my feelings compartmentalized, but you have me throwing shit all over the place. I can't think straight, I can't concentrate...I'm a fucking mess." I look over at Enzo who isn't paying attention to us. "Sorry, buddy."

"Well, maybe your girlfriend can help you sort it all out."

I give her a quizzical smile, but she doesn't return it. Her eyes are flat and cold. "I'm not sure what you're talking about."

"Well, Cam, imagine me calling you the other week, but it's not *you* who answers the phone. It's your girlfriend Lisa."

I scrub my hands down my face and groan. Fuck. My. Life. "Lisa is not my girlfriend—"

"So you admit she was there at your place at nine a.m.

307

while you were in the shower."

"It's a long story."

"Save it, Cameron. I don't need to hear it. In fact, I don't need anything from you."

"Dammit, no!" I say with a little too much bite. "I'm not going to let you think I cheated on you, Andie. I'm not your asshole ex." I breathe in through my nose. "Lisa came to San Francisco to plead her case. She wanted to get back together with me, but I told her no because I'm in love with you. *You*, Andie! She stayed the night in my guestroom because it was late and she didn't have a place to stay. She left the next morning. I don't know why she was answering my phone or telling you she was my girlfriend, because she's not and hasn't been for a long time. I have not touched another woman since you."

Andie sits down and absentmindedly rubs a scratch on the table with her finger. "I can't get involved with someone who doesn't want all of me, and that includes Enzo. I thought I could. I thought I could casually date someone, have some fun…maybe even a one-night stand, but I can't. I mean, you said so yourself, you don't want kids."

I throw my arms up in the air. "That was a moment of weakness on my part! I was pissed at Kiki for leaving me with three babies. I do want kids, eventually. Andie, I'm trying to tell you that I want to try and make us work. I'm not giving up on you…on us."

She's silent for a moment. "What does 'us' look like in your head?"

I sigh. "I don't know. We see each other exclusively when I'm in town."

She shakes her head and laughs, but there's no humor in it. "So basically when you're in town I'm your friend with benefits."

"No. I mean I could fly you and Enzo out to California too."

"And then what?"

"I can't think that far ahead, Andie. That's all I can give you right now."

"So, what's going on with the California locations anyway?"

"I'm hoping to get a new partner on board to take them over. Listen, I get it. It's frustrating as hell. I feel like a hamster on a wheel. I'm—"

She holds a hand up, cutting me off. "Cam, enough, please." She looks over at Enzo. "Two years ago I would have said hands-down yes to your offer. But it's not just about me anymore. If someone is going to be a part of our lives, then I want him all in. I want him to love us both unconditionally. I want him to love his job, work hard, but come home to us every night and recharge. I want *commitment*. I want someone who will trust me to catch him when he falls, and do the same for me in return."

I push away from the counter and pull her up, out of the chair. I lift her chin and seek out her lips. I've missed her taste so much, her petal-soft lips, her little moans.

She breaks the kiss. Her eyes begging me to have mercy on her.

"I *am* that guy."

A tear slips down her cheek. "No, you're not. I don't think you can ever be."

Chapter 41

Andie

A Month Later

I OPEN THE front door after someone continues to knock quite obnoxiously while I was in the bathroom. "Oh! Hey TJ, did I leave something at the office?"

"Hi Shorts, how are you?"

"Um…pretty good since I last saw you twenty minutes ago. Want to come in?"

"No can do, pretty lady. I'm here to take you to the airport."

"The airport? Why?"

"Can't say."

"I'm confused." I look behind me as Enzo toddles around the living room. "Are you feeling okay?"

"Right as rain. Come on, we're going to be late. I have a bag packed for you, so don't worry about that."

I fold my arms over my chest and smile playing along with his little game. "And where exactly am I going?"

"Can't say. But I'm super jealous. Ooh, I almost forgot,

you'll need this."

I sigh heavily in frustration as he hands me a dark blue passport book. "Haha, real funny. This looks pretty legit— did you make this, or is it off Etsy?"

A silver minivan turns onto the street squealing on two wheels. *What the hell? Is that Mandy?* Sure enough the driver side door busts open and Mandy comes barreling up the walkway. "I'm sorry, so sorry! Stupid mother-in-law insisted on telling me a story about some second cousin that died tragically from some nasty thing like gout, I don't really know I was half listening, but I was like Delores! I have *got* to go!" Mandy sucks in a deep breath. "So here I am!"

My jaw could be picked up off the ground. "*What are you doing here?*"

Mandy puts her fists on her hips. "Well, hello to you too!"

"I'm sorry. Hi, I'm so happy you're here, but what are you doing here?"

TJ waves the passport in my face. "Glad Thelma and Louise are back together again, but we gots to go!"

I grab the passport from his fingers. "Is this real? How did you get my picture for this? My birth certificate and social security card?"

"Remember when I was playing around with that camera and made you stand in front of the wall?"

"You told me we had to take head shots for a magazine piece."

"Please sister, like I would do a boring headshot where you can't smile. That was so the eighties." I look at him in confusion.

"I got your mama to give me the rest. So off you go! Where's my little butter bean?" Mandy pushes past me. "Twinnie, Auntie Mandy is here! You're going to come stay with me for a few days, maybe longer, we'll see. Grams and Grandpa can't wait to see you too!"

"Mama, doggie!"

"Yes, your mama will make sure to take your doggy too."

I snort as I cross my arms. "Auntie, not mama." I give her a stern look.

"Potato, po-tot-o."

"You guys! Seriously, what is going on?" I cry in exasperation as TJ pulls me down the sidewalk to his car. "I feel like this is some weird dream."

"Come on, Andie, get in the car. We're late for a very important date! Ooh, I'm getting some serious Alice vibes." He pushes me into the passenger seat.

"Wait!" I laugh as I get back up and hug Mandy and kiss Enzo. "I don't know what's going on but I'm either going to kiss you or kill you. Take care of my baby and Vader!"

I get in the car and wave goodbye to Mandy. I can hear her scream, "Bippity-boppity-boo, bitches!" as we pull away.

TJ PULLS ONTO the tarmac of a private airfield and drives up to a small jet.

"TJ, I'm seriously getting worried. What is going on? Are you coming with me?"

"Sadly, Shorts, no. My part in this ends here. God, I

wish I could. Here, take your bag and climb the stairs. Kiki and Sarah packed everything you could possibly need."

"I'm scared." I smile shakily at him and then back at the plane.

"Trust us on this one." He squeezes me into a hug. "Now get going before I start bawling." He shoves me roughly toward the stairs. I stumble before I regain my composure and glare at him over my shoulder. He blows me a kiss.

"Welcome, Ms. Daniels."

I look up to see a smiling flight attendant waiting for me at the top.

"Let me take your bag for you."

"Oh, okay, thank you. Actually, if you don't mind, can I keep it with me?"

"Sure, I'll just set it on the couch."

The couch? I step onto the plane and am blown away by the beautiful simple interior. This isn't like a regular commercial plane I've seen in pictures. I nervously wipe my hands on my jeans and sit down on a couch.

"Is this your first time flying?"

"Yes, ma'am."

"Well, don't worry about a thing. We have Captain Durham flying and he is the best of the best." She smiles graciously at me. "Can I get you a tea or coffee?"

"Um, just water please."

"Of course. We'll be leaving shortly, so you might want to get settled and buckle up. Bathrooms are at the back of the plane."

"Am I the only one on this flight?"

"Yes."

I look around at the empty plane feeling flustered. "Can you tell me where am I going?"

"Well, by law yes I'm supposed to, but it would ruin the surprise." She warmly smiles. "But honey, I'm a romantic at heart and my heart says to just go with it." She winks. "I'll be right back with your water." I'm quickly starting to panic because I've never flown before and I'm not quite sure what's going on.

She returns with my water. "I almost forgot to give you this." She hands me a gold envelope with one sheet of paper tucked inside. I take it out and read the four lines.

Satin sheets, appletinis
Dinner with me
The piña colada song
I'm ready.

I laugh despite my nerves over the lines that Marsha at the charity event said she wanted him to do. I hold the letter to my chest as tears leak out of my eyes. I take a deep shuddering breath.

He may say he's ready, but am I ready?

Chapter 42

Andie

I WALK DOWNHILL on the narrow cobblestone street following the directions the driver gave me. In heavily accented English he said, '*You'll know it when you see it.*' I turn a corner, careful not to get the heels Kiki packed for me stuck on a stone.

She and Sarah thought of everything from makeup to the most beautiful dresses a girl could dream to wear in a place like this. I chose a bright red silk dress that literally floats around my legs as I walk. She paired it with gold heels and accessories. All her notes and pictures were listed in alphabetical order and when to wear what with breakfast, lunch, dinner, with makeup diagrams matched to each outfit. There's no messing up with these two. My nerves are equally balanced out by my excitement. I can't believe I'm really here.

I turn the corner and am blown away by the sheer beauty as the town drops off into the cerulean blue waters down below. Yellow umbrellas dot the sand as families pack up their belongings, expired from a full day spent in the sea and the sun. I look at the brightly colored shops as I pass and sigh wishing I had more time to explore, but giddy excitement and nerves pushes me on toward my destination.

I remember the driver said to turn right at the blue shop on the corner. As soon as I do, I see it and smile. At the end of the short street is a large wooden door set into an old cream stucco building. The sign above the door reads, 'The Social Hour'." Standing next to the door, leaning casually against the wall, is none other than Cameron Forbes dressed in a white button-down and linen trousers looking completely relaxed. He smiles his devastatingly handsome, sinful smirk. I want to run to him, but I contain myself, not ready to concede to whatever this plan of his involves.

"*Buona sera*, Andie."

I smile like a loon despite telling myself to remain cool and calm. "Hi, Cam." I reach him and he pulls me to him.

"Welcome to Italy."

"I've always wanted to come here."

"I know," he whispers as he softly kisses the corner of my mouth. I want him to grab me and smash his lips to mine, but I need some answers first.

"This is beautiful and incredible…but what are we doing here?"

"Did you get my note?"

I quirk an eyebrow. "You really want to sip appletinis and listen to the piña colada song?"

"You forgot the most important detail…the satin sheets."

"Hmm."

He clasps his warm hand around mine. "I'm cashing in

your date with the most-wanted hunky romance cover model."

"Hunky, huh? Aren't I the one who's supposed to be cashing it in?"

"Semantics." He arches an eyebrow at me as he opens the wooden door. "You look beautiful by the way."

"Thank you," I murmur as I slip by him into a dark hallway. The smells coming from down the hall are mouth-watering. My stomach rumbles and I quickly clasp it to try and stop it.

"Hungry?" He chuckles.

"I was too nervous to eat anything on the plane." I smile ruefully at him.

We walk down the dimly lit stone hallway and turn the corner to the most magnificent little restaurant overlooking the ocean. It's all open to the sea and the air and I breathe it all in. The setting sun casts the ivory stone walls of the bistro in rosy golden light.

"Cam, this is…breathtaking."

He squeezes my hand as he leads me to a table with the most perfect views. Boats dot the harbor, birds swoop down for their dinner. I tear my gaze from the ocean and look around the quaint little place. "Where are all the other diners?"

"I rented it out for just you and me." He casually shrugs.

"Do you own this place?" I whisper as a waiter appears out of thin air and pours two glasses of red wine.

"Why are you whispering?" He smiles cheekily at me. "No, I don't own this place. I found this little 'hole in the wall' one summer when my friend Josh and I were traveling the coast during college. We decided to stay and waited tables here for the rest of the summer. This is where we came up with the plan for The Social Hour. I became friends with Marco, the owner, and asked if I could use his name, L'ora Sociale. He had taken Josh and I under his wing like we were his sons and said he would be honored. The rest is history." He pauses to take a sip of wine. "He tried to get me to come back here and run this place with his family, but I had bigger plans, bigger ideas. Really, I think he just wanted one of us to marry his daughter, but she was twelve at the time so that was a no-go. I finished school, got a small loan from my dad and roped Josh into partnering with me. That's how it all got started."

"That's amazing, Cam. I had no idea you got your idea for The Social Hour from here. This wine is so good by the way."

"It's a red blend from a vineyard in the Barolo region."

"I have no idea what that means, but it's good."

Cam chuckles as the waiter brings out the first course. Cheeses and meats with pasta dishes. It all looks and smells so amazing. A man in the corner starts to play the guitar and I'm entranced.

"How was your flight?"

"Hmm? Oh, scary as hell, but luckily I fell asleep pretty quickly. I slept through a majority of it."

"You can check that and Italy off of your never-have list."

I smile at him as I bite into the freshest bread I've ever tasted, the creamy cheese oozing off of it like butter.

By the time dessert arrives I feel like a stuffed pig. I

should have paced myself. I shouldn't have jumped out of the gate mowing down everything in sight. I groan as the waiter puts two silver dishes down in front of us. "*Signorina, posso presentarvi il cioccolato...er...gailato.*" The waiter blushes as he bows his head and backs away from the table.

I throw my head back and laugh as Cam's grin spreads across his handsome face.

"I'm never going to forgive Mandy, and I can't believe you made him say that." I smile, and despite my full stomach, I can never turn down chocolate gailato as I spoon the creamy cold concoction into my mouth.

Chapter 43

Cameron

MARCO, MY MENTOR and surrogate Italian father, came out to meet Andie and to say hello after we had dessert. I usually come back here at least once a year, and he was more than happy to help me try to win my *amo* back when I asked him for a favor. After the most incredible dinner with the most beautiful woman I asked her to take a walk with me down the hill to the beach.

Andie takes off her heels and I take them from her. I hold her hand as we walk in silence.

"So, Cam, you didn't really answer my question. What are we doing here? Don't get me wrong, I don't want to sound ungrateful, but we didn't exactly leave things great between us. I told you what I needed."

"I know. I had to work through some things before I could come back for you. Andie, this is my way of showing you that I'm ready."

"What are you ready for?"

"I want a relationship with you and Enzo. I want to be in

your lives. I want to be a part of it."

She sighs as she stops walking and looks up at me. "Cam, this..." She flops her arms at her sides looking helpless. "This is amazing, but it's not my reality. I don't fit into this world. I don't fit into *your* world."

"Says who?"

"Me!" Andie looks around desperately as she hugs herself, looking as vulnerable as the day I met her. "My life is a mess. My idiotic waste of space ex will probably reappear at some totally inconvenient time and I won't know how to handle him. I've gotten a lawyer involved, but he can't be my guard dog twenty-four-seven." She looks down the beach and starts walking again. I match her slow stride as she continues. "I'm a single mom, Cam. I'm not one of your supermodel girlfriends who lunches with her friends, or can jet off to Italy wearing the latest fashions at the drop of a dime. I usually have Cheerios stuck in my hair or dog slobber on my blouse. I hide behind my camera because socializing isn't exactly my thing." She sighs. "The truth is, I want it all. I *deserve* it all. I want you to say you'll move heaven and earth to be with me. To be with Enzo and me." She takes a deep breath. "I want what you can't give me."

I reach for her hand and pull her to a stop. I rub my hand along my jaw. "Are you done?"

"I think so."

"Come here." I gather her in my arms and tilt her chin up so that her hazel eyes are looking into mine. I cup her face in my hands. "Do you know what kind of woman I'm looking for?"

She slightly shakes her head no.

"I'm looking for someone who will stand by my side through thick and thin. I don't care if she's wearing a messy bun, or just got her hair styled at the salon. If she's got Cheerios in her hair, then so be it. It means we'll never go hungry." She snorts out a laugh as I smile and touch one of her curls. "I'm looking for a woman who doesn't mind me working late nights, but welcomes me home when I get back early. I want a woman who has a passion of her own that she wants to pursue. I'm looking for someone to be my partner, my lover and a place my heart can call home." A tear slips down her cheek. I lean in and kiss it away. I touch my forehead to hers as she shakily inhales. "Andie, it's you." I kiss her soft lips gently. "I've been looking for you, I just didn't know how badly I needed you. That insanely gorgeous woman who showed up in my bar looking for a job opened my eyes to what could be."

"But what about the bars?" She sniffles. "California?"

"I'm working on that."

"I can't do long distance. And it's not just me, there's Enzo too."

"I thought that was a given. When I say I need you, it means I need the both of you with me and whatever craziness that comes with it. I love *you*. I want it all with you and Enzo, Andie. I want lots of fucking babies with you. Whatever it takes, whatever that means, I want it al—"

She smashes her lips to mine as tears from her eyes moisten my cheeks. "I love you too."

I never gave up on you."

"Because you're stubborn and ornery."

"Because I love you. We're in this together."

Chapter 44

Andie

I PLACE MY hands over the cloth covering my eyes. "Come on, Cam, where are we going today?" I feel his breath on the shell of my ear and it makes me shiver.

"You don't know how badly I want to keep this blindfold on you and fuck you senseless right now," he growls in my ear. I swallow and my legs turn to jelly as his words wash over me causing me to stumble. He quickly wraps a hand around my waist helping me to stay upright. I can feel the Italian morning sunshine on my face as we walk down the sidewalk.

"*Ciao.*"

"Aren't people thinking this is weird? That I'm walking down the sidewalk with a bandana over my eyes? I feel like Sandra Bullock in *Bird Box.*"

"As long as you smile, it's totally normal."

I frown. "I really need a coffee. I'm cranky."

"I know." He chuckles as he stops me and pulls a door open. The smell of coffee hits my face like a blast of unbelievable fresh roasted goodness.

"Oh my god," I groan, "I love you."

"I love you too, even if you're declaring your love for me getting you into a coffee shop."

"Can't I take this darn thing off yet?"

"No." He orders two cappuccinos as I pretend to sulk silently next to him. He wraps an arm around me and I lean into his wall of muscle, my fingers gliding over his soft cotton tee. His fingers slide up and down my arm in a lazy pattern as we wait, and as simple as the touch is, it makes me feel like I'm cherished, that I'm his.

This past week has been incredible, exploring the coast of Italy, eating amazing food and of course getting to know each other intimately all over again. We can't seem to get enough of each other, and even though I miss Enzo like crazy, this break with just Cam and me was really what we needed. Enzo has been doing great with my parents and Mandy, and the last time I tried to call them, she bossily told me he's doing great and to enjoy my vacation time, don't call again until I'm home.

We walk back into the sunshine and head in another direction. I carefully take a sip of coffee as Cam slows to a stop and opens a car door for me. He takes my coffee and I feel my way onto the seat. "Cam, where are we going? This is driving me nuts!"

He laughs. "I know it is."

"You're evil."

"You'll regret that in a little bit."

I fold my arms over my chest as he speaks to the driver in Italian. I can't understand a word which drives me even crazier.

"I want to see the scenery," I pout.

"It's just a bunch of rocks and old buildings. Maybe an olive tree here and there. Ooh! That's cool!"

"What? What's cool?" I arch my neck as the wind from the open window blows against my skin.

"Oh, nothing, you missed it."

I turn toward him. "You are seriously going to pay for this."

He runs a finger down my arm and whispers seductively. "I love paybacks, *bellissimo*. I look forward to it."

I huff out a laugh. "You are sick in the head."

"Just fifteen more minutes and you can take it off."

We sit in silence for a bit, my hand in his. "Hey, Cam?"

"Yes?"

"I've had a really good time. You know, in case this next part is pretty awful. You've done so great up until this point."

He leans over and captures my lips in his. "Thanks, beautiful."

"And just so you know, whatever this is, even if it's total crap, I love you anyway."

"I'm trying not to be offended that you would think I would plan total crap, but I love you too."

"And even if—"

He places a finger on my lips. "Andie, ssh. We're here."

Chapter 45

Andie

THE CAR COMES to a stop. "Wait here." Cam gets out of the car and says something in Italian to the driver and then jogs around to my side. He opens the door and helps me out. He walks me forward and I trip over the curb.

"Watch the curb."

"You're terrible at this," I grumble as he pulls me forward and then stops.

"Whatever happens next, we're in this together."

I smile. "In this together." I hop on my feet in anticipation. "Come on, take it off!"

He places a quick kiss on my nose and then moves behind me. He unties the bandana and my hands reach up to help take it off. I stare dumbly, unable to comprehend what's in front of me.

"Surprise!" the crowd shouts. My hands move up to my mouth. "Oh my god, what are y'all doing here?"

My parents, Mandy and Deacon, TJ and Connor, Kiki and Tatum holding baby Drew and Chase, Lex and Sarah with Jax and the twins, Cam's parents. All our loved ones together.

"How did you..." I pivot to look at Cam and almost pass out. He's down on his knee holding a diamond in his finger.

"Oh my god," I whisper as tears run down my cheek.

"Anderson Leighton Daniels, you are my final destination, my forever. I want to share every minute of the day with you and Enzo. I promise to take care of you and love you both always and forever. Will you marry me?"

I nod yes as tears leak down my cheeks. "Yes, always and forever."

Everyone starts to cheer, TJ, Mandy, Kiki, and Sarah being the loudest.

Epilogue

Cameron and Andie

"YOU'RE PROBABLY WONDERING what happened next. I had all of our loved ones flown out a few days before to get ready for the wedding."

"I still can't believe you arranged all of that without me knowing. What if I hadn't said yes?"

"Please. I didn't have a doubt in my mind."

"You got lucky."

"Yep. I got lucky. Biggest gamble I've ever taken and I struck gold. I'm the luckiest guy in the world."

"Ah, you're layering that cheese sandwich pretty thick." I lean over and kiss him. "We got married that afternoon at the beautiful old church overlooking the sea. Kiki brought me one of her dresses, Sarah did my makeup, Mandy was my maid of honor, it was perfect. The flowers, the candles…it was so romantic and beautiful."

"Except for the glitter TJ threw all over. I'm still finding it in my luggage and other places."

I roll my eyes. "That sounds like a personal problem. It

was perfect."

"Enzo looked like a little stud in his matching tux."

"He did. You have TJ to thank for that."

"We celebrated with everyone on a trip to Tuscany afterward. It was pretty special."

"It really was magical. Even Deacon and Mandy had a good time. He's never been outside of Alabama."

"I've never heard someone pronounce Italian 'Eye-talyen' before."

"Clearly Inkdale, Alabama isn't very worldly."

"Maybe tonight we can go get Eye-talyen and then get some gailato...I caught that eyeroll."

"Thin ice, Mister."

"I went from cheese sandwiches to thin ice in a matter of minutes."

"I mean...you're a guy. It's pretty typical."

"I'm so proud of you."

"Don't try and butter my biscuits."

"I love it when you talk dirty...no but seriously, I'm really proud of you. Andie took the most amazing photographs in Italy, sent them off to a publisher and got a book deal. And Mandy helped write the copy for it. *A love story in Italy*. Who knew Mandy was such a sentimental romantic?"

"I did, she's been writing short stories ever since we were kids. She just couldn't find that spark to inspire her."

"You inspired her."

"*Italy* inspired her. I just helped with the visuals."

"So modest. Tomayto, tomahto. And Mason?"

"Ha. Mason showed up to a supervised court visit drunk. Once he sobered up he admitted he didn't want to be responsible for Enzo and signed his rights over. Have I told you how much I love you lately?"

"I love you more. Yup, Enzo is officially a Forbes. I love that little guy more than words can say. I never realized how much I needed him."

"And he needed you…and whatever happened to crazy brunch lady?"

"Crazy Kendra? Jesus. Last I heard she was prowling the Nashville singles scene. She'll get her hooks in some poor sucker."

"At least it wasn't my sucker."

"I feel like that wasn't quite a compliment…"

"Tell them the latest about The Social Hour."

"I closed down the California locations and sold the properties. I turned the Chicago location over to Allisson, the manager there, and am happy just being a silent partner. We just broke ground at the second location in Nashville. I convinced Connor to partner with me. Life is good."

"Life is so good. You ready to be a daddy for a second time?"

"Is it time?"

"I think Charleigh Forbes is going to give her brother and her cousins Chase and Drew a run for their money. Let me call TJ really quick and let him know. Oh, and I better call Mandy. She'll want to be there too."

"Great. Let me get the taser charged. *Why* is TJ going to be there again?"

"Because he's my doula."

"Shit. What on earth possessed you to choose TJ as your doula?"

"He's taken this role very seriously. He said after delivering Drew into this world, he just knew it was his part-time calling."

"I believe Dr. Rosen delivered Drew…"

"He's really good with the Lamaze breathing. He does this funny rap rendition."

"Yeah, I've heard it. Trust me, when you're in the moment, you're going to hate it. Is he going to wear that hideous outfit again? And we better make sure he doesn't have sage on him."

"Um…I'm not sure…should I be worried?"

"Nah…what could go wrong with him and Mandy in the delivery room?"

"I'm sensing sarcasm."

"Didn't he faint when Kiki gave birth to Drew? A nurse had to give him smelling salts off to the side. He missed the whole thing as I recall."

"I forgot about that. Anyway, at least I nixed the water birth."

"Jesus, this is not going to end well."

"Cam, it always ends well. In it together?"

He dips his chin and kisses my lips. "We've got this together…Forever."

Post Epilogue
The Food Choice Network

"I'M WORRIED THAT Paul has put too many chilis in his dish."

"Yes, Lindsey, but they're roasted, that should bring the heat down a little bit. Paul! Don't use too much man! Time is almost up!"

Paul looks at the camera irritably as sweat glistens his brow. He adds a garnish of pepper to his plate.

"Five four, three, two, one! Chefs, please step away from your dishes."

Paul backs away with his hands in the air. He wipes his hands on his dish towel and then shakes hands with Chef Bobby Flint.

"Paul, can you please tell us what your famous best dish is tonight using the ingredient risotto?" the show host asks.

Paul clears his throat. "Judges, I'm pleased to be here tonight." He nods his head toward the three judges. "This is my famous Paul's vegan spicy lemon mushroom risotto quinoa balls."

The judges fork into the moist balls.

"Wow! Paul's balls are spicy!" Judge Lindsey announces as she fans her mouth and then takes a big gulp of water.

"Wow, Paul...I don't know what to say. They're definitely...uh, moist." She drains her water glass. "Moist...balls." She coughs.

"Too spicy." Judge Michael wheezes as he coughs up the ball into a napkin. Paul blanches as he nervously fidgets next to Chef Bobby.

"This lemon mushroom combo...is that ancho I'm tasting?" The third judge chews thoughtfully.

"Yes, sir. I used a Carolina Reaper with ancho and jalapeño peppers."

"Jesus, Paul, are you trying to kill us?" Judge Michael's eyes water as a stage hand brings him more water.

"Thank you, Chef Paul." The host cues him to take a step back as Chef Bobby steps forward.

"Chef Bobby, you have been challenged to the same ingredients. What have you made for us?"

"Yes, thank you. Tonight, I have prepared for you a lemon mushroom risotto with ancho chile and parmesan cream sauce."

"Wow, this is amazing! The texture is creamy, just the right amount of heat." Judge Lindsey shoves another bite into her mouth. "I can't get enough!"

"Oh my god, this is so good. A Sauvignon blanc would be amazing with this. Can someone get me a glass?" Judge Michael looks around.

"I love the nuttiness of the parmesan blended eloquently with the earthiness of the mushrooms. It's like a symphony on my tongue. Well done."

"Judges, please take a moment to vote for Chef Paul's Spicy Balls or Chef Bobby's Symphony on the Tongue."

"You liked that eh?" Judge number three puffs up proudly.

"It was gold."

Paul grinds his teeth in annoyance as the three judges hand their votes to the host.

"And in a unanimous vote, the winner is…Chef Bobby Flint!" The crowd cheers.

"Paul, unfortunately we all agreed your balls were just too spicy." Judge Lindsey tries to keep a straight face, but snickers to the judge next to her. "Never thought I'd say that on live television."

"Thanks, Paul, for challenging me tonight to a vegan risotto meal." Bobby stretches a hand out to Paul, but he ignores it as he turns to the judges.

"My balls are perfect! They are round and delicate. They melt on your tongue! Stupid Chef Bobby Flint didn't even *make* balls!"

"I think Paul's crying…" Judge Lindsey whispers to Judge Michael.

"Paul—" Chef Bobby puts a hand on his shoulder as he worriedly looks over at the host.

"No! Don't *touch* me!" Paul screams hysterically. "First they took away Vriendly Vegans from me and now this! Paul's balls forever!" Paul screams into the camera before security tackles him to the ground and tasers him.

"Didn't see that one coming." Chef Bobby makes the cut motion with his hand as he steps away from a screaming Paul. "Jesus, dude, get a hold of yourself. It's just a fucking cooking show. Is Paul *crying?*"

Paul's Spicy Lemon Mushroom Quinoa Balls

1 cup of risotto

¼ cup of quinoa

1 cup chopped baby bella mushrooms

¼ cup of lemon juice

½ teaspoon of salt

A pinch of pepper

1 carrot pureed

15 ancho chilis chopped

1 Carolina Reaper finely chopped (wear protective mask and goggles)

4 jalapeños diced

1 white onion chopped

½ cup of hot sauce of your choice

Lemon zest

Cook risotto and quinoa.

Throw all ingredients into risotto and stir. Shape into cute little moist balls.

Bake in oven for thirty minutes at 425 degrees.

Sprinkle with parsley. Paul's balls should be springy to the touch. A fork should glide through them easily. If they are spongy, cook for fifteen more minutes.

Warning: Be careful. Paul's balls *are* spicy and probably should not be consumed without Helen's peanut butter tofu dip.

Also I made this recipe up. Try it at your own risk. ☺

The End

Read on for a sneak peek of Sophie Sinclair's upcoming standalone, *Lindsey Love Loves.*

Prologue

SMOKE BILLOWS UP blurring my vision as I gasp for fresh air. Bullets ricochet off the table above me and I scream Nick's name, shooting my hand out as I try to grasp his shirt, but I just grab air. Patrons are screaming as I curl into myself blocking out the sounds and the carnage around me. I can't breathe. Please God, I don't want to die alone under a café table.

Another loud bomb goes off as more people scream. I wrap my arms tightly around my knees and bury my head into them. I know I'm crying but I can't feel anything except a fiery heat in my ankle as I rock back and forth.

"Nick, please help me. Nick! Nick Elliot, please be alive. Please help me," I chant as I cry.

I can't see anything because of the smoke, but I hear people shouting, glass breaking, bullets lodging themselves into the café walls around me as sirens roar in the distance. Please let Nick and Patrick be alive. I don't want to survive this if they aren't.

I feel like hours have gone by, but in reality it's only been minutes. A woman at a table next to me starts wailing. Please make it stop. Nick, please make it stop. Suddenly a hand grabs my arm and I shriek. "Please don't kill me!"

"Shh, Lindsey, it's me. I've got you. Come on, we have

to get out of here. Quick," Nick whispers in my ear as he pulls me to his hard chest. "Come on, Lindsey, you've got to move your feet."

"I can't," I cry back. "It hurts. I think I've sprained my ankle."

Strong arms quickly lift me and I bury myself into his chest as I grip his t-shirt. "Whatever you do, keep your head down and your eyes closed," he says, his breath tickling my ear as we move.

I disobey him and look up and see the lifeless body of a man in body armor I can't ever unsee. "Oh my god, oh my god…" I mumble hysterically. "Where's Patrick?"

"Goddammit woman, do you ever listen to me? Close your eyes! He's safe."

I immediately close my eyes and say a prayer thanking God that both men are safe. Nick stops jogging as someone speaks to him harshly in French. He answers back, his tone just as severe, and then continues to jog. If I weren't freaking the fuck out I would have commented on how flawlessly the French language rolled off his tongue. But I can't think about that. I don't want to think about anything.

I whimper and Nick's arms tighten around me.

"I've got you, Lindsey. You're safe now. I've got you."

Acknowledgments

Oh my gosh, y'all, what a ride this has been! I can't believe it's over. I'm really going to miss writing these characters. I'm so thankful you loved them as much as I did and shouted them from the rooftops. A big thank-you to my four biggest fans, Allisson, Lisa, Julie, and Heather. Your support means the world to me. Thank you to all the bookstagrammers and readers who fell in love with the *Coffee Book* series. It's hard to believe this series has come to an end, and I'm forever grateful to those who have gone on this journey with me. Shout-out to Emily, Rachel, Molly, Brittni, Becky, Aundreya, Addie, Alexa, Brook, Wendy, Brandi, and Amanda. Thank you always for voicing your love. Thank you to my beta readers, Rachel, Becky, and Heather for your guidance. I can't list all my ARC readers, but thank you for being so excited to read this series, I love each and every one of you. To Michelle, for having to read and edit this thing a zillion times again, thank you for your support, this series wouldn't have been possible without you. I promise to work on my beat tags. Thank you to Stephany for tying up all the loose ends. To my family, for their support and insisting on reading the *Coffee Book* series, thank you and I love you. To my husband and kids for putting up with my: just give me one more paragraph, one more minute, one more second! Your patience made this book happen. To Josephine and Richard, thank you from the bottom of my heart for all your love and support.

About the Author

Sophie Sinclair lives with her husband, two daughters, and gaggle of animals in Davidson, NC.

CPSIA information can be obtained
at www.ICGtesting.com
Printed in the USA
JSHW011413020820
7049JS00006B/4